FACADE

For information:
Melodious Enterprises, P.O. Box 2400 Fort Lauderdale, Florida 33303

For information about personal appearances, please contact Melody Saleh at info@melodiousenterprises.com melody@melodysaleh.com

Cover: 17 Studio Book Design
Editor: Revision Division

ISBN: 978-1-7333897-0-9
ISBN: 978-1-7333897-1-6 (e-book)

The Unbroken Series
Book I - Facade - Release Date 12/31/2019
Book II - Deja Vu - Release 6/23/2020
Book III - C'est la vie - Release Date 12/1/2020

Revised 10/2020

For Shiela

INTRODUCTION

Welcome to *Facade,* where things aren't always as they appear. I hope you will become fast friends with the characters you meet along the way and come to love them as I have. I don't feel as if I wrote *Facade,* but your soon to be friends had a story to tell—I'm just their storyteller. Sometimes I couldn't type as fast as the movie played out in my head. I wrote the first chapter of Facade in 1990. Well, most of what appears as Chapter One here today. I had an idea and couldn't wait to get it down on paper. I let a few friends read it, who then hounded me to—FINISH already! In typical fashion, life got in the way.

Facade, it's mostly conversation because let's face it, that's how we interact. It's also fast-paced and packed full of drama. You'll learn about each of the four main characters as you work your way through the chapters. Their love interests and family, you'll discover more going into Book II. I have four wonderful women I want to introduce you to in this book; I don't want to introduce too many characters right away. I sometimes feel too much information can cloud your judgment. I'd rather you form your own opinions as you get to know them better, the same as if you met them in real life.

The lives of Amber, Dominque, Zya, and Debra can get messy. Their lives are complicated, beautiful, passionate, and very loving. I warn you; they have sex, and they fantasize about sex. One also unexpectedly explores an alternative life-style. At times their language can be colorful. I thought about changing that, but under the circumstances, the words I chose fits the situation. You will cheer them, and sometimes you might even yell at them. Keep a box of tissues handy as you may shed a tear or two along the way. They're not perfect—

they may do things you can't imagine, but don't give up on them. Remember, things are always as they appear.

When you've finished reading *Facade*, I hope you'll let me know what you think. I'd love to get your feedback, positive and/or negative. Constructive criticism is always welcome as I perfect my craft. Your encouragement keeps my fingertips on the keyboard so if you love it, I hope you'll share that with me too; and all your friends because lets face it—there's so many great books out there and by-word-of-mouth advertising is the best.

One of the kindest thing you can do for an author is leave a review. Even if you just want to leave a rating (stars), that's very helpful. Be honest, but please be kind. When we publish our work, we become vulnerable, putting ourselves out there. Don't abuse it. Some of the greatest author's first books did not become best sellers, so be helpful when commenting.

Here I am, now over 20 years later, finally introducing you to the beautiful and crazy lives who make up *Facade*. We've all dreamed of writing a book someday, well I've finally done it. *Facade* is the first of the planned trilogy, the Unbroken Series. I promise you won't wait long for book number two, *Deja Vu,* and the finale, *C'est la vie*. Your new friends have been busy answering some of the questions you're bound to have when you finish *Facade*. Just a reminder, these books are meant to be read in order. They are not standalone books.

ACKNOWLEDGMENTS

Facade has been a work in progress over the past 20+ years. So many people have helped these pages come to fruition. My husband, Ali for not only offering to help edit my grammar, but always encouraging me—even gently nudging me to the computer when necessary. My talented friend Nancy for beta reading my final draft, even if you might have gotten me into a little trouble. My daughter, Tiffany, for giving me both negative and positive feedback. You helped strengthen some of these characters and provide them with more backstory. Then you went back and reread the book and found even a few more minor fixes. My editor, Kimberly Hunt from Revision Division, for your guidance in character/plot development and copyediting. And this cover—WOW! Anjanee, you are so very talented. I can't wait to see what you come up with for the next books.

I have so many wonderful people in my support system who have encouraged me along the way. To name just a few, Tammy (TT), Linda, Cherie, Holly, Lisa, and many more. And last, but not least, I have to give a special THANK YOU to Shiela, for hounding me constantly these last 29+ years to *finish already*. You loved the first chapter I wrote so much; you kept *Facade* in the back of my mind. Thank you for never giving up.

Melody Saleh

FACADE

A Novel

CHAPTER ONE

Feeling out of control, Amber grabs the back of his neck. She can't believe she's doing this—her body is on autopilot. She encourages him, pushing him lower down her body. The need to feel his lips on her is past urgent.

His lips slowly travel over her flat, taut stomach, pausing to tease her navel with his tongue.

She continues to urge him, pushing his head even lower while pulling her hips up to meet him. Luckily for her, Fort Lauderdale beach is unusually quiet; there's no one else around.

With the most devilish grin on his face, he sits back on his heels, the waves gently rolling over his feet, and watches as her head thrashes back and forth.

It takes a moment to register as she can still feel his hands on her body, although he's not touching her. She opens her eyes; her face begging and pleading him, without uttering a single word.

He willingly complies as his hands glide over her breasts. Her white dress now drenched as the waves of the ocean match the intensity of the waves of heat within. With their eyes locked, he grabs both sides of the top of her dress and rips it open, causing her nipples to stand fully erect under the early morning sun and salty air. His intense gaze never leaves her eyes as he strokes her inner thigh with his fingertips.

She squirms, trying desperately to make his fingers touch her. Her hips undulate as his reach goes higher and higher. Just as she thinks he's gone as high as he can his lips take over the exploration causing her to buck and moan once his unexpected fiery breath washes over her.

Putting her legs over his shoulders, he lifts her hips high in the air and trails kisses everywhere but where he knows she really wants it. He's teasing—pulling back every time he gets a little closer.

So close, the need becomes so strong, she throws her legs farther apart, spreading them more now than she ever thought possible. The ocean waves crash behind him with the same fre-quency and intensity of her waves of desire. Unable to control herself anymore, she reaches down and grabs his head, pulling him up so they can join as one.

He leans back and pulls her up to him. Without hesitation, she reaches down and directs him into her. The heat is all-con-suming; the way Hell must feel—the sensation Heavenly.

She groans as their motions meet, pulling her towards him with increasing speed and intensity. The waves along the shore continue to increase in speed and strength, equaling those with-in her body, becoming of dangerous tidal proportions. She's riding higher, higher until she can see waves cresting, foaming at the very top…

Beep. Beep. Beep.

Oh, no, not now! Amber groans as she reaches for the

snooze button on her alarm clock.

Just a few more seconds, that's all I needed. She pulls the covers up over her head, hoping to fall back to sleep quickly and pick up where she left off. She tries desperately to get back, imagining the feel of his ripped and naked body against her along the water's edge. She can't get it back. Frustrated, she works harder—moving her hips in what she hopes is the same rhythm as in her dream. The harder she tries, the more awake she becomes.

Beep, Beep, Beep, Beep, nine minutes later she throws the covers off of her and hits the snooze button again. Amber sits up on the side of her bed in her damp silk pajamas, her head in her hands, rocking back and forth. Frustrated, she says aloud, "I just needed 30 more seconds. Timing, timing, it's all about timing!"

She can still feel his hands on her body. *How can that be?* She thinks as her hands randomly roam her torso. Her mind can't help but go back to where it was a few moments before. The intensity has faded, but the euphoria she felt takes over her mind.

Beep. Beep. Beep.

"Oh, shut up!" she screams at the alarm clock as she picks it up and throws it across the room.

Just before the clock hits the wall, Amber reads the display, 6:45 a.m.

"Oh great, not even enough time to settle for Buzz!" she says out loud as she walks into her bathroom and turns the cold-water knob to the extreme left, as far as it will go. She's getting used to these daily cold showers.

Later that day, Amber meets up with Debra and Zya at the gym for their Monday afternoon kickboxing class.

Amber hits the bag continuously as Debra holds it steady, using this opportunity to let out some frustration, pushing hard, hitting the bag with all her power, blow after blow. Her beautiful face twisted with annoyance. Her usually sparkling eyes look like daggers ready to stab at any moment and her long dark hair, which is typically tied back neatly, is sticking out in all directions.

As class ends and the girls leave the studio, Debra asks, "Wow Amber, who are you mad at? You punched that bag like you were beating the crap out of someone. I hope you're not mad at me."

Amber shakes her head and chuckles. "Deb, you would be the last person I could ever be angry at."

"Want to talk about it?" Zya asks.

"No, not really, but thanks."

"How about we stop for a glass of juice before we leave?" Debra asks.

They walk over to the counter and order their fruity concoctions. Once they find seats, Amber asks with a smirk, "Okay, think they have some vodka back there they can add for me?"

"What's gotten into you?" Debra asks. "You really beat that bag up pretty good today."

Looking up at her friends—her sisters, Amber's initial instinct is to brush it off. However, as she looks at two of her best friends sitting across from her looking worried, she realizes she has to tell them something.

"Okay, I keep having these wonderful erotic dreams every

night. It sounds like it should be a good thing, right? Well, just before I hit my peak and get some release, I wake up. Any time of the night, it doesn't matter. At first, it was kind of fun, but now it's frustrating. My poor vibrator, Buzz, is going to go on strike soon! I've tried everything, including meeting up with Buzz before bed; that only makes it worse. No matter what I do, as soon as I go off to dreamland, there is Mr. Wonderful, looking gorgeous and sexy, waiting to tease me again."

"Wait a minute," Zya asks. "Would this Mr. Wonderful be someone Debra and I might know?"

Blushing slightly, Amber responds, "Ever since I met him last month, I can't get him out of my head. I can't concentrate or stay focused on anything. Me, nose to the grindstone, nothing's going to get in my way; Miss Success Role Model of 2017—and I can't focus. I'm obsessed with this man, and I have no control over it. It's driving me crazy!"

Trying to be sympathetic, Debra states, "I'm not sure if I should feel sorry for you or jealous. Who exactly is this, Mr. Wonderful?"

Amber replies without looking up from her juice, "Patrick Simpson, *The Ethical Attorney;* the guy I wrote about in *South Florida Magazine* last month."

Debra responds, "Maybe you need to see what this is all about. Make up some excuse to call him and meet him for drinks. I'm sure you can do some follow-up work on that article. He could be a total jerk, and you just need some time with him to figure that out."

Amber looks down at her hands with a look of defeat on her face. "You're right, I should, and I've already considered it. Last week he brought in a client to resolve a lawsuit he has against NeoQuest. I was ruthless; it's in my nature when I'm backed up against a wall. I doubt he'll ever want to have anything to do with me. But I have tried. Every time I pick up the phone, I clam up. I know, I know," Amber says, shaking her head back and forth. "The gal who's never at a loss for words, who interviews Fortune 500 CEOs, kings, queens and princes, and rock star idols… but this guy makes my insides twist—I can't help it."

Zya, listening from the sidelines, adds her two cents. "Well, girl, it's time you make a fool of yourself. If you don't try, you'll never know. It's no good being obsessed—so in lust and in need of this man. You're going to go insane if you don't do something about it."

As Zya continues to persuade Amber to take the next step with Patrick, Amber reminisces on how far Zya has come. Just last month, this year's hottest new designer was crying hysterically in Amber's arms. Zya wasn't sure how she was going to make it since she finally broke it off with Doug for good; her on-again, off-again relationship for the last 17 years. More off, then on. In the past, Zya knew they would be on-again at some point. Zya is determined to let that loser go once and for all. It was bad enough the games he played with her emotions, but now he was disappointing their fourteen-year-old daughter, Ashanti.

"What do you have to lose by asking Patrick to meet you after work for a drink?" asks Zya.

"Here comes Dom, let's ask her." Debra adds.

Although it's unusually quiet for a Monday evening, Dominque can't help herself. She slows her walk to a strut as she passes through the tables—drinking in the looks and sideways glances. Her flaming red locks and long legs turning heads every which way.

"Hey girls. Amber, what's wrong, you look like you just lost your dog or something?" Dominque says, seeing the lost and frustrated look on Amber's face.

Amber flashes a weak smile. "Thanks, I needed that."

Debra interjects, "Remember that gorgeous hunk of the legal system Patrick, that Amber interviewed last month?"

Dominque nods her head with her eyes lighting on fire as they usually do when discussing hot men.

"Well, it appears our good friend here is seriously infatuated. It's affecting her every waking and sleeping,"—Debra winks at Amber—"moment. She's plagued by him doing wonderful things to her body at night in her dreams. We're trying to persuade her to make up an excuse and call him; maybe meet him for drinks. Don't you agree?"

Dominque, excited about helping, sits on the edge of her chair and replies, "Absolutely! Amber, you've got to take the bull by the horns and just go for it. But first, tell us all the details about these dreams. I remember how hot he looked in clothes; I bet he must look orgasmic naked."

Amber smiles and says, "Stop it, you guys. And yes, he has an incredible body. Or at least I think he does."

The girls laugh, and Dominque adds, "What have you got to lose? Just call him. If you don't, you're going to drive yourself, and us, crazy."

Shaking her head, Amber asks, "Yeah, and say what? I'm obsessed with you, and you may not know this, but we've made love at least seventy-five times already. I'm wondering if it's been good for you?"

Debra laughs, and adds, "You say that, and you will find out!"

Dominque shifts around in her seat. "What if he asks you to describe your seventy-five encounters? Would you be able to tell him all the details?"

With a big smile on her face, Amber replies, "I'd tell him, body language would be more appropriate than the English language in this situation."

The girls break out in hysterics.

"Sure you would. It sounds great, but when it comes down to it, you know you couldn't. Besides, I have one sexy man at home, and although I may think about seducing him daily, picturing in my mind all the wonderful things I'm going to do to him, I'd chicken out at the last second and put on my good little wife smile and let him lead me. You girls are a bad influence on me," Debra says as her eyes drop to her lap.

Both Amber and Dominque look at each other with confused expressions. "You mean to tell us, you've never seduced George?" Amber asks.

"I know what I'm getting you for Christmas—black leather with whips and chains," Dominque interrupts.

"Yeah, you do that, and I'll probably get divorced. His parents raised him as a good Catholic. He married me because he knew I was a sweet, Christian girl who dreamed of having a big house with a white picket fence, a dog, and lots of kids."

"So, what's wrong with having one of those sex swings hanging from the old oak instead of a tire?" Dominque asks while twirling her hair.

Debra's eyes open wide. "You have got to be kidding me!"

"Do you tell George what you fantasize about when you

masturbate?" Dominque asks.

"Fantasize? Masturbate? George and I don't do that. He would think that's ugly, or perverted even," replies Debra, feeling somewhat embarrassed.

"First, I'm sure George masturbates. And Debra, there's nothing wrong with exploring and knowing your body and pleasuring yourself," explains Amber.

"Don't ever feel ashamed of your beautiful body—it's all yours. You should explore and know every inch. How can you learn to receive pleasure if you're not sure how to give it to yourself? Debra, have you had an orgasm?" Zya asks.

"Of course I have," states Debra matter-of-factly. "Or, at least, I think so."

Dominque interjects, "If you're not sure, you probably haven't. How long have you two been married? Never mind, it doesn't matter—it's time for you to experience the big O."

They all laugh as Dominque forms an O with her lips.

Dominque looks down at the ground and back up several times with this guilty smile on her face before she answers. "Speaking of O's, this sexy hot guy came into the office today." Dominque turns to Amber and continues, "His name is Stewart Lewis. He works as a sales executive for Rizner Pharmaceuticals. Do you know him?"

"No, the name doesn't ring a bell. What did he want?"

"He came to get some articles we wrote last year about Dr. Jones's breakthrough in Alzheimer's research. He's going to pull the doc's heartstrings and tell him about the patients he's met. He's betting emotionally, he'll get him to agree to almost anything if they can get the drugs out quickly to patients and their families. This guy is real smooth. I know why he's been a top salesman at Rizner for the last ten years," replies Dominque.

"Sounds like you may have a new story to write, Amber," Zya states.

"Dom, why do you know so much about this, Stewart?"

Dominque blushes and again looks at her feet. "Well, I guess you could say he has the uncanny ability to sell just about anything."

The three other women say almost in unison, "You didn't?"

"I did! You have to see this guy—he's gorgeous. He's about five-foot, ten inches tall, one hundred sixty-five pounds of pure lean muscle; not an ounce of fat on his body. He has blonde hair with bright blonde streaks and styled intentionally messy —that just got out of bed look. And pools of baby blue you could drown in. And his smile—oh God, that smile!"

Dominque's face takes on a dreamy, I'm floating look as she continues to tell the girls about her afternoon. "He asked me if I had plans after work and I told him—I swear I did—I had to be at a kickboxing class by 7:00 p.m. He assured me we would just meet for a drink and talk. I wouldn't miss my class unless that is…I wanted to. So, I met him at Hot Chocolate's after work for a drink.

"When I got there, he was already seated with an open bottle of Perrier Jouet. He hoped I didn't mind, but he was hungry and figured me out to be a champagne kind of girl. It was five-thirty when I met him; he assured me we'd be done by 6:45 p.m. at the latest, with plenty of time for me to get here, which is only two blocks away.

"To make a long—sizzling story short, we had the most incredible dinner, and although I had promised myself I'd only

10

have one glass of champagne, he was ordering another bottle before I realized I had drunk four glasses. I stopped him from ordering another bottle, but I couldn't help myself and prevent him from doing anything else.

"He sat next to me on my side of the booth with his arm around me, peering into my eyes. Oh, those baby blues...they hypnotized me—he could have anything he wanted at that point. He looked so deeply into mine when he kissed my face with lips so soft and promising me if I missed my class, I'd still got a great workout—maybe even a better one. Next thing I knew, I was doing pelvic thrusts with him in the back seat of his car."

"In his car? You've got to be kidding me? This man wines and dines you then has sex with you in his car?" Zya asks.

"Well, if I must confess, it was me who couldn't wait. We started in the parking lot there, then finished after he parked here. Can someone please give me a ride back up to Hot Chocolate's to get my car?" Dominque asks as if she's done nothing wrong.

"That's it? Does he want to see you again? Did you get his phone number? Did you give him yours?" Zya asks, the protector of the group.

Amber interrupts as Dominque is about to answer. "It doesn't matter, just please tell me you were safe."

"Well, it all happened so fast, the champagne, his very talented hands. I didn't even think about it. When we were all done, I panicked, but somehow without missing a beat—or stroke, he took care of it. He's amazingly gifted."

Debra steps in, "Dom, I'm glad he thought of it, but you need to stop taking so many chances."

"One chance is one too many, if you ask me," Zya states firmly.

"Dom, I gave you some to put in your purse last week; where are they?" Amber asks.

"Oh, they're still there. I know you're right…it all just happened so fast. One minute I was coming to class no matter what. The next, I've had four glasses of champagne, and I can't get my panties down fast enough so I could cum on top of him; riding him like a bullfighter."

"Look, we're not your mothers, but we are your friends, and we love you—we care about you. You need to take this more seriously and be a proactive participant."

"Although the chance of dying from AIDS is greatly reduced, it's not worth the risk," adds Zya.

"We'd like to go to your wedding one day, not your funeral," Debra adds.

With tears threatening, Dominque says, "I know and I promise from here on out, I won't take any more chances." Dominque holds up three fingers. "Scout's honor."

Amber senses Dominque's unease, so she shifts the attention to Debra. "Okay, changing the subject, I'll make a deal with you Debra, I'll drum up the courage to call Patrick if you loosen up and become more adventurous in the bedroom with George—deal?"

"Deal," replies Debra. "I think I'll start tonight. I've got to run now though…time to put on the chauffeur cap. I have to pick Tracey up from dance in ten minutes. A mother's work is never done, but I love it!"

Debra kisses Amber on the cheek. "Thanks for the advice. I know you're right; it's just not how I was raised. I'll try to let myself go a little more. Who knows, maybe I'll surprise George and wear one of those slinky things I got as a wedding present. Thanks again, love ya."

As Debra gets up to leave, Amber reaches across the table and grabs her friend's hands. "I don't know what I'd do without you. You are my family—my sisters. I probably don't say it enough, but I want you to know, I love you, and I cherish—US."

Everyone gets a little teary-eyed as they nod in agreement. Their bond—friendship—sisterhood is unbreakable. They know how much this means to her. She has a sister, but in blood only, she wrote off years ago. To her, Brandy doesn't exist.

In the car on the way back to Hot Chocolate's, Dominque begins, "Amber, please don't judge me. I know I said I would wait before I slept with any other guys, but Stewart is different. This guy has serious long-term potential."

"I'm not judging you. I'm not you and I haven't walked in your shoes; it's not my place to judge. I just want you to be careful and use your head. Stewart may be a catch, but is he going to respect you? He knows you're a fun girl, and you like to have wild, kinky sex, but does he think *you* have long-term potential?" Amber asks.

"I don't know. But, if I hadn't had sex with him, he would have thought I was a tease. Or worse, a prude," Dominque responds.

"Better a tease or prude than a slut or whore," Amber says a little too quickly.

Dominque, red-faced, snaps her head towards Amber. "Are you calling me a slut?"

13

Amber instantly regrets what she said. "No, I know you're not a slut or a whore. I know you on the inside, but he doesn't. All he knows is the last three hours. I may not have the experience you do with men, but one thing know, a man's brain is an erogenous zone. Sex! Sex! Sex! That's all most of them think about. If a woman has sex with them too soon, they must be easy and sleep around. Most of them have serious ideas about the type of woman they want to marry. They don't want someone everybody else has had. Plus, after three or four dates, you may decide you have nothing in common." Amber stopped at a traffic light, turns facing Dominque, and says through gritted teeth, "What were you thinking? If you want to go out and have sex Dom—go for it; just be safe. If you're looking for love, trust me, you're going about all wrong."

CHAPTER TWO

S tewart steps out of the bathroom with a towel wrapped around him and finds Patrick drinking his coffee and reading the morning paper. "Hey, you never told me how it went at NeoQuest last month?"

"It went great. I finally worked out a deal for my client we could all live with. Man, those people at NeoQuest sure know how to drive a hard bargain. For a while there, I thought we hit a stone wall. That gal Amber stuck to her guns. Remember, she's the one that interviewed me last month. In the end, my client gave in."

Pouring himself a cup of coffee, Stewart responds, "I never doubted you could close the deal...wait, your client gave in? Never mind...I meant, what did you think about Amber? Isn't she hot?"

"Yeah, she's okay. Way too headstrong and opinionated for me, but she's cute."

Stewart reaches to feel Patrick's forehead. "Are you sick or something? Her deep brown eyes and those legs." Stewart bites down on his knuckle. "Those luscious lips and wow, what a body! Boy, what I wouldn't do to see what she has under that business suit. I would love to run my hands all over those firm round breasts."

Patrick, rising from his chair, flustered, refills his cup. "Is that all you ever think about—women and sex—sex and women? Is there anything else in your life? Hey, if you think she's so hot, then you go for her. I don't think you're her type though."

"I won't argue with you there. I like my women adventurous and passionate—willing to try anything, anywhere. She seems a bit too reserved for me. I leave those women for guys like you. If I taught all the women in the world how to have incredible sex, they would want me all the time, and there wouldn't be any left for you. Besides, I heard through the grapevine, it's you she has her sights on."

Almost choking on his coffee, Patrick replies, "What, me? You've got to be kidding. She had it out for me—she was out for blood. For a minute there, I thought her claws were coming out to strike. She's one tough lady. I think your grapevine has a bunch of sour grapes; she's not interested in me."

Stewart says, "Well, suit yourself. If you want to be a hermit for the rest of your life and let all those beautiful women pass you by, that's your choice. By the way, if you really don't want them, don't worry, I'll take care of them for you."

Patrick states matter-of-factly, "You can have all of them. They're nothing but bad news, anyway. Plus, I'm too busy with work."

"Well, I hate to leave this uplifting conversation, but I have to get ready. I have a rendezvous planned with Tammy. She just bought a 1997 red Ferrari, and she needs me to show her how to handle the stick," Stewart replies and motions the actions of a stick shift over the zipper of his jeans as he exits the room.

Patrick tries to concentrate on the financial section of the newspaper; however, he can't get the image of Amber out of his mind. She can't be interested in him. She was ruthless and determined—but beautiful. It's hard to imagine someone with such an angelic face can have a demonic demeanor and hellish tenacity. *She must have all kinds of men after her. What would she want with me?*

Patrick agitated at himself for allowing the thoughts of Amber to stir him, walks into his bedroom, and opens a steel box on his dresser. He pulls out a wrinkled, folded note and rereads the suicide letter from his father.

Patrick's mother died unexpectedly when he was four-years-old. Raising a child was hard—especially alone. Patrick's father remarried quickly, hoping to fill that void. He tried desperately to keep Patrick in a healthy home, so thought finding a mother figure for him was of the utmost importance. Little did he know, Mary Beth, his wife, wanted nothing more than someone to keep a roof over her head and food on the table. The bed was something she warmed with many others, day-in, and day-out, in front of Patrick. Patrick's father luckily found out exactly who she was by the time Patrick turned ten.

On the day of Patrick's graduation from law school, his dad left him the note. It was time for him to join his love—his Maggie, Patrick's mom. Swearing never to follow in his foot-steps; a woman will never shatter his life. Patrick strengthens his resolve to stop thinking about Amber.

His hands leave the small of her back and travel down to caress and explore her body, as his kisses burn a trail down her neck. Starting at the front of her throat, he works his way down to her firm peaks. His lips and tongue devour one, then the other, leaving her breathless.

She can't help but grind her hips into him—feeling his hard erection.

While his mouth explores above her waist, his fingertips search below. Slowly, running them up her inner thighs, they brush over the place where they meet then glide over her bare skin, teasing along the edges of her thong. The tips so close to where the fire burns brightest, causing sounds to escape her she's never heard before. Her body squirms and contorts in ways she never thought possible.

Amber awakens again from a deep slumber, trying to focus on the clock when she realizes—it's 3:00 a.m. She gets out of bed, pacing her bedroom.

Speaking to nobody, "This is getting to be ridiculous. I have to do something. If I don't, I'm going to go out of my mind. Why is he doing this to me?"

After throwing off her damp pajamas, Amber jumps in the shower, turning only the cold knob, never touching hot. "I should just call him," she says aloud to no one. "He's probably not interested, but at least I can put this to rest and get some peace—and sleep. Oh Lord, what is happening to me?"

Driving into the office the same day, Amber plans her strategy. She can't pick up the phone and say, *Patrick, it's Amber. Remember from NeoQuest?* She has to find out if he's interested. She needs to sound mysterious and sexy. Something that drives him as crazy as he's making her. Amber parks and quickly crosses the parking lot into her office. She has a desk full of work, but maybe Dominque can help, so she invites her out for lunch to help strategize.

After a hectic morning, Amber awaits Dominque in their favorite diner down the street, The Black Olive. Amber hesitates to order a glass of wine, but then decides that might be just what she needs.

"Hey, thanks for meeting me," Amber says, smiling as she hugs Dominque.

Pointing to the glass of wine sitting in front of Amber, Dominque states, "I'll have what she's having," to the waiter.

Without small talk, Dom gets right to it. "I have some news for you about Patrick. It looks like you can put him out of your mind. According to Stewart, his roommate, he has someone else after him. Stewart told tell me, the same time I found out he's a jerk, he got roses at his office yesterday. Get a load of this note she sent with them,"

Roses are red
Violets are blue
Oh baby, the things
I'm going to do to you

"It's signed, '*Your Fantasy.*' Stewart can't believe it. He was wondering if he was gay or something, the way he avoids women. Anyway, sorry, honey, but maybe now you'll have some peace."

Amber shifts in her seat, eyes darting around the room.

"That's nice to know. Maybe it's for the best."

Dominick reaches for Amber's hand and asks, "Are you all right? You've been dreaming about this guy for over a month now. Can you really give up that easily?"

Unable to look Dominque in the eye, Amber quickly changes the subject. "Yes, I can. And don't worry, I'm perfectly fine. So, why is Stewart a jerk?"

Dominque cuts her off. "Wait a minute. You've been driving yourself crazy over this guy. Not sleeping at night or able to concentrate at work, and you want to talk about Stewart? This seems awfully strange. What's up?"

Dominque notices a satisfied smirk on Amber's face. "Hold on a second…are you his secret fantasy? Did you send those roses?"

Amber says, feeling unsure, "Do you think it was a bit too forward?"

Dominque, very excited, says, "Shut the front door! I can't believe you did it. That's great! Why didn't you tell me?"

Amber straightens up in her seat. "In case I chickened out, I didn't want to tell anyone. I figured I would have a little fun with him first. You know, be mysterious, increase his curiosity. It felt great sending them—a bit in control. I want to drive him a little crazy. You think he liked them?"

"Are you kidding? Stewart said he blushed when he read the card and insisted he didn't know who they were from. He brought them home and put them on the dining room table, and the card went right into his shirt pocket. I think you definitely roused his curiosity. Stewart told me Tuesday is Patrick's birthday, and they're hiring a stripper from Ladies-Ladies-Ladies to come to his office. Why don't you disguise yourself and take her place? What a great way to seduce him, and he won't even know it's you."

"I don't know where you come up with these harebrained ideas. There's absolutely no way, no way at all, I can do something like that," Amber answers shaking her head.

"Why not? You can remain anonymous and run your hands all over his body and drive him nuts. He'll never know it's you. You *can* do it. I've seen that determined look on your face. Those times when come hell or high water, you do what you have to do. You've got this."

Amber still shaking her head, matter-of-factly replies, "No, not gonna happen."

"I can disguise you so good even you won't recognize yourself. Think of it as your opportunity to act in a role—the seductress."

"Dom, thanks for the support, and yes, it is a great idea, but I can't do it. I'm no actress."

"Will you at least let me put a wig on you, maybe some blue or green contacts. I can do your make-up so you can at least see how well I can disguise you." Dom not giving up continues to sell Amber on the idea.

"Will that make you happy?"

Dominque enthusiastically nods.

"Okay, but no promises, all right?"

"Deal. Oh, this is going to be so much fun," Dominque replies, clapping her hands together.

Amber takes Dominque's hand in hers across the table. "Okay, your turn to spill, what happened?"

Dominque's eyes pools as she takes a deep breath. "I prefer not to talk about it if that's okay. I messed up...again. Can we just leave it at that? I promise I'm going to go slower from now on."

Amber replies, "I'm sorry he hurt you, but I'm glad to hear you may have learned a little something. And yes, I'll drop it— for now."

❧

Disguised as a conservative secretary in a business suit, black wire-rim glasses, and her wig swept up in a bun, she arrives at Patrick's office promptly at 4:00 p.m. Stewart meets her in the lobby.

"Hi, I'm Stewart."

"Hi, I'm Candy from Ladies-Ladies-Ladies. You hired me as a birthday present for Mr. Patrick Simpson."

Stewart, pleased as he checks Candy out from head to toe, nods in satisfaction. "Oh, yeah, he's in the conference room. We're all in there for his little surprise."

"Before I start, and not to create problems, is his wife or girlfriend present?"

"Patrick? Please, he doesn't have one of those. In fact, this is a test to see if you can boil his blood; or find out if he has any."

She has taken the role of Candy in her mind. She reminds herself, *I'm a stripper. I do this for a living—and I'm very, very good at it.*

"Oh, I think I can handle that," Candy replies with a twinkle in her eye.

"Take my recorder into the conference room and get everyone to make a lot of noise. I'll pretend to be from one of the other offices complaining. When I take my glasses off, press play, okay?"

"This is going to be great. He's probably going to kill me, but it's going to be *so* worth it." Stewart excitingly goes into the conference room to ready everyone for Candy.

Once the noise level gets loud, Candy barges into the conference room, red-faced and angry. "Excuse me. Do you have to be so loud? It's still business hours, and some of us are still working. Who's in charge here?"

Patrick says a bit embarrassed, "I am. My name is Patrick, this is my office. I'm sorry for being too loud; we'll try to keep it down."

Stewart steps forward to explain. "It's his birthday, and we surprised him with a little get together. Would you like a drink?"

Candy, never taking her eyes off Patrick, says, "I know it's close to quitting time, but some of us have work to do and can't socialize yet. Your party here is keeping me from meeting an important deadline. Unless you plan on writing my boss's speech for tomorrow night, I suggest you quiet down or take your party elsewhere."

Patrick, agitated with her tone of voice. "Wait a minute. I'm very sorry if we're a little loud, but don't you think you're being rude?"

She backs Patrick into a chair at the head of the table. "You think I'm rude? You're the one who's not thinking about others."

She turns to leave, but abruptly spins back and kisses him on the mouth, then pushes him down into the chair. "And another thing, did you know you have the sexiest eyes?"

Candy straddles him and gives him another passionate kiss

as she throws her glasses across the room and pulls the barrette out that holds the blonde trusses up.

Patrick, unsure of what's happening or how to react, sits back. His eyes are as enormous as saucers—his mouth agape.

Stewart starts the tape player as Toni Braxton starts seductively singing about how her man makes her feel.

Candy gets up from Patrick's lap and moves behind the chair. Running her fingers down his chest, she unbuttons his shirt while kissing his neck.

Patrick tries to remain composed on the outside, however, the blush on his cheeks tells all.

The crowd is going crazy and egging Candy on further and further, helping her step into her role.

After spinning his chair away from the table, she pulls her jacket down to her elbows and instructs Patrick to remove it for her.

As he reaches out with his hand, she playfully smacks it, then wags her finger, instructing him, teeth only—no hands allowed.

Still blushing, Patrick grips the collar with his teeth and pulls it down to her wrists.

Candy wraps the jacket around the back of Patrick's head. With the sleeve in each hand, she straddles him again and pulls his head into her chest. She grabs his head on either side, shaking her shoulders with his face buried in her cleavage. After he comes up for air, she instructs him to unbutton her shirt. Again he needs to be reminded, no hands. As he unbuttons her silk blouse with his teeth, she braces herself by grabbing his head again and leans back so he can reach the next one. The farther she bends, the more she undulates her hips, grinding against him and causing a commotion from the onlookers. He may fool everyone around him, being so calm and collected, but she knows exactly what she's doing to him.

With all the buttons unfastened, she turns around on his lap and allows him to pull it off again with his teeth. She spins back around and looking him square in the eyes, seductively sways her hips to the music, running her hands over her breasts and stomach. She turns away from him and strokes her buttocks and legs, slightly lifting her skirt; bending over, giving him a full view.

Unable to contain himself, he reaches out to touch her silky skin.

Playfully, she slaps his hand then slowly twists her skirt around so the button and zipper face front. Candy places Patrick's hands on her hips while she runs her fingers along his lips.

He kisses her finger at first, and then she slowly pushes it into his mouth. Taking her cue, he sucks on it as she pulls it free, locking eyes with her.

Her moist finger moves to her button, motioning him to do his duty.

This creates quite a commotion from the other people around the room and brings a deep blush to Patrick's face. For a moment there, he forgot they're not alone.

Patrick smirks as he obediently unbuttons her skirt, kissing her softly on her abdomen, when he's done. Looking up into her eyes, he can't help but think there is something familiar about her—he can't place her.

She gently grabs the back of his head and seductively sways her hips from side to side, guiding his mouth to the end of the zipper, just below her navel.

Patrick pulls it down very slowly, then takes in the exposed skin by letting the tip of his tongue slip out just above her panty line.

Candy pulls his head up, locking her gaze with him as her skirt to falls to the ground. She turns around again and steps out of her skirt. She bends over at her hips, reaching for her skirt.

Unable to stop himself, Patrick reaches out and strokes her bare cheeks.

Candy spins around and grabs his hands playfully, scolding him. She turns around, facing away, and lowers her hips into his lap; grinding into him before she sits back, resting her head on his shoulder. She grabs his hands and directs them from the top of her panties up and over her breasts seductively with the music.

Candy closes her eyes and blocks out everyone in the room except for Patrick. While still in control of his hands, she re-traces her steps across her breasts, then moves them across her abdomen, then down the top of her thighs. Not willing to give up control, she pulls them inward, then slowly up—how high will she go?

Just as he thinks she's going to run them up to her moist core, she brings them to her mouth, where she playfully sucks on his index finger. As her head still rests against his shoulder, he watches as she slowly sucks down to his knuckle, then pulls it back out—again and again.

Patrick breath is heavy and deep in her ear. He whispers, "You're driving me nuts."

Before she loses control, she sits up and bends forward,

again driving her hips into him. She thrusts her hips forward and back several times, rocking against his hard erection.

In a split second, he grabs the back of her bra, and with one hand, unfastens it.

She grabs the front just in time before it falls, revealing herself.

The crowd cheers, "Take it off! Take it off!"

She looks over her shoulder at Patrick, who raises one eyebrow.

He grabs her bra from her hands, revealing her perfect, natural round breasts. He pulls her back to him and whispers, "We have to entertain them." He leans her back against him and grabs her chin pulling her lips towards his, he kisses her passionately.

She gives in as one of his hands cups her breast, gently trapping her nipple between two fingers.. He wraps his other arms around her waist, pulling her tighter up against him.

Trying to gain her composure, Candy stands up and reaches for her jacket. She removes a can of whipped cream and a small jar of cherries. She locks his gaze as she puts whipped cream around her nipples and pulls out two cherries. She places the cherries on the tip of each nipple and instructs him to eat them. "Make sure you clean your plate now," Candy instructs as she lowers herself down into his lap.

As he dives in for dessert, she sways back and forth and side to side to the music, making it impossible for him to complete the task, causing him to get whipped cream all over his face and creating a roar from the others in the room.

Patrick grabs her on her upper back and engulfs as much of her breast as possible in his mouth.

She can't help but let out a gasp and moan quietly.

Patrick is aware of her passion, as much as she can feel his throbbing. As he continues to remove all the whipped cream from one breast, he presses her hips harder into him—his hardness pressing up, meeting her with each beat of the music.

After Patrick removes the cherry, he's not allowed to remove any of the whipped cream from her other breast. She stands up and steps towards the conference table, then turns and lies back on it. She spreads her legs and motions him with her finger, inviting him in.

Without missing a beat, Patrick steps forward and pulls her by the legs, so she slides up against the tightness in his pants. Forgetting they're not alone, he slowly grinds his hips into her as he lowers his head to lick the whipped cream from her other breast. He devours all the cream, nibbling gently on her nipple as if the cherry were still there.

Candy wraps her legs around his hips and pulls herself as close as she can up against him.

He suddenly feels the instant heat pulsating against him. He grabs the back of her head and pulls her up to him, willing them to become one. After looking deeply into her beautiful blue eyes, he grabs the back of her head and kisses her passionately. Slowly at first, then deeper while continuing to grind into her.

Trying to catch her breath, Candy pushes him away.

Patrick, with a twinkle in his eyes, notices the whipped cream can and takes charge. He instructs Candy to lay back on the table so he can make a circle around her belly button.

She's not sure if they would allow this if she were a real stripper. But then again, most of what they've done would never be allowed in a strip club.

He slowly removes the cream from her belly button using his tongue. His tongue darts a little south a few times, and she feels as if she's going to lose control—he's driving her when she should be doing the steering.

As she regains control, the music fades, and the crowd claps and cheers.

She quickly pushes Patrick away and states, "I'm sorry, sir, but remember, I have my boss's speech to write. Do you think you can keep the noise level down now?"

Candy picks up her clothes and licks the remaining whipped cream from Patrick's mouth before passionately kissing him one last time. She looks into his dark brown eyes and winks before exiting towards the lobby.

Once safely inside the lobby restroom, she stops to enjoy the passion she feels and relive what just took place. She can still feel his hands on her body—on her breasts—his hot wet tongue. Elated with joy and a smile that won't quit, she quickly dresses. *That's something he won't soon forget.*

Stewart slaps an embarrassed and blushing Patrick on the back. "Patrick, I'm proud of you, man. I didn't think you had it in you. If you had the chance, I bet you would have done her right there on the table. Did you forget we were there?"

Patrick sits down and grabs his head. "Yeah, I guess I got a little carried away. Who was she? She looks familiar."

Stewart, raising his glass and toasting his friend, loudly proclaims, "Happy birthday, Patrick. I'll call tomorrow and see if we can get her back again for an encore."

Patrick, blushing, excuses himself to get away by himself for a few moments. No one has aroused him like that in years.

He'd almost forgotten how it felt. Patrick retreats to the men's lobby restroom to regain his composure.

Still, in disguise, Candy emerges from the ladies' room and catches sight of the back of Patrick as the door closes behind him. Her body is still tingling from the fire he ignited, so she follows him in.

Hearing the door open and assuming it was Stewart, Patrick says, "Man, I can't believe you guys did that to me. What kind of birthday gift was that? You send me the most beautiful, sexy, incredible woman in the world to tease me for ten minutes, and then she leaves."

"Maybe I haven't left yet," Candy responds.

Patrick spins around in disbelief to find Candy leaning against the wall just inside the door.

"Thank you for the compliment, you're not so bad yourself," Candy says, batting her eyes.

"I'm sorry, I didn't know it was you," stumbles Patrick as his cheeks flush bright red.

She is flattered by his reaction. "You know, I had a hard time remembering there were other people in the room. If the music hadn't stopped, we might have ended up with more than we both bargained for."

"I'm sorry the circumstances weren't different. I would've liked to continue. You are one expert seductress," Patrick says, stepping closer, drinking her in from head to toe.

"You're just full of compliments today, aren't you? Maybe one day, when you least expect it—we'll pick up right where we left off," she replies as she turns and exits the men's room just before he can reach her.

"Maybe?" blurts Patrick going after her. "I want to see you

again. Let's have dinner. Can I call you?"

As she steps onto the elevator, she turns facing him. "Let's leave the ending as a fantasy for now." She leans outside the elevator and kisses him on the cheek. "We'll see each other again, I promise," she says as the elevator doors close.

Her kiss leaves a burning imprint. By the time he comes back to reality, she's gone, but not before he locks eyes one last time with the most beautiful woman he has ever seen. He can't shake it, but he knows her from somewhere.

Patrick rushes back into the conference room. "Stewart, tell me who she is. I have to see her again," Patrick begs as he paces back and forth.

"I told you, she's from Ladies, Ladies, Ladies. I'll call tomorrow and see what I can find out. Calm down, man, she's just a stripper. You really need to get out more."

The next morning, a stunned Stewart visits Patrick at his office. "Patrick, you will not believe this, I called about your stripper, Candy. It appears they don't have anyone by that name there. They didn't send a stripper yesterday. Someone canceled the order I placed. I don't have the slightest clue who your mystery woman is. Whoever she is, she must have a thing for you to go to all that trouble."

Getting out from behind his chair, Patrick paces. "You mean to tell me she isn't a stripper? She was so good—so sexy. Stewart, we've got to find her."

"And how do you suggest we go about that, Don Juan? Have another birthday party for you and hope she finds out? She told you you'd see her again soon," Stewart responds.

Not paying attention to Stewart, Patrick stops and says,

"Who did you tell you were getting me a stripper? She has to be someone you told or a friend of someone who knew."

"A lot of people. You with a half-naked, sexy woman... everyone wanted to see that. I know I didn't tell her. I've never seen her before in my life," Stewart responds, frustrated.

Patrick says while pacing, "She must be a friend of someone you told."

Patrick's secretary gently knocks then opens his door to notify him a package is being delivered, only he can sign.

The deliveryman hands Patrick, now speechless, the package and clipboard. "Please sign here."

"Must be a late birthday present," Stewart says.

Patrick dismisses his secretary and begins opening the box on his desk. Inside is musky scented tissue paper wrapped around the black thong panty from his mysterious stripper with a note that reads:

Not sure who enjoyed your birthday more, you or me.
Is fantasy better than reality? Hope not.
I'm looking forward to finding out for sure one day.
Signed, Candy

CHAPTER THREE

A tall, blond man walks over to Amber, Zya, and Dominque. "Hey, great party and congratulations Zya, you're very talented, you deserve all this." Looking at Amber and Dominque, "I'm surprised to see you girls here tonight."

"Hi, Sonny, Great to see you too. We wouldn't miss this for the world. Zya's success is something we all admire and celebrate. Why wouldn't we be here tonight?" Amber asks, puzzled.

"I thought you would be with Debra. You guys are still good friends, aren't you?"

"We're the best of friends. She couldn't make it tonight; she had a special night planned for her husband. Tonight's his birthday," answers Amber, all smiles.

"I guess you didn't hear," Sonny replies.

"Hear what?" Amber asks.

"The big accident tonight on I-95 with a semi-truck."

The girls shake their heads in unison.

"I could be wrong, but I'm pretty sure Debra's husband George was one of the three that died," Sonny mumbles.

Amber's face immediately drains of all color, as her knees

buckle under her.

Sonny reaches out his arm and steading her.

Zya and Dominque stare at him in disbelief.

Zya speaks first, alarmed, "This can't be, not George. There has to be some mistake. I just saw George two days ago. He's fine—he can't be dead."

"I'm sorry to be the one to tell you. Please give Debra my best. Her husband George was an okay guy," Sonny says, bowing his head as he walks away.

"Why didn't she call us?" Amber asks, looking at Zya and Dominque.

"I don't know. We better get our butts over there pronto." Zya grabs Amber's arm and heads for the door. "That girl needs us now."

"Wait—you can't leave. This party is for you. You're the guest of honor," Dominque exclaims.

"Girl—watch me! These people are here today, gone tomorrow. They love you when you're on top, then they can't be bothered when you hit rock bottom. Debra is my friend, no matter where I am, I'll be there for her."

The girls rush outside as Zya yells for the valet to please get her car immediately—it's an emergency. All three sit somberly and quietly as Zya maneuvers around the evening traffic to Debra's house.

Debra rushes to the door when she sees the headlights from Zya's car.

Amber is the first one to her, greeting her with a hug. "I'm so sorry," Amber says.

"Oh, me too," replies Debra, a bit too quickly. "I wish you had called before coming over. George should have been home

34

by now; I guess he's running late. I'm afraid you guys can't stay. It wouldn't be a very romantic dinner with five of us. I hope you understand." Debra is in shock, or she doesn't know yet.

"We won't be long, I promise. Can we just come inside for a few minutes?" Amber asks.

Debra steps aside, allowing the three of them in. Candles are burning on the dining room table that's beautifully set with Debra's fine china and crystal glasses. The candles have burned to the bottom, and there's a bottle of champagne sitting in a bucket, forming a large condensation ring on the wood table. In the middle of the table sits a small gift, wrapped in teal paper with a big frilly bow. The music is playing softly in the background, and the roast she has made for dinner fills the house with a delicious aroma.

"Debra, come sit next with me on the sofa. I need to talk to you a minute," Amber says.

All four women sit in the living room.

Debra sits fidgeting next to Amber. She looks out the window every time she hears a car drive by. Debra's eyes dart around, looking none of them in the eye.

"Honey, has anyone called tonight?"

"I've had a few calls, but I've let the machine pick them up," Debra says, looking down at her hands.

"Who called you?" Zya asks.

"Just some people—wrong number," Debra answers, quickly.

"What did they say?" Amber asks.

"It's not important. They got the wrong number, so it doesn't matter. Where is George?"

Debra gets up from the couch and goes to look out the window. "I should probably call him, but I don't want him talking on his cell while he's driving. That's how so many accidents happen, you know? I'll wait a few more minutes, and then I'll try," Debra says as she walks over to the dining room table and picks up her cell phone, looking at it, willing for George to call.

"Debra, please humor me and tell me what these people said…the wrong numbers?"

Debra, frustrated now, turns on her heel and heads to the bathroom. As she leaves the room, she says, "Listen for yourself if you're that interested. I'm telling you, they've got the wrong number."

Amber gets up and hits the play button on the answering machine. The first message, 5:10 p.m., "Mrs. Harris, this is Sergeant Lee from the Florida Highway Patrol. Please call me at 555-1510 as soon as possible, please—it's urgent."

The second message, 5:30 p.m., "Mrs. Harris, this is Sergeant Lee again from the Florida Highway Patrol. It's of the utmost importance that you call me back immediately at 555-1510."

The third message, 6 p.m., "Mrs. Harris, this is Sergeant Lee again, ma'am I must speak to you regarding an accident this evening. I'm sending over two officers to speak with you. They should be there within the next thirty minutes."

Amber looks at the clock and sees it's 8:30 p.m. Surely, they've been here by now.

Amber jumps as the doorbell rings.

Debra comes rushing out of the bathroom. "Don't answer that. If it's those officers again, don't answer it. They have the wrong person."

Zya stands up and puts her arms around Debra's shoulders as she passes, stopping her. Zya whispers to her, "It's okay honey, let Amber tell them that." Zya looks over at Amber, and faintly smiles.

Amber slips out the door to greet the two officers. "Are you Mrs. Harris?" the first one asks.

"No, I'm her best friend, Amber. Debra—Mrs. Harris seems in shock right now. I believe she knows something has happened, but she doesn't want to believe it. If you come in and tell her, her husband has been killed, then...then…" Amber puts her hands to her face when she hears herself say the word *killed*. Overcome with emotion, she sobs uncontrollably.

One officer replies, "I understand. You don't need to say anymore. If it's any comfort, her husband died instantly; he didn't suffer."

Amber nods as the tears continue to stream down her face.

"Someone will need to tell Mrs. Harris. We can come in and tell her ourselves if it would be easier for you."

"No, no, I'll tell her. I'm here with her other two best friends, and we'll tell her. We'll stay with her tonight," Amber whispers.

"We'll come back tomorrow afternoon if that's okay, and we can answer any questions she may have."

"Thank you, officers, that would be great. Thanks."

Amber wipes her eyes and nose, trying to regain her composure as she watches the officers walk down the driveway.

She opens the door, looking down, and closes it softly behind her. Before moving in, she looks up at Debra.

Debra's eyes pleading, please, they have the wrong person?

"I'm so sorry Debra," Amber blubbers out as she walks over and wraps her arms around her.

Dominque and Zya join in.

Debra does nothing. She just stands there—frozen.

"No! No! George is fine! He got stuck at work. It happens all the time. He'll be home soon. He's okay," Debra demands.

"No, he's not okay, George was killed…" Amber's voice trails off.

"Stop it! Stop it right now! Please leave! I want you all to leave my house this instant! I won't listen to this! George will be home any minute. You just wait and see." Debra storms to the front door, opening it for them to leave.

"We're not going anywhere. I know it's so unfair, but Debra, they don't have the wrong person. George isn't coming home," Amber says as she closes it.

"Why are you doing this to me? I thought you were my friends. I thought you loved me. Why are you hurting me like this?" Debra begs, looking upon all three of their tear-streaked faces.

"The officer said he didn't suffer—it was instantaneous; he felt nothing."

"No! No! It can't be!" Debra sobs as she sinks to the floor. Sitting back on her heels with her hands in front of her, she bangs on the carpet with her fists and says, "Today is his birthday. I have a surprise for him. He has to come home. I have to tell him—he needs to know."

Amber joins her on the floor while Dominque and Zya look on in desperation. Amber takes Debra's hands in hers.

Debra's tear-filled eyes look into Amber's.

"Why don't you tell me what George needs to know?"

Debra rolls off her heels onto her side, lying down in a fetal position. "He's going to be a daddy again. We're having a baby. We did it, we're pregnant," Debra answers as she sobs uncontrollably.

Amber lies down on the floor in front of Debra and puts one arm over her shoulders.

Not a dry eye in the house when this should be a joyous occasion. George and Debra had been trying to get pregnant again for the last five years. After their daughter Tracey was born six years ago, they hadn't been able to conceive. They both wanted another baby so badly.

After several minutes, Zya wipes her eyes, stands up, and says, "Now would be a good time for a stiff drink. I think even I need one. I'll get four glasses."

Dominque stands up and follows her into the kitchen. "I'll get the vodka from the freezer."

Amber moves Debra's hair out of her eyes and says, "Let's get off the floor and sit on the couch."

Debra's face is somber and pale. Her eyes are sunken with dark rings underneath. Debra looks as if she's aged ten years. Her face is devoid of all emotion.

Zya hands Debra a drink and says, "Here, honey, drink this, it will help."

"Do you think that is such a good idea?" Amber asks quietly, motioning to her own belly, reminding Zya about Debra's pregnancy.

"Under the circumstances, I think she needs this, and it may help calm her nerves," Zya answers.

Debra takes the glass and, after looking at their faces for a moment, tilts it back and drains it in one gulp.

Dominque breaks down the romantic dinner table while Zya pours everyone, except herself, a second drink.

Debra gulps down the second vodka as she did the first and feels its numbing effect. "What am I going to do?" she helplessly asks Amber.

"You're going to take it one day at a time, for starters. I know everything seems hopeless right now, but you have to believe me, you're going to be all right. We are going to be here for you, no matter what. You need it—you got it. We are in this together. You're not doing this alone."

Debra covers her face and begins sobbing again while dropping her head in Amber's lap.

Amber moves the hair out of her face and whispers, "It's going to be okay, I promise. It's going to be okay."

After three shots of vodka and gallons of tears, Debra finally falls asleep in exhaustion.

Amber, not wanting to leave Debra's side, calls her sister Megan. Tracey was spending the night with her aunt. Not the best way to break the news, but Amber feels it's better if Megan knows earlier rather than later.

"Hi, Megan, it's Amber."

"Oh, hi, how are you?"

"I'm all right."

"Are you sure you're all right, you sound as if you've been crying?"

"I'm so sorry to tell you this over the phone…George was killed in a traffic accident tonight."

"Oh my God, NO! Debra! How's Debra?"

"She's exhausted and sleeping right now. I don't know for how long, but she's resting for now," Amber replies.

"I'll be right over. I'll be there in a few minutes," Megan states.

"Megan, I know you want to be here, and if you want, I'll come over there and stay with Tracey. I think it might be easier for Debra to face Tracey in the morning. She's still in shock."

"I don't know what to say." Megan's tears start flowing as she looks over at Tracey, sleeping peacefully on the couch. She envisions Tracey having a good dream right now—she's smiling. "Are you going to stay with her tonight?"

"Yes, Zya, Dominque, and I are all here."

"As much as I want to be there right now for her, I'll stay here and let Tracey sleep. I'll bring her home in the morning."

"Okay, that's a plan. Can you text me when you're on your way?"

"Sure, do you want me to say anything to Tracey? She's a smart girl, you know—she'll know something's up."

"Yes, she is, but I'm sure Debra will want to tell her."

"Okay, I'll do my best. Anything else I can do?"

"I don't think so. But if there are any friends or anyone you think should know, will you call them? But please ask them not to call Debra right now. She needs a few days, and we'll contact everyone with the arrangements once they're made."

"Sure, I can do that. George has some buddies who will want to know, I'll call them in the morning."

"Thanks, Megan. We'll see you in the morning."

Amber hangs up the phone as fresh tears flow. She can't help but see George's smiling face in her mind. George was always smiling—always happy. Old fashioned at times, but George could always make you laugh no matter what. That man was in love with life, Debra and Tracey...so in love with everyone. George will be sorely missed. She can't even imagine how much hurt and pain Debra must feel right now.

"Here, looks like you need this," Zya says as she hands Amber a glass of wine.

"Thanks, you're right. I need all the numbing I can get right now." Amber slumps down into the couch, taking a large drink.

Zya slowly shakes her head. "We're going to have to help Debra through this as much as possible. She's going to need to deal with this the easiest and best way she can, you know."

"I know. I'm not sure exactly how to help her; I've never dealt with this before, but I know we will do everything we can for her."

"Oh, I don't doubt we'll bend over backward for her. What I'm trying to say…the baby. It's bad enough she's lost George; if she loses this baby, it will be a double whammy for her. We have to help her deal with the stress and make sure she takes care of herself."

Amber sits up. "You're right. You know I didn't even think about that, but you're right. Maybe tomorrow we should call her OB and let him know what's going on. Maybe he has some suggestions."

"I tell you what, I'll call her OB tomorrow, if you call Dr. Phelps."

"Brian Phelps, yes, I should call him. He said if there is ever anything I need to call him. I don't know if he can squeeze her in, but I'm sure he can recommend someone."

"Don't you dare let him push her off on someone else. He's the best there is, and he owes you big time. His practice wouldn't be what it is today if it wasn't for that article you wrote about him two years ago. You better believe that man owes you, and the least he can do is help Debra," Zya states.

"I'll call him tomorrow. If there is any way he can fit Debra into his schedule, he will. I know he will."

"Amber, Amber, wake up! George didn't come home yet! Where do you think he could be?" Debra is shaking Amber from her sleep on the couch, asking for George.

"Debra, honey, don't you remember? George isn't coming home."

"Not coming home? George always comes home. Did he have a meeting or something?"

Amber puts her arms around Debra's shoulders and hugs her tightly. They rock back and forth as Amber smooths her hair and says, "George isn't ever coming back home, I'm so sorry. George is gone."

Debra sobs again, repeating, "No! No!"

"Dr. Phelps, hi, it's Amber Fiore from NeoQuest Enterprises."

"Oh yes, my angel from heaven. The beautiful brunette I can thank for my sixty-hour, seven-day work weeks," Brian replies, chuckling.

"Do I sense a bit of hostility from your newfound success?"

"Absolutely not! Your article turned my one-digit client practice into a high two-digit one. I have no complaints. Remember what they say, be careful what you wish for. So, what can I do for you?"

"Remember when you told me if there was ever anything I

needed…don't hesitate to ask?"

"Did I say that? Are you sure? Just kidding, of course I remember, how can I help you?"

"I would never take you up on your offer, except it's for someone very special to me. My good friend Debra lost her husband yesterday to that horrific tractor-trailer accident on I-95. I know people deal with loss all the time, and she'll be okay, but she just found out she's pregnant. She and her husband had been trying for a few years. They have one child. A daughter Tracey—she's six, but they had been trying for a while for another one. Yesterday was her husband's birthday. He didn't know about the pregnancy, she was going to surprise him with it at dinner. I know you're very busy, but please, please can you help her? If she loses this baby now after losing her husband, she'll be devastated. She's in shock and forgets he's gone. She keeps asks me when he's coming home."

"Amber, calm down and take a deep breath. I'm not seeing any new patients right now, however, I will see Debra for you. I'll do what I can to help. Promise me, you won't tell a soul I'm seeing her, okay?"

"Okay." Amber wipes her eyes. "Thank you—thank you so much. When should I bring her?"

Looking through his appointment book, he replies, "Well, I definitely have no time during regular office hours, but you can bring her by this evening around 6:30 p.m. Will that work for you?"

"Yes! And Dr. Phelps, thank you."

"My pleasure, she sounds like someone very close to you."

"She is. I feel so much better knowing you'll talk with her."

"Then I'll see you and Debra…"

"Harris, Debra Harris," Amber states. "This evening at 6:30. Again, thank you."

As Dr. Brian Phelps hangs up the phone, he can't help but think he knows that name, Debra Harris. Where does he know that name from? After a few minutes of thought, he gives up. It will come to him, eventually.

☙

"I spoke with Debra's OB today, Dr. Francisco. He was very nice and understanding. He called in a prescription for her to take if she needs it. It's a tranquilizer. He feels it's the safest one to use. But only if Debra needs it," Zya tells Amber on the phone.

"Did Dr. Francisco know Debra was pregnant?"

"Yeah, he spoke with Debra the day she took the pregnancy test. Debra has an appointment to see him tomorrow morning at ten."

"I'm not sure Mr. Freeman is going to be so understanding about me taking time off right now I'm under deadline. I'm working on that development boom downtown; how boring," Amber states.

"Don't worry about it, I was planning on taking her myself."

"How can you take her? I know you're under pressure to get your spring line done before the end of this month. Do I need to remind you, fall is just around the corner?"

Zya laughs into the receiver. "Thank you, Mom. No, I don't need reminding what day it is. I can't explain it, but last week I dreamed my entire spring line. It was like the only way my brain would cooperate was to lose some sleep. I've got all the designs roughly sketched out, and Stan is helping me with fabric choices and final drawings. I'm okay in that department. I mean it—I'm not just flapping my gums. I can take some time and help, so don't worry about me. In fact, let's make it clear right now…any appointments or responsibilities to help Debra during working hours, I get, okay?"

"Are you sure?" Amber asks.

"Yes, I'm sure."

"You get the working days, and I'll take nights and weekends."

"Oh, girl, don't you dare leave Dominque out. We know her nights are pretty much taken up,"—Zya snickers—"but I bet she can help on the weekends. I can help too, but you get first dibs."

"Okay, it's settled. I spoke with Dr. Phelps today, and he has agreed to see Debra at 6:30 p.m. tonight."

"Tonight! Isn't that too soon?"

"You may think so, but Dr. Phelps is famous for his unique ways of handling bereavement, and he believes in speaking with the widowed ASAP."

"Well, I sure hope he knows what he's doing. He does any more harm to my girl, and I'm going to have to open up a can of *whup-ass* on him!"

Amber laughs and says, "I don't doubt you would do just that. But trust me, Dr. Phelps is an expert."

Amber pulls up to the small cottage-office of Dr. Brian

Phelps, Psychiatrist. His office connects to his home off Broward Boulevard. It's a busy street heading west, however this far east, where it almost ends, many small homes are now businesses.

Debra stares out the window, watching a little girl and her mom walking their dog along the sidewalk. The girl looks up and waves. She waves back as tears start streaming down her face.

Dr. Phelps comes to the door after Amber gently knocks.

After an affection hug with Amber, he extends his hand to Debra. "Hi, I'm Dr. Phelps, but please call me Brian; Dr. Phelps makes me feel so old."

In his practice, seeing the bereaved shortly after their loss, he's used to seeing his patients at their worst. However, this cold, almost zombie-like woman standing before him, is like nothing he's seen before. She's beyond numb and shock; her sunken eyes and pale skin make her look almost dead herself. He's sure there is probably a beautiful woman under there. His job is to find her.

Forcing a smile, she says, "Okay."

He escorts the ladies into his office.

"Debra, first, I would like to extend my sincerest sympathy. I know you're having a tough time and it probably seems strange to be meeting with me so soon. Expressing your feelings and discussing your recent tragedy is the last thing on your mind, and that's okay."

She nods her head and wipes the tears from her face.

"Our time together will be a two-way street. I am not one of those doctors who just sit there and let you talk. I want to know what you think, and I'll give you my thoughts. Instead of thinking about this as a doctor-client relationship, I'm hoping we'll be able to meet as any two friends and discuss any issues you're dealing with. I won't take up too much of your time tonight, but I would like to explain a few things about the grieving process to you. First, there is no right or wrong way to feel right now. However you feel, is perfectly normal. Not feeling anything right now is also okay. There are many steps going through the grieving process. There is no right or wrong way, or time limit; you do what's right for you. No two people are going to handle it the same. You are going to get all kinds of advice; some helpful and some, not so much; and hopefully, all kinds of support. People mean well, but aren't sure how to show it."

She sobs uncontrollably and puts her hands to her face, saying between sobs, "I'm sorry. I'm so sorry."

"Please don't apologize, crying is very healing. Never be afraid to cry."

"Thank you," she mumbles as she regains some control and blows her nose.

"I have something for you." He pulls out a box and inside is a beautiful pink taffeta covered book. "This is a journal. It's not homework—it isn't something you have to do. It's just my gift to you. Some of my patients have found writing in one very helpful in the healing process. Others have found it time-consuming and of no use. If it's helpful to you, please use it."

"What do I write in it?" she asks, with tear-stained cheeks.

"Anything you want to. You can write what you feel, what you think you feel, you can even write things you want to say to other people but can't. Heck, you can use it to write recipes if you want."

She gives him a faint smile.

"It's whatever you want it to be, or not to be, it's up to you."

"Thank you. I can't promise I'll use it, but I do appreciate it."

"Please, no promises. If it helps, I'm glad to give it."

He gets a glimpse of her beautiful smile. His heart beats faster, and he feels as if someone has punched him in the chest. Déjà vu?

After being lost in his thoughts, he shakes it off. "Amber, if you don't mind, I'd like to speak with Debra for just a few minutes alone."

"Oh, okay, I'll wait in the lobby."

Amber looks at Debra for the cue it's okay to leave.

"It's okay," Debra says, motioning for Amber to wait for her in the lobby.

"I want to assure you I take my doctor-client confidentiality privilege seriously. However, if I feel there's something of grave concern I need to discuss with your support system, who is that person?"

Brian is trying to figure out why this grieving widow sitting in front of him is making his palms sweat and his heart pound. Has he met her before?

"What kind of grave concern are you talking about?"

"Anything I feel that puts you in immediate physical danger."

"I guess that person would be Amber. I have a sister, Megan, but I think Amber would be the better choice. And Megan would agree. Amber is like a sister too."

"So, do I have your permission to discuss ways to help you

through this process with her?"

"Oh, of course, you can. But you won't talk about specifics, will you? I mean, Amber and I are close, but there are things even she doesn't know."

"I promise, only if I feel it's an emergency or helpful coping skills for you. Everything you say in this room, or over the phone, will be held in the strictest of confidence. Okay?"

"Okay," Debra replies, nodding.

"Before I bring Amber back in, is there anything you want to talk about?"

A long silence before Debra finally speaks. "I don't know how I feel right now or if I feel right," Debra replies more like a question than a statement.

"That's perfectly normal—you are experiencing shock; the body's way of dealing with something greater than what you can handle. Your body will only let you deal with fractions of this a little at a time. You can expect to feel great sadness and loss; and at other times nothing at all. It's your body's way of controlling how much emotional pain you deal with at any one time. How often or how long they last, these periods of grief or numbness, will depend entirely on you. I understand you're pregnant."

Crying again and looking into her hands fussing with the used tissue, Debra nods.

"Do you want to talk about that?"

Through her tears, Debra tries to make sense. "I want to…"—sobbing—"to be…"—sobbing—"happy." More crying into her hands. "I'm sorry, Dr. Phelps, I mean Brian…"—more sobs— "I'm not sure I can right now."

"That's all right, and please again, don't apologize for crying. I'm glad to see you letting the grief out. That way I know you're not holding back on me."

A brief smile flashes across her face as she wipes her eyes.

Brian reaches out for the Kleenex box next to his chair and hands it to her.

"Thank you." Debra takes a tissue, pauses, and then takes another one.

"George and I have been trying for the last five years to have another child. We were just about coming to terms that we may never have another one when I got pregnant." Debra sobs hard again; however, she says, "He didn't know. I didn't get the chance to tell him. I wanted it to be perfect; I wanted it to be the right time. He doesn't know—he doesn't know we're going to have a baby." Debra continues to sob into her hands.

Without giving it much thought, Brian gets up and sits down next to her on the couch. He puts his arms around her and holds her close to his chest as her sobs turn into howls. *George, her husband's name was George—no, it can't be.*

After a few minutes, and she quiets, Brian realizes what he's done. He cares about this woman—but that's crazy. He's feeling grief because of her pain. But he just met her.

Debra sits up, wiping her face as Brian stands and walks to the back of his desk.

"I'm sorry, I don't know what came over me. I know no more apologizing. Thank you. Thank you for helping me."

Trying to regain his composure and remain professional, Brian responds, "No need to thank me. Why don't we call it quits for today, unless, of course, there is something else you want to talk about?"

Sensing a slight coolness in him, Debra responds, "No, I

don't need anything right now."

"Okay, great. Please use the journal if you need it, and I'll speak with Amber for a few minutes if you don't mind."

Brian opens the door for Debra as she responds, "No, that's okay; take all the time you need."

"Amber, would you mind giving me a few minutes?" Brian asks.

"Not at all," replies Amber. "Deb, I'll be right out."

Debra nods and sits down.

"Is everything okay?" asks Amber, a little confused over the cold vibes bouncing off him.

"Yes, everything is fine. Debra's in shock, but that's to be expected. Amber, I know you're aware of how busy my practice is, so I'm afraid I'm going to have to recommend another therapist for Debra. I know I owe you the favor, but I think she'll be better off with a different psychiatrist."

"What do you mean, another one? You're the best?"

"Thank you for that vote of confidence, but in Debra's case, I don't think I'm the best choice. I have some colleagues I know will be able to help her. I'll make some calls and see who can squeeze her in."

"Please, Dr. Phelps, Debra is my closest friend—she needs you. Can you help her through the hardest parts? Later, if you still feel she should see someone else, then we'll look for a replacement?"

Brian knows seeing this patient will not be good. There is something about this woman—he can't put his finger on it. It's their first session together, and he already broke the rules.

"Okay, but we have to agree, if I think she needs a fresh approach, you'll support my decision to bring in another colleague."

Amber agrees, a bit bewildered, as she stands up and shakes Brian's hand.

CHAPTER FOUR

"Hi Debra, won't you please come in and have a seat." Teddy Randover, George and Debra's attorney, greets her at his office for the estate proceedings. Teddy's office is Old English style, with cherry wood bookcases, a matching desk, and credenza. Leather chairs and a couch form a sitting area away from Teddy's chunky traditional desk. The dark wood might seem gloomy in most offices, but not Teddy's. Being on the eighteenth-floor and two blocks from the ocean, the two large picture windows frame the perfect view of the deep blue Atlantic.

Teddy fits well in his environment. A distinguished gentleman in his late fifties always dressed impeccably in a black or gray Armani suit and brightly colored Italian silk tie. Teddy is very traditional, yet he knows how to relax in an old pair of jeans and a T-shirt. Teddy's wife, Sylvia, is friendly and lively; she swears she fell in love with the relaxed Teddy, not the lawyer. She even insists he leaves the lawyer persona outside when he gets home.

"Debra, I know this is very difficult for you. Please, if at any time you want me to stop, or go back over anything, let me know. My time is yours; we'll go however fast or slow you want, okay?"

"Okay," Debra whispers.

Somehow she's been able to pull herself together for to-day's meeting. Her face still bears the signs of deep grief with swollen eyes from hours upon hours of crying, she managed some make-up, fixed her hair, and her eyes are dry—at least for the moment. She doesn't care how she looks, but she knew it was important for her to pull herself together; George would have wanted that. Instead of picking out a dull black pantsuit to match her mood, Debra wore a silk light pink shell dress with matching strappy sandals. When she looked at her reflection before leaving the house, she knew George was smiling down on her.

"First, before we go over the paperwork, George left this video for you. He insisted it be the first thing you see when you came here. George has always had a video here for you since the day he knew you two were going to marry. He recently brought me an updated one—just last week. Are you ready?"

Tears spring into Debra's eyes as she nods. *Leave it to George to be prepared...even for this.*

The video starts with George sitting in his home office, working at his desk. The camera zooms in for a closeup, and George looks up at the camera.

"Oh, I guess the zoom button works," George says, chuckling as he lifts the remote, so it's visible.

Wet streaks instantly appear down Debra's cheeks as she sees George's beautiful smile.

"Hi honey, I know if you're watching this, I must no longer be with you. Many times, I berated myself for being so anal about these videos, but I'm glad I did them. The last video was about three years ago, and I felt I needed a new one. Maybe this is what they call a mid-life crisis. Next week is my fortieth birthday, and I guess I just feel I need to get things in order. There's so much I want to say to you, and I'm sure it won't come out in the right order, but you know me, I plunge ahead and reorganize later."

George's chuckle at himself gets a smile from Debra. As she watches his face and smile, her chest fills up with that incredible warm fuzzy feeling she affectionately calls the *Georgy bear* effect. She can't help herself; her hand reaches out, caressing his cheek on the screen.

"Debra, on this day, you and I have been married for twelve years, seven months, one week, one day and"—looking at his watch—"almost two hours. I won't get as precise on our time together, but you've been a part of my life for over fifteen years now. As I sit here and think about turning forty, I realize I've spent most of my adulthood enjoying what most men dream of—the perfect wife and friend.

"When I was a kid, I used to think men just got married, bought the house, had a few kids, got a dog, and then one day retired. When I met you, I knew all those things were possible and much more. You are the one person who compliments me —you complete my sentences because we're so much alike. You are the one who makes me whole. You make my life worth living.

"We've made some ambitious plans for our future. I was going to write that book finally, take a trip to Europe, and one day sail around the world. I hope we got to do some of that. Even if we haven't, I wouldn't change a thing. If I had a choice of living to be ninety-years old without you or only living a short while with you, I'm glad we fell in love. My life of ninety years would be nothing compared to the life I have with you.

"I know this is very difficult for you, and you wish you could be with me, but please try to remember all we had and don't dwell on the things we didn't get to do. Remember all the love and wonderful times we've had. Tracey needs you. You need to be strong and help her. You're a terrific mother and her best friend. You'll help her get through this, remember her daddy, and all the wonderful times we've had.

"I can't be with you anymore, but I'll be watching over you from above. There is a part of me inside you right now. A part you'll always have, no matter what."

As Debra hears these words, her face twists in anguish, and she says, "He knew. How did he know?"

Teddy pauses the video and says, "Knew what, Debra?"

"About the baby—I didn't get the chance to tell him…he already knew."

"I'm not sure I understand what you're saying," Teddy says, confused.

"I'm pregnant. I didn't tell George right away because I wanted to surprise him. I was waiting for the right time. I was going to tell him over dinner on his birthday."

Teddy sits down next to Debra on the couch and puts his arm around her shoulder. Looking into Debra's eyes, he says, "Debra, I'm not sure that's what George meant—and we'll never know for sure. Maybe he means you have his heart, and you always will. Or maybe, in some strange way, he knew about the baby. What I do know is George had to—needed to record a new video for you."

Debra wipes her eyes and blows her nose.

"Are you okay to continue?" Teddy asks.

Debra nods, dabbing at her eyes.

"Debra, I want you to be happy. I know that sounds like the furthest thing from your mind right now, but trust me, in time you'll be happy again. It's said, there's only one person for us; how fortunate we are when we find that special someone. But I think some people have more than one soul mate. They deserve a second chance—someone like you. We both know that you could stay single if you want to, honoring my life and my death. I don't want you to do that. You touched my life in so many ways, it would be a shame for you not to touch someone else's. Oh, I know I can never be replaced, come on this is me, George Harris here!" George chuckles. "But seriously, don't mourn my death too long. Life is a gift—please live yours to the fullest. Don't close up and shut people out. Teach Tracey about love; show her by example.

"I've loved you since the day we met, and I always will. I know you'll love me forever and a day and I'm not asking you to stop, I'm just want you to be happy. Try to smile every day, especially now, for me, please. Remember, I'm watching you… I'll know when you do."

The corners of Debra's mouth involuntarily do just that at George's words and his bright smile on the screen.

"I see that…I knew you could do it. Baby, I love you and miss you, and I thank God for what we have. Be happy."

Fresh tears start streaming as the screen turns to snow.

"Debra, you okay?"

"Yes, I'm all right. I would love some water if you don't mind."

"Not at all, I'll be right back."

Teddy fills a glass with ice and water from for her.

59

"Can we continue?"

"Yes, please," she says as she takes the glass, sipping from it.

"First, I'd like to talk about the funeral arrangements. George left me instructions on your behalf if you like." Debra nods.

"He wants to be cremated, however, he understood your wish for a burial, so long as you don't have an open casket. As far as how to dress him, he said to bury him naked; he wants to go out the same way he came in."

Debra smiles. "I guess another reason not to have an open casket."

Teddy winks at Debra. "He would like his favorite song *Born to Be Wild,* playing at his celebration of life."

As Debra listens to Teddy, her emotions spin out of control. Seeing his face today is so painful, yet her heart swells thinking about what a wonderful loving man he was.

"Yes, please make the arrangements, and of course, I'll do whatever George wants, but with one small exception. I know George wants to be buried naked, but I'd like to give the mortician George's lucky silk boxers. I think it's more fitting for George than his birthday suit."

Smiling, Teddy responds, "Sure. I won't go into detail now about the specifics of George's estate, but I want to put your mind at ease and let you know you'll have no financial worries for the rest of your life. George has also taken care of Tracey's college and other expenses and, there's plenty for the new one's future as well."

"Thank you," Debra says as she rises to shake Teddy's hand.

Teddy shakes hers in return and kisses her on the cheek. "Take good care of yourself. You have Tracey and this one to think about now," Teddy says, as he walks her out of his office.

"Thanks—I will. Or, I promise I'll try." She gives Teddy a weak smile. "It's a shame George will never get to meet this one," she says, rubbing her abdomen.

On a hot and humid mid-June morning, Debra attempts to drag herself out of bed to get ready for what she perceives to be one of the hardest days of her life. George's funeral service starts in less than four hours. *I hope I have enough make-up to cover the bags under my eyes.*

Lying in bed, she looks over at George's side and rubs her hand over his pillow. Tears roll down her cheek as she imagines her Prince Charming lying beside her. Wiping them, she rolls over and gets out of bed. She needs to put a smile on and keep it together for Tracey. She pushes herself off the bed and rushes to the bathroom, lifting the lid of the toilet just in time. *Morning sickness—of course, why not add that to today's misery?*

Amber arrives an hour before the service to ride with Debra and Tracey to the church. Debra opens the front door and watches her approach with a big bag in her arms.

"Hi honey, how are you doing?" Amber asks, hugging Debra.

"As well as can be expected. I've been throwing up all morning. Probably morning sickness, but it might be nerves too. Anyway, as much as I am dreading this, I am also looking forward to celebrating his life today. For me, I'm not saying goodbye, I'm saying thank you."

Amber's eyes pool as she watches her best friend. She can't imagine how she feels. "Well, if it's any consolation, you look great. The blue in your dress matches your eyes perfectly. I can barely see the deep circles under them," Amber says, chuckling.

Debra smiles and says, "It was George's favorite. He said it made me look young and carefree. I thought he might want to see me wearing it today."

Tracey comes rushing out of her room. "I'm not going! Daddy is coming home soon, and I want to be here when he does," she says defiantly.

Debra's heart swells as she scoops her up in her arms. "Honey, we talked about this last night. Daddy is not here with us anymore—he's up in heaven with God and all the pretty angels. He's got important business to do there and promises he'll be waiting for us when we get there."

"I want to go now! I want to see Daddy now!"

"You will, one day…but not yet. He misses us terribly, but he says we have important things to do here. Daddy told me you're going to grow up to be a beautiful, strong woman who will make a difference in this world," Debra says, trying to reassure Tracey.

"I don't want to grow up! I just want my daddy," Tracey says through tears, burying her face in Debra's shoulder.

"I know honey; I want to see him too. It's tough, but I promise it'll get easier. We'll always love Daddy, and he'll always love us. We'll never forget him—I promise."

Debra takes Tracey back into her room to get her dressed

for the service. Amber watches in awe of how natural mother-hood is for Debra. Amber could never have that patience.

As Debra, Tracey, and Amber prepare to leave for the service, Amber picks up the big bag.

"What's in the bag?" Debra asks.

"George made me promise him I would get the tackiest, most colorful jackets, scarves, and sweaters I could find and bring them to his funeral. He said if anyone dares come dressed in black, I'm to give them something colorful to wear."

"When did George make you promise this?" Debra asks, confused.

"When Tracey was born, I didn't want to talk about it, but he made me listen, and promise. He wanted a celebration...to remember the good times." Amber hands the bag to the chauffeur and steps into the limo with Debra and Tracey.

As they arrive at the church, they're overjoyed to see hundreds of people milling around outside the church, mostly dressed in bright, cheerful colors.

Amber squeezes Debra's hand and says, "Everybody loved George—he touched so many lives."

Teddy greets them and escorts them into the church before the guests enter.

Debra looks over the beautiful photos of her late husband; some even make her giggle. There's one with George's face all covered with food. That picture was taken as Tracey was just starting to eat solids. She refused to eat, and just when Debra was beyond exasperation, George turned it into a game. He grabbed his food and started shoveling it into his mouth, getting it everywhere. Tracey laughed so hard, she had difficulty catching her breath. It did the trick, though; she soon grabbed her food and started shoving it in her mouth.

There were pictures of them together in the Caribbean. George got way too much sun one day, and when he came out of the bathroom to go to dinner, he had on a red shirt and pants. He somehow fashioned antennas out of red napkins and coat hangers and had big red oven mitts on his hands. He came out and said, 'If I'm going to look like a lobster, then by-golly, I might as well be one.' Debra never found out how he got his hands on those things.

One of Debra's favorite pictures was there, even though it was posed. Teddy knew how much she loved it and made sure it was there. Debra touches George's cheek on it and whispers, "I love you."

Debra turns to Teddy as he asks, "Ready?"

She nods as they're ushered to a nearby waiting room.

The doors to the church open as the guests fill the pews. It's standing room only as many guests line up along the side and back walls.

After seating Debra and Tracey, the priest begins George's celebration. Debra hears nothing. Her wet eyes are glued on her favorite photo of George.

Teddy, taking over to give the eulogy. "I'm sure I don't have to tell you about George's sense of humor. This envelope wasn't to be opened until I got up here. It seems he triple taped, and super glued it shut. You got me George."

The room fills with gentle laughter.

"Ah-Ha!" Finally succeeding, Teddy reads, "Welcome, family, friends, colleagues, and everyone else, as we celebrate George Harris—me. The biggest and most wonderful miracle is life. Ever wonder how it's possible for a man and a woman together to create that wonder? I have many times. Every time I looked into my daughter, Tracey's face, I couldn't help but think, I helped make her—she's a part of me.

"We have many choices how we live our lives. My philosophy has always been to enjoy every day as if it were our last. And most importantly, leave a legacy behind. I've always been an off-the-cuff kind of guy, so I'd like my good friend Teddy, he's the one reading this for me, to blurt out the first word that comes to mind when he thinks of me."

"Witty," Teddy answers, smiling.

Continuing to read George's eulogy. "George is asking for anyone else to shout out one word that best described him."

"Loving."

"Kind."

"Generous."

"Unselfish."

"Remarkable."

"Giving."

"Funny."

"Loyal."

"Gifted."

They shout words out from all over the church.

During a slight pause, Tracey says in barely a whisper, "Daddy."

Teddy wiping his eyes continues, "I've tried hard to leave this world a better place. I hope I've succeeded. My life has truly been extraordinary sharing it with my beautiful wife, my best friend Debra, and the world's prettiest, smartest and sweetest daughter, Tracey. To have known and laughed with all of you has made me a better person. I'm truly thankful for the time I had with all of you and for everything you've shared with me. I am blessed for the life I have lived.

"Before you leave today to go to the beach and release motivational messages in balloons in celebration of my life, I would like to fulfill one last wish for my Tracey. Missy, can you please come forward? You see Tracey, I promised you one day we would get a dog; in case I hadn't fulfilled that wish for you, I think today should be that day. Meet Bear, your new puppy."

Amber, Dominque, and Zya finish their Monday evening kickboxing class in exhaustion.

"Wow, Dom, I've never seen you so worked up. You got some pent-up frustrations in there or what?" Zya asks.

"I don't know—I'm just so angry!" Dominque screams.

"That bag was definitely a substitute for something!"

Amber adds, "Yeah, I know what you mean. I think we are all going through the stages of grieving. We're angry thinking about Debra. This should be one of the happiest times in her life, and she's dealing with losing George. I think we are all in disbelief and angry we can't take away her pain."

Changing the subject quickly before the tears start, Amber says, "I'm famished. Can we get a snack at the café before we leave? I think we all deserve it."

"You go ahead without me," Zya says. "Ramadan started last month, and I still have another hour before sundown."

Amber asks, "Zya, I thought you were revisiting being Muslim since you and Doug are finished?"

"I need to keep up appearances for Ashanti—for now."

Dominque interrupts, "You mean you can't eat anything during the day?"

"That's right, we fast throughout the day; but we eat until our hearts' content after sundown until dawn. It's for twenty-eight days, a moon cycle, and then we celebrate *Eid*. Then we feast all day!"

"So, explain to me again why you starve yourself every day for an entire month every year?" Amber asks.

"Ramadan is the most sacred month of the year. It's when we burn away our sins. A time when the Prophet Muhammad opened the gates of Heaven and closed the gates to Hell. It is also a time for us to appreciate our blessings and remember those who are less fortunate.

"At night, when we eat, we try to feed someone who isn't as blessed. Ashanti and I go down to the local food bank and bring a big pot of whatever we've made that night and share it with the homeless. We've also been collecting clothes, shoes, blankets…whatever the homeless need.

"On the last day of Ramadan, I bring a check for the total profits *Label Zya* earned during the holiday.

"The first day of *Eid*, the breaking of the fast is in a few days. We'll spend the morning cooking a feast we take to the food bank for all to enjoy. This is the best part of being Muslim—the part I know is teaching Ashanti the most valuable lessons. It's one of the main reasons I'm keeping up appearances. You should come with us sometime."

"I would love to go. I've helped serve Thanksgiving and Christmas dinner there. Feels great to take time out to help others. Count me in," Amber says.

"Great, I'll let you know what the date is so you can put it on your calendar. I want to get Debra involved too. I think she needs this; needs to feel like she's making a difference. What do you think?"

"I think I need to become Muslim," adds Dominque. "I'm having such a hard time losing this last ten pounds. I bet not eating would help."

"Wait." Amber looks over at Zya and says, "First, I think getting Debra involved is an excellent idea. You can count me in on getting her there. Second." She turns, looking Dominque in the eye, and adds, "Dom, lose ten pounds, where?"

Zya adds, "You know, your pinky was starting to look a little chubby, but I didn't want to say anything."

"No really, I need to lose ten pounds. You know the camera adds at least that, and I know that's why I'm not getting any callbacks. I was born to model, so I'll do whatever it takes to make that happen."

Zya and Amber look at each other. "I think you look perfect just the way you are," Amber states.

"I think you could gain a few, if you ask me," Zya adds.

"Oh well, maybe I should skip the treat at the café too. Thanks anyway, but I think I'm going home to jog on my treadmill for an hour," Dominque responds, not hearing a word Amber or Zya said.

Dominque turns on her heel and leaves while Zya and Amber look at each other in disbelief.

"Did she just say she was going to work out more?" Zya asks.

"We need to keep an eye on her. I think she's getting a little carried away with this modeling thing."

"I agree. I was planning on asking her to walk the catwalk

at my show next month in Milan. Do you think that's a good idea?"

"Are you kidding? She would love you for it. Maybe she will get it out of her system once and for all and come back to reality."

"Yeah, I was thinking her flaming red hair and pale skin would be dynamite modeling my wedding gown that closes my show. It's a big deal; I hope she's up for it."

"Call me crazy, but why don't we all go with you to Milan? It would be great for Debra, and I'm sure her mother would love to spend some quality time with Tracey. What do you think?"

"I think it's a great idea! Let me see if I can upgrade my room to a suite so we can all stay together. It will be like a week-long slumber party."

"Good afternoon, Miss Freshman," Zya says, greeting her daughter Ashanti on the first day of high school. Zya glows as she looks at her beautiful fourteen-year-old daughter with her smooth almond-colored skin and silky, long brown hair. *Well, at least Doug was good at something.*

"Hi, Mom."

"How was your first day?"

"It was great. I'm going to join the debate team, and swimming tryouts are next week. I want to help out at the nursing home down the street one afternoon a week too. I hope I can fit everything in."

"And still get your homework done?" Zya adds.

Ashanti smiles. "Yes, Mom, I promise I'll keep everything

prioritized. There just never seems to be enough hours in the days."

"Welcome to my world."

Ashanti kisses her mom on the cheek and runs upstairs. Zya watches her leave as the phone rings—it's Doug. Zya contemplates not answering, but he'll then call Ashanti on her cell phone and get her that way.

"Hello, Doug," Zya says with her pinched lips.

"Hey baby, I was thinking about you and thought I would give you a ring and tell you how much I miss you."

"That's nice, Doug, but I told you we're through. I can't keep doing this back and forth. One minute you want to be a loving father and companion, and the next, you want your freedom. Please, stop calling me—it's over!"

"But baby, that's what I'm calling to tell you. I'm different now, really," he says, trying to convince her.

"And how many times have I heard that before? Doug, please don't make this any harder than it already is."

"I was hoping you would have dinner with me tonight, and I could do this properly. However, here goes…Zya, I'm ready to settle down; will you marry me?"

Shocked and speechless, Zya stares out into space. She loves Doug, always has, and probably always will. She snaps back to reality; she's been down this road before. "Doug, the last thing I want to do is hurt your feelings. I'm sorry, but no, I won't marry you. I know you're saying the words, but you don't really mean them. Please, let's try to be civil for Ashanti."

"Well, if you cared at all about our daughter, you would say yes so I can come back home, and we could be one big happy family again," he angrily replies.

Zya's eyes tear with rage. "I am hanging up now, Doug. I'm done with your games and your manipulation. I know how much I love Ashanti, that's all that matters. And in fact, it's the reason I'm saying no to you. I don't want her to think this is the way men should treat women they say they love. Goodbye, Doug. Don't contact me again."

After slamming the phone down, Zya rests her head in her hands, letting the tears she's been holding back, flow.

She doesn't see Ashanti at the top of the stairs turn and amble back to her bedroom.

"Debra dear." Debra's mom, Alice, tries to wake her. "I've dropped Tracey off at school for you, and here's a cup of decaf coffee with that flavored creamer you like so much. Come on, dear, it's time to get up."

Debra groans then looks at her mom before she pulls the covers over her head. "Thanks, Mom, but I just want to sleep. Will you pick up Tracey after school for me?"

"No—I won't! It's time you stopped feeling sorry for yourself and got out of bed. I've sat by and watched you now for the last two weeks, and I can't stand by anymore."

Debra pulls the covers back from her slitted eyes as they meet her mom's.

Alice's face softens. "I'm sorry, honey, I didn't mean to yell. It's breaking my heart to see you hurting so much. I know what it's like to lose your husband—the man you love; but life must go on. Do it for Tracey. Do it for the baby."

"Mom, we've been over this already, I need more time,

please just leave me alone."

"No, Debra, I will not leave you alone, and I will not take care of Tracey for you anymore. Call it tough love, but it's time you take care of her yourself. How do you think she feels seeing her mom like this? Have you asked her how's she's feeling? George is looking down on you right now—very disappointed."

Alice gets up to leave the room as Debra throws the covers off her and springs up behind her mom. "Don't you dare tell me how George is feeling right now. He's not allowed to have any feelings—he left me. He left me to take care of Tracey and to raise this baby all by myself. Let him be disappointed. Hell, he can be downright mad for all I care. Maybe then he'll know exactly how I feel." Debra, seeing her mom's stricken face, breaks down, and falls to her knees.

"It's all right, sweetheart. Get mad, curse out the world, and George, if it makes you feel better. Do something besides sleep all day, please. I love you, and I can't bear to see you like this anymore. At least take a shower and let me cook you some breakfast. You have your appointment with Dr. Phelps today, remember."

"Mom, I just don't think I can go on. I don't know how I'm going to do all this—I can't do it. Why did he leave me? Why did God take my George from me?"

Debra's sobs continue as Alice rocks her back and forth like she did when she was a child.

Brian's jerky movements around the office reveal his agitation. He's short with everyone from his secretary to the poor delivery man. He knows it has to do with his next appointment, Debra Harris. When Amber brought her to his office a few weeks ago, he didn't recognize her. But now, seeing her again…he didn't think he would except in his dreams.

"Dr. Phelps, your eleven o'clock is here."

"Thank you, Miss Sanders. Please ask her to take a seat. I'll be right out."

Brian straightens his tie and puts on his jacket as then stops to get a glass of water. His throat is dry, and his palms are sweaty. *Oh, this is ridiculous!*

He goes to the outer door and greets Debra. "Mrs. Harris, sorry to keep you waiting. Please come in and take a seat, won't you?"

Brian's eyes focus on the deep circles under her eyes. Her golden hair today looks like straw. And her dress looks two sizes too big.

Brian meets her mother Alice's eyes, the same deep blue as Debra's, in the waiting room, pleading with him to help.

"Please, call me Debra," she says, as she tries to smile.

Brian feels a little flush inside at the sight of upturned lips. *I have to stop this! I'm a professional—I have to get a grip!*

"Debra, it's been a few weeks since we first met; how are you doing? Anything specifically you want to discuss?"

"Specifically? I can't get myself out of bed in the morning and get dressed; the most basic of human actions. I guess, specifically, tell me how to deal with all this. How am I going to raise Tracey and this baby all by myself? Am I crazy to think I can?" Tears stream down her cheeks as she pleads with him.

Brian resists the urge to run around his desk and gather her up in his arms and say, Everything is going to be okay. You're not alone—I'm here.

Swallowing hard, he says, "Debra, I know your world has been turned upside down, and although you can't see how you'll be able to go on, you will. You're still in shock—disbelief. What should be a joyous time, enjoying your pregnancy, is like a bad dream; one you wish you could wake from. Be easy on yourself and take it one day at a time. Anything happen this morning to make you feel you can't do this?"

"Get out of bed and take Tracey to school. If it weren't for my appointment with you today, I'd still be there. My mom is helping, but I should be there for Tracey. I know she's grieving too, and I'm being selfish, only thinking about myself," Debra states as more tears stream down her cheeks.

Brian hands the tissue box to her. "It's great you have your mother close by to help. Maybe tomorrow morning, you can get Tracey dressed and ready for school? Why not take it one step at a time and see what you can add back into your life each day?"

"I'll try. I haven't started using the journal you gave me yet."

"That's all right, remember I gave it for you to use only if you want to. It's not homework, just something to help you channel your thoughts should the need arise. I have a colleague who specializes in child psychology. It might help if Tracey had someone to speak to and share her feelings with."

Debra is crying again. "I should be the one helping her. I'm her mom; I'm the one she's supposed to be talking to."

Brian comes around and sits in the chair next to Debra. He wants to wrap his arms around her and protect her, instead he gently holds her hand in his. "Debra, you'll be able to talk to Tracey about this soon. For now, don't be so hard on yourself. You're not being selfish—you're grieving. You're not superwoman, and you shouldn't think you have to be. Right now, let's focus on getting you slowly back into your normal routine, one small step at a time."

Debra nods her head in agreement.

"I'm sure your mother and friends are already telling you this…you look as if you've lost a lot of weight. Not sure your OB will be happy about that. It's understandable, but let's add that to today's list. How about enjoying a sandwich with Tracey when she gets home from school? This would be a wonderful opportunity for her to share with you if she's ready. Kids are funny that way, don't push it. Sharing a few quiet moments with mom might be what she needs right now."

Brian goes into professional mode blocking out the effect this woman has on him and continues to explain to Debra some ideas and tips to help Tracey through her grief.

Debra nods and tries to take it all in. This feels right to her; this might actually help distract her from her own feelings.

"I know we've spent the majority of this session talking about Tracey and how you can help her. Is there anything else you want to talk about?"

"I'm afraid to say it out loud because of what it might mean. I keep having this dream I'm falling into this bottomless, black pit. I never hit bottom, but as I float downwards, I keep thinking I'm at peace now—the pain's gone. I think about Tracey and the baby for a fleeting moment, but then say to myself, they'll be better off. I don't want to wake up because then I'll have to face everything again; I just want to keep floating.

What does it mean?"

Brian, biting his lip and wrinkling his brow, says, "We can sometimes translate dreams into issues we're dealing with. Don't take them literally. Most likely, you're feeling over-whelmed and your mind and heart might need a little break. How about I prescribe you a very low-dose antidepressant to help you get through this?"

Debra adamantly shakes her head back and forth. "No pills! I don't want to do anything that might hurt the baby."

"How about I give you the prescription, and you talk to your obstetrician about it, what's his name?"

"Dr. Francisco, Anthony Francisco. I'll ask him about it. If he thinks it's safe, then I promise I'll take it. I've always been against tranquilizers and anti-depressants; I never could under-stand why anyone would need them. I guess I'm finding out."

Brian writes out the prescription and hands it to Debra as they walk out into the waiting room.

After Debra and her mother leave his office, he asks, "Miss Sanders, can you please get Dr. Anthony Francisco on the phone for me right away?"

CHAPTER FIVE

"How did you get Debra to come along with us?" Dominque asks.

"I'll tell you if you tell me how you got Zya to agree to relax a few days before her big fashion show next month and join us?"

"She told me on the phone the other day how guilty she feels about spending all her time working and not much with Ashanti. I told her this would be a great, short two-day trip where she could devote her time and energy to Ashanti. It could help make up for these past few months—and the next few weeks. It worked, although I think she brought her laptop with her. If she did, I'll hide it."

Amber, laughing while she finishes packing, replies, "Well, my story for Debra is not that far off from yours. She's been in such a funk—sleeping all the time. I kind of guilted her and told her George would want her to be a mother to Tracey; mourning time is over. Go away for the weekend and spend some time with your daughter. Oh boy, you should have seen the look on her face, but it worked. In fact, we're late! We need to get a move on and pick them up. Zya and Ashanti left an hour ago."

The ride to Holiday Isle is quiet. Debra sleeps the whole way down while Tracey reads a book.

Amber could see her in the rear-view mirror, glancing over at her mom from time to time. That feeling of helplessness seeing the concerned look on Tracey's face. If only there was something she could do to help her snap out of it.

Dominque opens her car door and jumps out, yelling, "Last one to the tiki bar for a Miami Vice is a rotten egg."

Debra slowly opens her eyes and looks over at Tracey, who is smiling at her. "Hi, beautiful; ready for some fun?"

Tracey nods enthusiastically as she frees herself from the seat belt and jumps out of the car.

"Debra, why don't you catch up with Dominque and make sure she doesn't get into any trouble so soon on our trip. I'll go check us in. Come on, Tracey, I'll let you jump on the beds. You didn't hear that, right Debra?"

Smiling, Debra heads out towards the water to the music and noise of the popular Holiday Isle tiki bar.

Dominque spots Zya at a table with her laptop open. "Hey lady, you here for some fun in the sun and quality time with your daughter?"

Zya looks up, guilt written all over her face. Chuckling, she responds, "Yeah, yeah, yeah, Ashanti found herself a friend already, and they're playing in the pool. Besides, I need to put the finishing touches on some accessories for my show."

Zya looks over at Ashanti in the pool and waves to her. "Looks like my daughter is okay with me not being around, after all."

"Did you see any hot guys yet? Anybody you think has potential?" Dominque asks.

"Actually, I've seen quite a few hot bods, but they all seem to be interested in that gorgeous blonde at the end of the bar. I've seen her shoot down six hunks within the last hour. Not sure what her gig is, but she didn't come here for the men, that's for sure," Zya replies.

"Well, that means there's more for us!" Dominque says, heading to the bar. She yells her order to the bartender when she still four steps away. A Miami-Vice; a frozen mixture of a piña colada and rum runner; she orders it with a 151 floater. She spots Debra on her way heading over to the bar, so she adds, "Make that one, very strong; and one virgin, please."

The gorgeous blonde at the end of the bar looks over in their direction and smiles brightly.

Dominque waves and says hi.

The blonde lifts her drink and nods.

After jumping on the beds and racing around the room trying to get Tracey into her swimsuit, she and Amber finally emerge to join the others by the pool. Amber, already exhausted, wishes she had Tracey's energy as she runs ahead of her.

"Where's Ashanti?" Tracey asks.

"She's found a friend. They're playing in the pool."

Tracey looks over at the pool and sees Ashanti waving at her, calling her name. Tracey looks at her mom, who nods, it's okay, and runs off at full throttle. Tracey took swimming lessons when she was barely a year old. Now she's a fish.

"Didn't take Ashanti long to find a BFF," Amber states.

"No, not that girl," replies Zya. "That girl could make friends with a fly. In fact, I've seen her do it."

All the girls laugh, and even Debra looks up with a smile

on her face.

The blonde walks over to the table and says, "Excuse me, but it seems my daughter Stacey, and yours, have become inseparable. My name is Tina." She extends her hand to Zya.

The woman before them is drop-dead gorgeous. Her dark tan plays perfectly with her bleak-blond, long, thick hair. She has it up in a messy bun. Her blue-gray eyes are warm and friendly.

Zya instantly likes her. Being an expert judge of character, Zya decides this woman is okay in her book. "Hi, I'm Zya. They seem to have hit it off, haven't they?"

Amber introduces and invites her to join them. "I will, but only if you let me get the next round," Tina responds.

"Next round? I'm already one behind you. Better get me a shot of Tequila to catch up," Amber states, as she motions the waitress over to the table.

Dominque can't help herself. She walks over to their table and after introducing herself, she asks, "Tina, Zya told me you've been hit on by some real hunks, and you've brushed them all off. What gives? I don't see a wedding ring on your finger."

"Not my type—I prefer the soft touch of a woman over a man," Tina answers, glancing over at Zya.

Dominque, who is sipping her drink, almost chokes. "Please don't take this the wrong way, but you're so beautiful. You don't look like a dyke. In fact, I'd say you look the complete opposite."

Laughing, Tina replies, "That's a typical stereotype. If it's uncomfortable for you, I'll be happy to go back to my end of the bar, but drinks are still on me."

"Oh no, no," Amber quickly replies. "Please excuse my friend; she can be unfiltered at times. We would love for you to stay. I have to warn you though, we will be checking out the hotties."

"That's all right by me. I've always been able to appreciate the opposite sex...I just don't choose to play with them."

After an afternoon of laughter and way too many cocktails, the girls call it a night. They invite Tina and Stacey to join them the next day, snorkeling at John Pennekamp.

"We'd love to join you. That was our plan for tomorrow anyway," Tina replies, smiling at Zya.

Zya groans at the thought of seeing the slimy critters she'll encounter while Ashanti jumps up and down with Stacey, all excited about their upcoming adventure.

"You'll have to excuse our African beauty here. She's a bit squeamish about the fishes in the deep blue sea," Amber says.

Ashanti interrupts and says, "Oh, Mom, you don't need to worry. I'll teach you how to snorkel. You'll love it."

Zya nods, not convincingly. "Yeah, okay, we'll see."

"What a beautiful day," Amber says as she stretches her arms out, tilting her face up to the sun.

"Yeah, too bad Dom didn't come with us," Zya adds.

Whispering so the kids cannot hear, Amber replies, "I think Dom had her fun last night. She's probably still in bed."

Zya rolls her eyes as her daughter comes over to help her with her mask and snorkel.

"Mom, remember to keep looking down. If you look in front of you, you'll breathe in water from the end of the snorkel here," Ashanti instructs her mom, pointing to the top of the snorkel.

"Am I really going to do this?" Zya asks.

"Yes, you are," Amber, Tina, and Ashanti all respond together.

They wade out to where they are waist high in the water. Ashanti and Stacey snorkel like fish in the water.

Debra, still looking somewhat like a zombie, helps Tracey get a feel for it.

Tina asks Zya, "Ready to try this?"

"No, but I have a feeling you're all going to make me, anyway. So, I might as well get it over with."

Zya floats on top of the water and looks down into the water. At the exact moment, a large barracuda swims about four feet away. "Oh my gosh, no way, I can't do this. Did you see that thing?" Zya says, scared and trying to scamper out of the water.

"Whoa, whoa, whoa," Amber says. "Zya, yes, we all saw it, and I can tell you, it's not going to hurt you. Seeing a barracuda is a good thing."

Zya looks at her with a question mark on her face as Amber explains, "You can be sure there are no sharks or other large predators around."

Ashanti swims over to Zya. "Come on, Mom, if I can do it, so can you."

Zya nervously agrees and while holding Ashanti's hand, floats back on top of the water, looking down as instructed.

Still fearful, she slowly relaxes as they drift across the

beautiful coral reef, taking in all the colorful fish. A teal and purple parrotfish to her right and a funny looking one, which she later finds out is a triggerfish, swims right past her. She marvels at how they all get along. Different kinds, swimming around together, like one big happy family. Just as she finishes that thought, she catches sight of a very serious tiny black and white Sergeant Major darting out from under the rocks, trying to scare away a blue tang more than ten times its size. She laughs, forgetting she's underwater, and begins choking. Lifting her head, she spits out the water and continues to laugh. Zya decides she can learn to like the little creatures in the sea after all.

At the dinner table that evening, Ashanti brags, "I can't believe you went snorkeling today, Mom."

"Well, I guess that means you owe me something now, don't you?" Zya responds, narrowing her eyes at her daughter.

"Oh, come on, tell me you didn't have fun?" Amber asks.

"Maybe a little." Zya replies, looking at her glass of tea, smiling.

A group of young men walk by the table as they leave the restaurant. One comes over to Dominque and whispers something in her ear, making her face drain of all color. As she looks up, she sees a familiar face in the group. She gets up to excuse herself as another young man smiles at her. Dominque darts towards the restroom with Amber following closely behind.

"What was that all about?" Amber asks.

"I think I might have had a little too much to drink last night. I didn't remember until just now. I may have been with a few of those guys in that group," Dominque says, ashamed.

"What! Dominque, why do you do this to yourself?" Amber asks a little louder than she should.

Leaning over the sink, she splashes cold water on her face. "The alcohol; I guess I got a little carried away."

"What did that guy whisper in your ear?"

Tears spring into her eyes, Dominque responds, "He told me his other buddies feel left out. Can we have another round tonight? I'm so embarrassed."

Hugging Dominque, Amber responds, "Well, I promise you, I'm not letting you out of my sight for the rest of the weekend."

Forcing a smile, Dominque nods as they make their way back to the table.

☯

"Please, Mom, can Stacey spend the night in our room? Please?" Ashanti begs.

"Oh, all right," replies Zya. "Under one condition."

"Anything."

"You must have lots of fun, but try to get some sleep."

Zya looks over as Tina nods her approval.

The kids run off ahead as they leave the restaurant.

"We better hurry and make sure they don't ransack your room," Zya says to Tina.

While the girls get the necessities for Stacey to spend the night, Tina pulls out a nice bottle of white wine.

"And now for dessert…"

Tina pours about two inches of liquid in one glass, and as she pours another one, Zya stops her. "I don't drink."

"Oh, how about some orange juice?" Tina asks.

Zya nods as Tina pours a small amount for her in a glass. Tina raises hers to Zya's and toasts, "To new friends."

"To new friends," Zya replies.

"Mom, can we head over to our room? We want to play electric banking Monopoly?" Ashanti asks.

"Sure, but make sure you bolt the door behind you don't take one step outside that door, understood?"

"Got it, thanks, Mom."

The girls, giggling, rush out of the room with Tina looking outside the window to make sure they get there—three doors down.

Zya rubs her shoulder and neck, feeling the tightness and stress of working twelve-plus hours every day, seven days a week for the last two months.

"You all right?" Tina asks.

"Yes, just my shoulders are tight."

"Here, let me. In another life, I was a masseuse."

Tina walks behind Zya and starts rubbing her shoulders. "Wow, I'll say, you have some serious knots. You know, neck and shoulder massages are a must for anyone who looms over a computer, sewing machine, and a sketch pad all day."

"Yeah, I know, there never seems to be enough time," Zya replies.

"I think I brought some oil with me," Tina says as she walks into the bathroom. "Yep, I did. Lucky for you, take off your shirt."

Zya looks uncertainly into Tina's eyes. "Oh, come on, I'm not going to bite you."

Cautiously, Zya removes her shirt, leaving her bra. Tina rubs oil on her shoulders.

"At least take down your bra straps unless you want me to get oil all over them."

Zya takes her arms out of her straps, leaving her bra in place.

Tina immediately goes to work on a knot on Zya's left shoulder. Gently at first, then goes a little deeper, little by little.

Zya closes her eyes and can't help but relax. She can feel the knots in her shoulders as Tina works on them—patiently and expertly, staying with one as long as Zya can stand it, and then moving to another.

Tina motions Zya to sit backward in the chair, straddling it. Tina pulls up another chair behind Zya's and continues to massage her shoulders and neck more gently now as most of the knots are gone.

Zya is in total bliss; she has forgotten how good it feels to get a massage.

Slowly and expertly, Tina moves her hands down the center of Zya's back, working gently between each disc as she moves down to her lower back. Finding more knots and tension, Tina continues to work on Zya's lower back, using trigger points to help release them. Tina feels Zya relax deeper, taking longer, deeper breaths. She asks Zya to rest her arms on the top of the chair so she can work on her shoulder blades.

Zya tenses as Tina releases the back of her bra, but soon relaxes again as she expertly works her magic over and around her shoulder blades. Zya's mind goes blank as she feels herself drifting off to sleep.

Tina rubs her hands all along Zya's back, taking big strokes up the center, over her shoulders and down on her sides. Tina's touch is much gentler now.

Zya is a little embarrassed as Tina's fingers gently glide along the outside of her breasts on her downward stroke. She doesn't squirm or fidget—to her dismay, her mind screams for her to continue.

Tina pauses for a moment. Just as Zya raises her head to look back at her, she feels Tina's body gently press up against her back. Tina's hard nipples against her as her hands gently stroke her arms.

Zya's lack of protest urges Tina to continue gently stroking the sides of Zya's neck first with her fingers than with gentle kisses.

Zya feels light-headed, aroused, and confused, but mostly—in bliss.

While placing small little kisses down her shoulder onto Zya's back, Tina's hands stroke along Zya's abdomen, feeling her tense up slightly at her gentle touch.

A moan escapes from Zya. She hasn't felt like this in so long. She knows she should stop her, but she doesn't want to.

Tina's hands gently brush against Zya's hard nipples as they come up to stroke her upper chest.

Zya gasps gently—Tina's touch has started a fire deep inside; she feels like she's going to burn up. Tina's body is firm and hot up against her back, without thinking, Zya reaches behind, her touching Tina.

Tina gently takes her hand, swings it back in front and up over her shoulder, and gently kisses her palm. Tina's other hand reaches down and cups her breast. She places little kisses down her fingers until she reaches the tip on her index finger. After one last kiss, she wraps her lips around the finger and gently sucks on it, pulling it ever so slowly from her mouth.

Simultaneously, her thumb finds Zya's nipple and, with a little pressure, flicks back and forth across it.

Zya's head thrashes back and forth. Her toes are tingling as her breath comes in short bursts. Zya has never felt like this before; nobody has ever explored her body like this or ignited a forest fire within her. Zya pushes her hips backward, grinding into Tina while she places her hand on the seat between her legs.

Tina takes her cue and kisses her ear lobes—nibbling gently while her hand moves lower, stroking her abdomen. Her other hand expertly releases the button and begins lowering the zipper of her shorts.

Zya is now grinding her hips furiously—raising them towards Tina's hand as it slips down the front of her panties; stopping millimeters above pleasure center to tease her.

Zya continues to moan and thrash her head from side to side; all this teasing is driving her crazy. Focusing her mind on Tina's hand inside her panties, she doesn't realize her other one is sliding up her inner thigh inside her shorts until it touches her. The sudden unexpected touch sends shivers from her toes all the way up her spine. She can't take it anymore; she feels as if she's going to explode.

Tina, sensing Zya's height of passion, takes both hands and gently glides them up and down inside Zya's inner thighs—giving her a chance to cool off.

Zya is confused and aroused; not sure if this is right—but enjoying it too much to put a stop to it.

Taking her right hand, she gently lifts Zya's chin so she can kiss the hollow of her neck as her head falls back onto Tina's shoulder. She continues placing soft kisses until she finally finds her luscious lips.

Zya returns her kiss feverishly—deeply—passionately.

Tina backs away, slightly nudging Zya to slow down, stroking Zya's quivering lips with her tongue. She gently nibbles on her lower lip, alternating between kisses and gentle biting. Tina's other hand gently removes Zya's hand from the seat between her legs. Tina's kisses get deeper as Zya reaches behind her—willing to touch Tina's skin. Their tongues intertwine as they moan and gasp with excitement.

Tina's hand quickly goes back to stroke the fire between Zya's legs as her hips raise up towards her fingers, urging them to their target. Tina teases and play everywhere except where she knows Zya wants her to go until Tina can't help herself anymore. In one swift movement, her finger slips between Zya's moist, hot lips. The wetness and heat, shocking at first, drives Tina to search out the entrance to Zya's moist center. Her finger searches just inside, stopping to explore all the nerve endings, causing Zya's body to become electrified—tingling all over. Once Tina senses Zya is close to orgasm, she sends her over the edge adding a deep passionate kiss.

Zya's hips buck as she screams through each wave that comes crashing down, one after the other, willing the feeling to never end as every inch of her body comes alive. Zya rides the waves up and down many times before finally, exhausted and completely at peace, she gently rests her head back on Tina's shoulder.

They sit like this for a few moments, Tina's arms wrapped around her while Zya's arms rest on top of hers.

Reality creeps into Zya's mind as it hits her what has just happened. Not only has that been the first time she has ever experienced multiple orgasms, she's never been with a women before. The thought has never crossed her mind. Zya has never been attracted to women; she didn't think she was attracted to Tina. This gorgeous woman accomplished something even Zya couldn't do. She read about what it would feel like, failing the many times she tried to achieve it for herself.

"Are you okay?" Tina asks.

Not able to look directly into Tina's eyes, she replies, "Yes. Great. Confused. Nervous. I've never been with a woman before. I didn't expect this to happen."

"Yeah, me too. Don't get me wrong, you're gorgeous, intelligent, funny and so damn sexy, but I usually go for the tomboyish woman. And that, you are not."

Chuckling, Zya adds, "Well, I guess that makes two of us. I usually go for the gender with their biggest brain between their legs."

Both laughing, Tina pours a little more dessert wine in her glass.

Zya takes the bottle from her hands, pouring some in another glass.

Tina raises her glass and says, "Here's to trying something a little different, I think?"

Zya gulps her wine down in one swallow and sheepishly looks at Tina.

"Just so you know, I didn't plan this. You seemed pretty tense. Why don't we go with the flow and see what happens, okay?" Tina says, sensing Zya's discomfort.

"Okay, but…" Zya stammers.

Tina pulls the cover back on her bed. After jumping in on one side, she pats the bed next to her. "How bout you come lay next to me."

"What about the kids? Won't they wonder where I am?"

"Let me take care of that."

Tina dials their room.

A giggly Ashanti answers. "Jeff's Pool Hall, Eight Ball speaking."

"Ha, ha, ha, very funny, listen, your mom and I were watching TV, and she's crashed. I hate to wake her up. Think she would want me to, or should I let her sleep?" Tina asks.

"Oh, let her stay there. She's been working so hard; she needs the sleep. We promise to go to sleep and we've bolted the door. We will not go out for anything—promise."

"Okay, we'll you know we're just a few doors down. Call here if you need anything, okay? And no room service either. If you want something, I'll order it and bring it down to you."

"We're good. We've been eating the ice cream snack bites mom brought. I bought the White House. Now I'm trying to get South Beach. Stacey got all the airports." Ashanti fills Tina in on their Monopoly game.

"Have fun and let me know if you need anything."

"Okay. Thanks, good night."

"Good night," Tina says as she hangs up the phone. "All taken care of. Now, will you join me, please?" Tina again asks, patting the empty side of the bed.

Zya lies down, facing away from her. Tina spoons behind her; their bodies fit together perfectly. Within minutes, Zya is in a deep sleep.

"What's going on?" Stacey asks.

"My mom fell asleep in your room, so she's going to stay there tonight," Ashanti replies.

With a worried look on Stacey's face, she asks, "Does your mom have a boyfriend?"

"No, not right now. She broke up with my dad again, but she's done that a few times over the years. She says he won't marry her, but I swear he asked her on the phone the other day and she turned him down. I'm still hoping they'll get married one day. We'll see. Why do you ask?"

"Oh, no reason," Stacey says, looking away from Ashanti.

"You don't think they went out to the bar and picked up some hotties, do you?"

"Oh no, I can promise you, my mom did not do that."

Dominque and Amber walk into the hotel lobby, finding it overflowing by a large gathering of people waiting to check in —most young and male. Dominque hurries over to a bellhop stressing over a full load of luggage and inquires about the group.

"Speed boat races tomorrow, they come in tonight and leave tomorrow. Great business for the hotel—lots of work for me," he says as he pulls the overflowing cart toward the elevators.

"Oh, come on, Amber, let's go out to the tiki bar for one drink. Who knows, you might find yourself a hunk to help you keep your bed warm," Dominque pleads.

"One drink and no, I will not leave you alone—not for one-second," Amber replies, as the two head into the balmy night towards the loud tiki bar.

They look around the bar for a seat when the group of

young men they saw in the restaurant earlier greets them. Already a few drinks down the hatch, they're loud and obnoxious. As soon as they see Dominque, the one who whispered in her ear stands up and shouts, "Hey Red Hot, how about you come over here and plant yourself right on my lap. I'm hard for you, baby. Bring your friend too, I'll do her next," he says, grabbing his crotch.

Embarrassed, Dominque turns away.

Amber, with a sweet smile, walks up to the drunken jerk. With her lips close to his, she softly strokes the back of his head and whispers, "Honey, if you can handle me, you can have me." She holds his head as she brings her right knee up into his groin, causing him to double over in pain. "Didn't think so. Have a good night anyway."

Amber strolls away, hooking her arm into Dominque's as they make their way through the crowd to the other side of the bar.

"Oh shit! She's coming this way—gotta go," Stewart says to Patrick.

Stewart, upon seeing Dominque, was looking forward to rolling around with her again—she was a lot of fun. That was until he heard the remarks from the drunken group of frat boys. A few of them have already enjoyed her company. No, thank you. He has enough problems as it is. An STD he can do without. He slinks away from the bar, leaving Patrick looking deeply into his drink.

Amber doesn't recognize Patrick in his T-shirt, shorts, and baseball cap. He's pulled the cap lower, covering the upper part of his face. He just wants to be left alone and enjoy a quiet moment and a few drinks before he calls it a night.

"Oh my gosh, Amber, I can't believe you did that!" Dominque shouts.

"He was a total jerk, and his comments were uncalled for—he deserved it," Amber spits out.

"Yeah, he'll be waking up with a sore crotch tomorrow morning and won't remember how he got it. Certainly not the way he planned!" Dominque snickers.

Both girls laugh as Amber waves the bartender over and orders drinks.

"Amber, you haven't said much about Mr. Ethical Attorney lately; have you gotten up the courage to call him yet?"

"No, I've picked up the phone many times, even dialed all but his last number, and then I chicken out at the last second. Why is it, I can be self-assured and aggressive with everything in my life except him?" Amber asks, shaking her head.

"Maybe all of those unbelievable fantasies you're having are getting in your way. Have you ever had that kind of sex with anyone?"

"You know, that's the strange part, I haven't. I never even knew I had it in me. I've thought about writing some of these down and selling them to romance novelists," Amber chuckles, trying to lighten the mood.

"Well, if you ask me, you need to call him. Hey, why don't you practice on one of these guys here? You can pretend they're him," Dominque states, a little too loudly.

Patrick turns to the girls, recognizing their voices. Lifting his cap, he says, "Amber?"

CHAPTER SIX

Patrick made reservations at Johnny V's on Las Olas Boulevard with plans to stroll along the avenue and grab ice cream at Kilwin's. Tonight would be the first proper date with Amber, by his definition, complete with an elegant dinner. Since their chance meeting in Holiday Isle, they have met up for coffee occasionally. She still doesn't know how much of her and Dominque's conversation he heard.

He can't believe how nervous he is. He's already changed his shirt four times. *This is crazy* he says to himself as he grabs his keys and heads out the door.

With sweaty palms, Patrick buzzes Amber's bell on the directory. Without saying, 'hello,' or, 'who's there,' the door buzzes, allowing him entry.

Shaking his hands out, taking deep breaths, he wills himself to calm down as he waits for the elevator.

Her door is ajar, "Hello, anybody home?"

Amber, with the phone at her ear, motions him in. "Honey, calm down, I'm sure everything's going to be all right. Your doctor said bed rest, and to remain calm. Please listen to him and relax."

Debra has just called Amber to tell her she started bleeding.

Although she's panicking, her doctor isn't too concerned.

"I'm such an idiot! How can I be so stupid—so selfish? I've spent this last month in my own little world, not taking care of Tracey, or this little one; least of all—myself. Oh, Amber, if I lose this baby, I don't know what I'll do."

"Deep breaths—you're not stupid and you're the most unselfish person I know. Don't be so hard on yourself. I'm sure everything's going to be fine. Your doctor said this happens sometimes, so don't be alarmed. Do you want me to cancel my date and come over?"

"Absolutely not," Debra says, wiping the tears from her face. "You've been looking forward to this for way too long. Please do it for me; go out and have a great time. Don't worry about me. I promise I'll keep my feet up and watch a movie with Tracey tonight. You better call me in the morning, though —I want details."

While looking at Patrick, she responds, "Okay, but please call me if you need anything. I'm sure Patrick will understand why I have my phone with me."

"Everything all right?" he asks as Amber hangs up.

She pauses, looking out into space. Coming back to earth, she says, "Yes, I'm sorry. Can you give me ten minutes to finish getting ready?"

"No problem; take all the time you need."

"Thanks. Help yourself to the wine I opened."

"Can I pour you a glass?" he asks.

"No, thanks. I want to keep a cool head tonight."

"In that case, do you have a large beer mug I can pour some wine into for you?" Patrick asks, laughing.

"Ha, Ha, Ha, I'm easy—but not that easy."

Patrick blushing goes into the kitchen to pour himself a glass of wine. He looks up in time to catch Amber's reflection in her dresser mirror as she pulls her dress over her head. He can't help but notice how silky smooth her skin is and her long, toned legs that seem to go on forever. *God, she is perfect,* he whispers to himself as the wine spills over the top of his glass.

"Shit," Patrick exclaims as he looks around for a dishrag or paper towel.

"Everything okay?" Amber asks as she comes out of her bedroom, pulling her clingy dress down her thighs.

"Clumsy me; guess I thought I was pouring into a big ole beer mug after all." Patrick looks sheepishly at Amber.

"Paper towels are under the sink. I'll be out in a minute," Amber says as she turns away with a grin on her face.

Amber turns, pulling the pins out of her hair as she re-enters her bedroom.

Patrick can't help but watch the curve of her lower back and the slight sway of her hips as she retreats. He picks up the wine glass and empties its contents in three large gulps, struggling to get a grip.

He's sitting on the couch, looking down at his hands, pleading for them to stop sweating, when Amber emerges. "Sorry to keep you waiting. Ready?"

Patrick lifts his head, unable to speak, or stand—she takes his breath away. Her long, thick hair begs for his fingers to run through it. Her full, pouty lips smile in anticipation of him kissing them. Her breasts rise and fall with every breath. After what seems like an eternity, Patrick catches himself and stands up.

"Oh yes, absolutely. No problem waiting—definitely worth

it," he mumbles reaching for the doorknob for her.

Amber notices the effect she has had on him—exactly as planned. So what if the dress cost four-hundred dollars and the last-minute deep hair conditioning, sixty. Seeing how much the results are effecting him…priceless.

After ordering a platter of assorted cheeses and wine, Patrick asks, "I hope I'm not prying, everything okay with your friend Debra?"

"Do you know Debra?" Amber asks.

"In passing, I've played racquetball with her husband, George, and a doctor friend of mine."

"They'd been trying for years to have another child, and now, Debra's pregnant. She kept it a secret, revealing it as a special surprise for her late husband, George's fortieth birthday. She even bought a silver rattle with *Daddy's Special Birthday Surprise* engraved on it. She wrapped it, waiting for him on the dining room table." Sadness washes away the smile on her face as her eyes water. "He was killed on the way home that night in a terrible accident on I-95."

"Oh my, I had no idea. I'm so sorry, I know you two are close," Patrick says, concerned.

"Thanks. George's death has been hard on her; she hasn't taken the best care of herself. Sleeping a lot, which I'm sure is partly because of depression and being pregnant; plus she's not eating. She's twelve weeks now and just started spotting. Her doctor says it's probably normal, but he's scheduled an ultrasound for Monday anyway—just to be sure."

"If you need to be with her, I understand. In fact, I'll be happy to drive you over there myself."

"That's sweet, and thank you, but she emphatically told me *NO.* In no uncertain terms am I to show up at her door tonight. She wants me to have a good time and not worry about her."

Lifting his glass to toast, Patrick responds, "To Debra. May life's road smooth out for her from here on."

"Here—here," Amber adds.

Amber isn't sure if it's the delicious wine, candied walnuts, exotic cheeses, or the Portobello pancake she just devoured, but she's feeling light-headed, almost as if she's floating. Everything is turning out perfectly.

She looks up as Patrick walks back to the table. Her eyes drink in his broad shoulders, his casual glide across the carpet, and those deep soulful brown eyes. She watches with territorial pride as every woman he passes turns or glances at him.

"What's with that sly smile on your face?" he asks as he sits down.

Quickly regaining control, she says, "Oh nothing, just thinking about the night we ran into each other in Holiday Isle."

Smiling, Patrick adds, "Yeah, that was perfect, wasn't it? Almost like it was meant to be."

Standing up, Patrick reaches out for Amber's hand. "Shall we?"

Exiting the restaurant, Patrick unknowingly keeps his hand in Amber's as they walk the block down to the sweet smells of Kilwin's for dessert.

Patrick halts, seeing a familiar face across the street. *No, it couldn't be.* He looks back at Amber, confused.

"What? You look like you've seen a ghost," she says.

He looks back again, but the familiar face across the street is now gone. "Wow, that's really strange. I know you're standing right here, but I swear I just saw you across the street. I guess too much wine."

Amber quickly grabs him by the sleeve and leads him into the chocolate shop. *Don't freak out. There's no way she's here. Breathe, just breathe....* She lets the delicious smell fill her nostrils. "Oh, I couldn't possibly."

"Oh, yes, you can. You hardly ate anything. I'm sure you were saving yourself for this," Patrick says as he extends his arm down the length of showcases filled three shelves high with every chocolate delight imaginable.

"All right, but just one piece."

"Okay—I get to pick it out."

Patrick paces in front of the chocolates, looking at Amber and contemplating the various options in front of him. After several attempts, he finally picks the perfect one—a dark-chocolate caramel cluster with walnuts inside.

"My favorite, how did you know?"

"ESP, my dear Watson," Patrick replies as he winks. "I saw how much you enjoyed the candied walnuts at dinner, so I took a wild guess. Thought you might like this too."

Patrick hands her the candy and takes his chocolate ice-cream waffle cone as they exit onto the Boulevard.

Amber takes a few bites of the candy, intending to put the rest away for later, but ends up eating all of it—it's so delicious. As she pops the last bite into her mouth, she remembers Patrick's sighting. Shivers run down her spine as the memories flood back. She hasn't thought of her in so long, almost forgetting she exists.

Patrick shares how much he loves the Boulevard and points

out a grassy area explaining that's where they have movies under the stars. They walk over to look at the elephant structures, playfully bouncing their heads up and down on their springs in the gentle breeze.

She knows all this, but she lets him be her tour guide anyway. Plus, it gets her mind back off *her*.

"So, she likes chocolate and elephants, but not ice cream," Patrick says playfully.

"I like ice cream," Amber protests.

"Really, prove it."

Patrick puts his cone in front of her. Amber looks into his eyes defiantly and, never losing his gaze, takes a long, slow lick. As she pulls away, Patrick reaches forward to wipe some off the top of her lip with his thumb. Without thinking, he leans down and whisks it away with a kiss instead.

Amber's knees buckle as Patrick's hand reaches behind her lower back, pulling her closer.

Dropping the cone onto the ground, he places his other hand under her chin, raising it enough to kiss her gently on the lips.

Amber pulls back, her heart pounding—her body tingling. It's better than her dreams.

Patrick discretely adjusts himself and picks up the cone in search of a garbage can.

His tongue expertly circles her hard nipple as his hand nudges her thighs apart. She can feel his hardness against her as he slowly grinds his hips in rhythm with hers. She moves her hips further down; her body begging for him to enter. He gets close, very close, and then pulls back, teasing her unmercifully. Moaning loudly, she moves her hands down to his buttocks, pulling him to her. "Take me now! Take me now!" she shouts to him.

He moves closer, and in one swift thrust of her hips, she engulfs him. His breath heavy, he quickly matches the height and intensity of her thrusts. Pushing in faster and deeper, causing her moans to grow louder—her labored breathing coming in quick gasps. She feels her toes begin to tingle, every nerve ending alive—it's happening! It's finally happening!

Ring. Ring. Ring. Amber opens her eyes wide as the sound of her cell phone by her pillow wakes her up. It's Debra.

"Are you okay?" Amber asks, out of breath.

"I'm fine. The question is, how are you? Did I interrupt something?"

Frustrated, she throws herself back into her pillow then throwing the covers off her sweaty body. "Nothing that won't happen again tonight."

"You didn't—You aren't?" Debra stutters.

"Oh, no. I really like him. My body wanted to, but my head kept cool and said goodnight to him at the door."

"So tell me all the details," Debra asks.

"Before I do, has the bleeding stopped? You sound better."

"No, I'm still spotting a little, but it is definitely lighter. Tracey, my dear daughter, brought me cereal and orange juice in bed. I begged for coffee, but she told me caffeine was not good for the baby."

Laughing with Debra, Amber replies, "You gotta love them youngins," she says in a southern drawl. "Every once in a while, they surprise you, don't they?"

"Yes, they do. Maybe one day you'll find out for yourself," Debra replies sheepishly.

"Oh, I don't know if I'm the motherly type. I love kids— everybody else's. I love your kid, and your soon to be addition…and Ashanti," Amber fumbles.

"Oh, you'd make an incredible mom. I asked you to be Tracey's godmother because I know you would take great care of her if anything ever happens to me. I hope you'll be godmother to this new little one too?"

"Oh, Debra," Amber replies, her eyes watering. "I'm honored. Yes, yes, of course, I will. Nothing is ever going to happen to you, but yes, you know you can count on me."

After wiping her eyes, Amber shares the evening's details with Debra, explaining every tidbit about the elephants, ice cream, and the kiss. Good thing he took her back home shortly after that. She may not have been able to say no otherwise. She left him at the door with a sweet peck on the lips. Had she allowed him in, she knows he'd still be there. That's what her body wanted; luckily her brain knew it was too soon. She didn't want to be another notch in anyone's belt.

"What time is your appointment with Dr. Francisco tomorrow?" Amber asks, trying to get Patrick out of her head.

"Three o'clock—I'm meeting with Dr. Phelps right before at one-thirty. I asked Dr. Francisco if I should cancel, and he told me to keep the appointment."

"Want some company?" Amber asks.

"Oh, that would be great. Can get off work?" Debra asks.

"Zya has insisted on taking over the afternoon appointments, but I'm sure there is some research work I can do downtown tomorrow afternoon, so don't worry about it. I'll bring my laptop and do some of it at Dr. Phelps's office. I'll pick you up at one."

Brian's morning has been especially trying. His receptionist is out sick, his car wouldn't start, and he has no idea how to make that stupid contraption spit out his elixir.

Debra and Amber enter the lobby as he slams down his cup full of light brown liquid. He turns around sheepishly. "Sorry, ladies, I can't seem to make this thing work."

"Here, let me," says Debra as she calmly takes the cup out of his hand. The feel of her touch is almost more than he can bear. She smiles at him, causing his heart to skip a beat. Swallowing hard, he turns and walks into his office, *Breathe—just breathe,* he tells himself.

Ten minutes later, Debra knocks on his door with steam rising from his mug. "I'm not sure if you want cream or sugar," Debra states as she sets the mug down in front of him.

"No, black is perfect. Thank you, thank you so much."

He sips the sweet brew as the aroma fills his nostrils. The coffee is even better than what Miss Sanders makes. He looks up and sees Debra smiling at him.

"Funny, you just reminded me of George. He did the same thing when I brought him his coffee," Debra says with a loving smile on her face.

"Well, you're smiling, so I'm glad to see this memory makes you happy, not sad," Brian says as he puts his coffee down, willing his heart to slow down.

"It's been two months…George wouldn't want me to continue like this. Amber said he's looking down on me, wagging his finger at me. He did that a lot whenever I was doing something he didn't like. Always making a funny joke or comment, and then he'd wag his finger at me. He had a way of using wit and humor to express his displeasure. I really miss him," Debra says, her eyes lowering to her lap.

"I'm glad to see you're dealing with this better now. So, tell me where do you want to be, let's say...in the next month, or so?"

"Well, first, I have an ultrasound with Dr. Francisco right after I leave here. I've had a little scare, so I want to be sure everything's okay with the baby. He mentioned giving me something to help calm my nerves. I figured he's been talking to you, but I told him I'd like to try to do this on my own— without any drugs. I know I have them if I need them.

"Last time we talked about feeling numb and me falling into a black hole, never touching bottom—feeling weightless. I'm sure that startled you as much as it did me. When I go to sleep at night now, I imagine myself stepping over the hole to the other side where Tracey is waiting for me with a bunch of flowers. Behind her is a baby carriage with the baby I'm carrying now safely inside.

"The dreams are still coming, but not every night like they were. And when they do, I wake up and think about my babies on the other side as I drift back to sleep. This baby, and my beautiful Tracey, are George's legacy. He's going to be remembered for a lot of things, but most importantly for the incredible children he helped bring into this world."

Watching Debra, Brian gets a sense of the incredibly strong woman she is. George used to brag about what an outstanding woman his wife was, and how he's probably biased. He wasn't at all—she really is as amazing as he said.

He's glad to see a little sparkle in her eyes, and her hair is looking much better. Her skin doesn't look as pale and gray, and her cheeks are a little pink today. He can see she's taken the time to put on make-up, and her shoes match today.

As she continues, he zones out. His eyes find the hollow of her throat, and he watches it move up and down with each syllable. His eyes slide down to the top button of her blouse, imagining his fingers opening it, kissing her softly between her breasts...

"Dr. Phelps, is everything okay?" Debra asks, a little alarmed.

She'd been talking nonstop for over thirty minutes, and he can't remember half of what she said. "Sorry, I imagined your daughter on the other side of the hole—they're yellow daisies in her hand, right?"

Smiling, Debra responds, "Why yes they were. They're one of my favorites. I want to paint a cluster of them and put it in my study at home. I've thought about doing it for a while, but now I've given myself a goal to have it finished by the end of the month. Our anniversary is in early October, so I want to give this gift to myself. He was my sunshine, and his personality reminds me of the color yellow. He made me feel the way the sun does, all warm inside. I'm hoping to exercise again too. Dr. Francisco will have to approve it, but I'd like to get back into jogging and swimming again."

"Well, it sounds like you have a lot to keep you busy; that's great."

"Oh, and I started writing in the journal you gave me. You were right—it helps. I write when I'm at my saddest. I tell

George how much I miss him and share my feelings with him. It's almost as if he's there listening to me. Thank you. I didn't think I would use it, but now I can't imagine not having it."

"My pleasure, I'm delighted to hear it's helping. If I'd known you liked yellow so much, I would have given you that color instead."

"I like pink too, it's very girly. So, same time, same day next week?"

"You got it unless there's anything else you want to talk about?"

"No, I'm good. I need to get over to the hospital."

Debra gets up from her seat, as does Brian. "Thanks for the coffee; it was delicious."

"My pleasure," Debra answers.

Without giving it any thought, Debra walks around his desk and gives him a big hug and a light kiss on the cheek. Friendly in nature, but it has a much stronger effect on him.

He breathes in her sweet perfume as her lips lightly brush his cheek. The nerves along his arms tingle; the kiss lingering as he watches her leave.

He drops into his chair, annoyed about his inability to concentrate. He's daydreaming about making love to her while she's pouring her heart out to him. She's paying for him to seduce her in his mind.

"So, how did it go?" Amber asks as they exit Brian's office.

"Really great, I'm glad you recommended him. He's so easy to talk to. I find myself wanting to say things to him I would never tell a perfect stranger. He doesn't judge; nothing seems to startle him. I even told him, seeing him today made me want to put on make-up and look my best for the first time since George's death. Once the words escaped my mouth, I regretted them, thinking he might misunderstand. He didn't even flinch."

"Debra, do you think Dr. Phelps is cute?" Amber asks, seeing the flushed look on Debra's face.

"Yes, he is handsome, but I would never even think—I couldn't…George has only been gone two months," Debra responds, alarmed at Amber's implication.

"Calm down, Debra, you're pregnant—your hormones are raging. Didn't you say you were lusting after George almost every night when you were carrying Tracey?"

"Yeah, I suppose you're right. Okay. I have thought about it, but it's always George's face is see—not Dr. Phelps's. It's strange, but he kind of reminds me of George a bit. Maybe it's wishful thinking."

"Maybe, but don't beat yourself up for being human—and a woman. Maybe we need to stop by the purple store and pick you up a little something to get you through the nights," Amber chuckles.

"Hey, I just wanted to call and give you the news from the ultrasound. The baby looks good, strong heartbeat, and we think it's a boy. The placenta is a little low, partially covering the cervix, so they want Debra to stay on bed rest for the next few weeks and see if it moves," Amber says, updating Dominque.

Dominque, out of breath, responds, "That's great news. Please give her a big hug for me. Can I come over and help with Tracey?"

"I'm putting a schedule together, so let me know what nights you can help."

"Can I get back to you? I gotta run now, five more miles to go."

"Five more miles? Didn't you run ten miles this morning?" Amber asks, stunned.

"Yes, but I still can't get these last five pounds off. Zya's show is next week. Gotta run, literally," Dominque says as she hangs.

Amber hangs up and dials Debra. "How much do you think Dominque weighs?"

"Soaking wet, maybe a hundred pounds. She's starting to look so thin lately—almost sickly. I bet if it wasn't for her height, she could probably wear children's clothes. She's what, five foot eleven?"

"Yeah, almost six feet. She's trying to lose five pounds in time for Zya's show next week. I'm just trying to imagine where she's going to lose it from," Amber replies.

"Think she's becoming a little too obsessed with her weight?" Debra asks, concerned.

"Yeah, but it's probably nerves. You know she's wearing the wedding dress at the end of Zya's show. She probably just wants to look perfect."

Stewart ducks, hoping Dominque doesn't notice him as she runs past him on A1A. Her phone rings at the perfect time, allowing him to slip by sight unseen. He loves running along the beach in the late afternoon. The honeys are all out—most of them wearing their short running tops and tight mini shorts, some even in bikinis. God, he loves living in South Florida. As a sexy brunette gets close enough so he can see her nipples straining against the spandex, he almost forgets the important call he needs to make before five.

Slowing to a walk, he pulls out his phone and dials the number from memory. A woman answers, "Hello."

"Hi, I'm sorry, I'm trying to reach Dr. Adams. Is this his office number?" Stewart asks, a bit confused.

"Sorry, no, you must have dialed wrong," The woman responds in a sexy, cat-like voice.

"I'm sorry," Stewart says, still out of breath and breathing hard from his run.

"I'm not; I usually have to pay fifty dollars an hour to hear someone breathe like this on the phone. Call anytime—it's my pleasure." She hangs up, leaving Stewart dumbfounded.

He looks down at his phone and adds the number to his contact list, naming it *Phone Sex.*

Patrick puts the champagne bucket and glasses out by the hot tub. He tests the water to make sure it's warm enough, but not too hot. Tonight, he's not chickening out. They've been spending almost every evening together. Her kisses turn his insides upside down. He's never felt this way—it's scary. He turns to mush; he's like putty in her hands. If a kiss effect shim this way, he's sure making love to her will bring all defenses down. One side of his brain says, 'Go for it man. She wants you just as much as you want her—how will you know if you don't do it?' The other side says, 'Run—and don't look back.

You made a promise—keep it.' The gambling side won out; she's worth the risk. If things get too heavy, he can always back away.

He rushes back inside, looks at the clock, ten more minutes, and she'll be here. He tacks the sign on the front door to meet him around back.

Stewart left for the night, so he has plenty of time to relax and enjoy Amber's luscious body. Grabbing the plate of chocolate-covered strawberries, he slips out the back and into the hot tub.

Closing his eyes, he leans his head back imaging Amber's naked body causing a throbbing between his legs, straining against his shorts. Hesitating at first, he eventually slips them off and puts them on the edge of the hot tub. She'll see them and know he's naked.

He panics imagining finally making love to Amber, wondering if he should take this chance. His equipment is operating perfectly now, but what if when he sees her, his nerves get the best of him causing things to go soft? He grabs a napkin and puts it over his eyes. Maybe if he can't see her at first, it will be okay.

The bushes beside the house rustle. His heart leaps. "Round back," he says. "I've been waiting for you."

He hears her footsteps as she enters, making tiny splash noises as he pictures her slowly approaching him.

Within seconds, her hands are on his chest…she must be as eager to get this first time out of the way.

He pulls her to him, kissing her neck as her legs wrap around his hips.

Her hands expertly guide him into her.

No time to be afraid; he stays hard as he instinctively buries himself inside; her muscles quivering and grabbing him as he pulls out, begging for him to come back.

Her moans get louder, overpowering the music.

The tension building up to tonight, along with the intense heat between them, gets the best of him. He can feel himself slipping over the edge. Quickly, he rips off the napkin and finds her lips and kisses her passionately.

She's pumping him like a madwoman—screaming, "I'm coming! I'm coming!"

Patrick realizes just as he peaks, exploding inside her—it's not Amber. He opens his eyes and finds one of Stewart's nymphs, Isabel, riding him like a bronco.

The bushes move behind her—it's Amber! He sees the tears streaming down as her cheeks, as she turns and walks away.

"Wait, wait, Amber! It's not what you think!"

CHAPTER SEVEN

Before rushing to the airport for her show, Zya calls Amber with last-minute instructions. "Reservations are all set. I'm heading out now. You, Debra, and Dominque are flying over to meet me next Thursday on the twenty-third. Debra can cancel, without penalty, if her doctor advises her not to travel. A car will wait at the airport to take you to the hotel. And don't forget your bathing suits. I have a nice, relaxing three-day trip planned for us on the French Riviera after the show."

"This sounds terrific. Thank you so much for treating us. You know you didn't have to, we were coming to cheer you on no matter what. It's going to be so much fun! Debra is seeing her doctor today. Cross your fingers he says okay and she can come too," Amber excitedly replies.

"I'm crossing my fingers and toes as we speak. Gotta run; I need to call Stan and make sure all my designs get packed in their crates and out the door today. See you soon."

After a long overnight flight direct from Miami, the three ladies emerge from the airport to an awaiting limo. The driver's sign reads Zya's Dream Girls.

"That's us!" Dominque squeals. "I'm so glad Zya put us in business class. Those seats were unbelievable."

"Yeah, I agree," replies Debra. "That was very nice of her. I slept pretty much most of the night. My internal clock is a little mixed up right now, but I feel good; even for being almost sixteen weeks," Debra adds, rubbing her belly.

The girls are speed away to the City Center in Milan along Piazza della Repubblica to the Prince Di Savoia historic hotel. Debra kicks back and closes her eyes for a little additional shut-eye during their hour-long commute, while Dominque excitedly looks at everything they pass.

"Who knows Amber, maybe you'll run into Patrick on this trip too," Dominque says sarcastically without looking away from the window.

"I hope not! If I do, I'll spit in his face!" Amber retorts venomously.

Debra, opening her eyes, looks directly at Amber. "Did I miss something?"

Looking down into her hands in her lap, Amber explains, "No, nothing really. Just Mr. Right turned out to be…you can't be any more Mr. Wrong."

"What happened?" both Dominque and Debra ask at the same time.

"After we had that romantic dinner and ice cream moment on Las Olas, Patrick and I got together a few more times. We were having so much, but it seemed we were hesitant about taking the next step—or so I thought. We even kidded about the three-date rule on our third official date.

"When it came time to ask him in, I chickened out, and he

seemed a bit relieved. Boy, that man is quite an actor! Anyway, that night, we talked about a lot of things, including hot tubs and how much we both enjoy soaking at the end of a long day with a glass of wine. So, he sends me this note the next day, inviting me to a rendezvous at his house to relax in the hot tub —any day, my choice. I knew where this was going so I texted him and told him I'd bring the wine and to expect me at six o'clock the next night.

"I was running a little late, then again, maybe that was karma. I arrived to hear loud moaning and some girl screaming, '*I'm coming! I'm coming!*' As I got closer, I realized some slut was sitting on the lap of Mr. Right, like she was bucking a bronco."

"Oh my gosh Amber, I'm so sorry. Did he say anything?" Debra asks.

"Oh yeah, he probably thought I wasn't going to show. He seemed shocked when he realized he was wrong and I caught him with my replacement. He's left me messages, emails and even sent me flowers, but I'm not interested. Thank God I found out before I had sex with him."

"What did he say?" Dominque asks.

"I don't know. I haven't listened to his voice mails or read his texts and emails. He's not worth my time or effort. Humph, men—I can't believe I was actually falling for him."

"Well, I'm sure there'll be plenty of hot Italian men running around here; you'll have your choice..." Dominque trails off with a devilish grin on her face.

"And don't forget about the French Riviera too," adds Amber with a determined look on her face.

"What?" Dominque and Debra ask in unison.

"Oh, didn't I tell you? After the show, Zya is taking us on a three-day trip to the French Riviera to enjoy the beach. I hope you brought two-piece bikinis because we're going topless," Amber adds cheerfully, glad to get the subject off Patrick.

"Oh, I don't know, Amber. I thought I was going poolside in my suit, not the French Riviera," Debra nervously states.

"Oh, and if I had told you, you would have found some way to get out of coming on this trip. And let's face it girl, you need it more than anyone."

"Okay, but I insist on going shopping while we are still in Milan," replies Debra.

"Yeah, me too," adds Dominque.

They usher the girls into the marble hotel lobby, where an elderly gentleman introduces himself as their concierge. Anything they need during their stay, all they have to do is ask.

He flashes their room cards and asks them to follow. He bypasses the elevators and takes them to the far corner on the first floor to a room with a metal plaque that reads: *Royal Suite.*

"Signoras, if you please." He motions the three ladies into a lavish sitting room with wood floors and silk paneling. "There is a deluxe room connected through here." He opens the door revealing another smaller, and as elegant room.

"This is my room," Dominque exclaims as she runs into the dwelling space and throws herself on the bed.

"That was easy," Amber says, as they turn to look at the rest of their suite.

"Your companion, Zya, has arranged for spa treatments for you this morning at eleven. I've taken the liberty and ordered a few refreshments, which will arrive momentarily. Signora Zya will join you for dinner this evening at Acanto. If there is anything else I can do for you, again, please ask."

As he turns to leave, Amber shakes his hand cleverly, passing him a folded American twenty-dollar bill.

"Can you believe this?" Dominque asks, as she strolls into the larger room.

"Not too shabby, huh?" Amber replies.

A gentle knock on the door sends Dominque swirling across the floor. A young girl pushes in a shiny cart with a lavish spread of fruit and fresh pastries. Large pitchers of orange and tomato juice and a large pot of coffee finish the buffet.

"Wow, this looks wonderful. I wish I could indulge, but I'm going to have to pass," Dominque says as she runs off into her room, closing the door behind her.

"What's up with that?" Debra asks.

"She believes she still needs to lose weight. I'm glad the show is this Saturday, so she'll start eating again," answers Amber.

Twenty minutes later, after Debra and Amber have made a dent in their morning treat, Dominque comes into the room wearing a big fluffy robe.

"Are you two ready?" she asks, super excited.

"I will be in two minutes," Amber says as she throws off her clothes on her way to the closet for a fluffy robe of her own.

She throws one over to Debra. "Come on, pokey; time's a wastin."

Smiling, Debra says, "Go on up; I'll be there in five minutes—promise."

Debra goes into the bathroom to undress, and just as she has expected, she's spotting again.

She finds the spa hoping to see Amber and to tell her what's happening. The lovely Italian assistant informs her Amber is already in session and cannot be disturbed unless it's an emergency.

"It's okay. I have to cancel my appointment."

"I'm sorry to hear that. Is everything okay?" the young girl asks.

Debra explains her pregnancy and the scare she has been through with the spotting starting again.

"No worries. You could not have had the stone massage or anti-jet lag treatments scheduled for you, anyway. We do, however, have a neck and shoulders soothing treatment I can offer you. Roberto is your masseuse."

Out of the back, a handsome and well-built dark-haired man comes up to the desk and reaches for Debra's hand. He kisses the back of it, then motions her to follow him.

Before she can reply, he's already ten steps ahead of her.

He turns and motions for her to sit in the chair, facing the back, cradling her chin in the opening. "Not to worry Signora Debra, I will be gentle and help you relax. I'm sure you tired after long flight. You will be safe."

Debra sits in the chair as instructed. It's like she has no control over what she does—she's on autopilot.

Roberto rubs the back of Debra's neck gently. Before long she relaxes, lengthening her neck as he expertly rubs away the stress and tension. He continues to massage her shoulders, pushing the robe down slightly, gaining access to skin. Forty-five minutes later, Debra wakes from a light slumber.

"You like?" Roberto asks.

"I think I slept through most of it. I'm sorry."

"That is good. Here, drink." Roberto hands her a glass of water with a mint leaf and a slice of cucumber in it. "Good for you to drink water. You come back and see me again, okay?" Roberto asks in his thick Italian accent.

"Oh, I will." Debra gets up and reaches her hand into her pocket to tip him.

"Oh, please Signora, the only thing I will accept from you is room number so I might give you tour of my lovely city of Milan."

Blushing, Debra replies, "I'm so very flattered, and thank you, however, I have to decline. I'm here with my friends only for a few days—female bonding time. I wouldn't want to abandon them."

"No problem, please, I insist you include them." Taking Debra's hand in his, kissing it lightly while never breaking eye contact. "Signora, I will be at the Café Brek at two this afternoon. I would love to show you and your friends the Milan tourists never see. Promise to have you back here by six in time to ready yourself for your planned dinner with Signora Zya."

Roberto turns on his heels and leaves.

Debra's heart is beating so fast. Dazed by how romantic he is, she mentally brushes it off as she makes her way down to their suite. *How does he know what our plans are this evening?*

"Yes! We'd love to go! The spotting is very light, right?" Amber asks as Debra explains the offer presented to them.

"Wait a minute. We don't even know this guy. He could be a rapist, or a serial killer, for all we know," Debra adds.

"Really, with hands so gentle he put you to sleep? Let's find out a little about your romantic Italian."

Amber dials the spa, "Hi, I'm a little embarrassed; however, a good friend of mine told me to ask about a male masseuse…"

Interrupting Amber, the young lady on the phone says, "You must mean Roberto; he is our only male masseuse here. Would you like to book an appointment with him? He's booked up for the next few weeks; however, I could put you on the waitlist if you like?"

"Booked up already?" Amber asks, surprised.

"Oh yes, people come from all over Milan—all of Italy; some even from other countries to see him. He has the best hands in all of Europe."

"Oh, his wife must be one lucky lady?" Amber's statement comes out as a question.

"Oh, Roberto is not married. He gets proposals all the time, but he has not settled down. One lady will be lucky one day to have him," the young girl dreamingly states.

Amber thanks the girl and hangs up. "Well, your serial killer seems to have the best hands in all of Europe; he's very well-known and very much single. So, what time do we meet him?"

Roberto's ear-to-ear grin is proof of how happy he is to see Debra and Amber arrive for their Milan tour.

While kissing Debra's hand, his eyes lock onto hers. His eyes don't leave until Amber interrupts by thrusting her hand to him, introducing herself.

"Nice to meet you, Signora Amber, so glad you could make it. Where is your flame-head friend?" he asks.

"She is at the gym, I think. Running off those last few pounds she believes she has to lose so she can be svelte for Zya's show," Amber answers.

"You American gals, we will never understand you. Why you want to be so skinny? We like curves—not bones," Roberto explains thoughtfully.

Chuckling as they walk down the street, Amber pinches her waist and replies, "Well, that certainly makes me feel better."

"If I might," Roberto asks Debra.

She nods, not sure what she's agreeing to.

"You Signora," he says, looking at Amber. "You are beautiful girl,"

Amber blushes.

"But you are too thin. Your lovely friend Debra here, she is perfect. I hope not to embarrass you." Now looking at Debra, he continues, "She has such wonderful curves. Her hips are full and round. Her breasts firm and full too."

At this, Debra's eyes widen in surprise. "Well, thank you, Roberto. Now, where are we heading first?" she asks, quickly changing the subject.

Roberto points the ladies in the direction of the Duomo district to the Palazzo Reale. In his thick Italian accent and broken English, "Signora, it has been long time since Milan honor Signor Dali. I wish to take you to Galleria to show you, if you like?"

Both Amber and Debra nod in excitement as they journey towards the City Center.

After spending more than an hour enjoying the incredible

art and exhibition of Dali, they head towards the La Scala district, where Roberto points out the opera theater and the Palazzo Marino. From there, they proceed to the Monte Napoleone district, where the most famous fashion designers have shops along Montenapo.

Amber and Debra make their way down the high-fashion street window-shopping at Bulgari, Versace, Giorgio Armani, Bottega Veneta, and Dior. At Louis Vuitton, Debra falls in love with a leopard print scarf on one of the store mannequins. Even with firm persuasion from Amber to make the purchase, Debra passes.

"Signoras, I make promise to return you in time for dinner with Signora Zya, please." He motions for the ladies to return to the Principe Di Savoia.

At 7 p.m. sharp, the ladies present themselves to the maître d in the Acanto dining room, who escorts them to their table, joining Zya and Tina.

Not sure whether to comment on Tina's presence or the magnificent wood and steel sculpture hanging above their heads, Dominque jumps right in, "Tina, how wonderful for you to join us; are you involved with Milan's Fashion Week?"

"No, actually I had some free time, so Zya invited me to join you in this romantic city." Glancing over at Zya, Tina puts her hand on top of hers.

Zya quickly pulls her hand away. "Tina just finished a huge project, so I thought maybe she could use the break."

Tina understanding Zya isn't ready to let her friends in on their relationship. "Yeah, Zya was nice enough to let me tag along. I'm crashing on the couch in her room."

Zya told Amber they would all be sharing a room. She understands it's actually Zya who's staying with Tina. Seeing the distress on her friend's beautiful face, Amber says, "Well, we're glad you could join us. I'm sure Zya can use all the help she can get for her big day." Looking over at Dominque and Debra, she adds, "Did you know Tina is a production artist?"

Debra and Dominque's confused faces relax.

"I didn't know that. You *think* you're going to get some rest and relaxation, but I'm warning you—she's a drill sergeant," Dominque says, chuckling, pointing to Zya.

Amber looks over at Zya, watching as her shoulders relax; the tension broken. "Are you getting nervous yet?"

"Me—nervous?" With an anxious chuckle, she says, "Maybe just a bit. I can't believe there's so much still to do. The production itself is much bigger than anything I have ever had to handle."

Tina smiles, "I'm happy to help in any way I can."

Looking into Tina's eyes says, "Thank you again for everything you've done—and are doing for me. I don't know how I could have done it all. There is still so much I have to do. Did I already say that?"

"Did I mention drill sergeant?" Dominque adds.

Laughing, Debra adds, "Yes, you did. If there is anything any of us can do to help, don't hesitate to ask. Maybe even Dom can pull herself away from the gym long enough to help."

All eyes are on Dominque now as she stutters her explanation. "I want to look perfect for the show. I went in today for the fitting of the wedding gown. It is unbelievably gorgeous! And I think it might hang a little nicer if I can just lose a few more pounds."

Zya responds, "Oh, so you're the one who came in today

for her fitting. My girls told me they refuse to alter that dress anymore, so don't worry about it. That gown has a lot of intricate lacework on it; we don't have time for another alteration."

"And, thanks, everyone." Zya motions to everyone around the table. "I appreciate the offer, but I invited you here to celebrate this incredible moment with me. You are to enjoy yourselves—and that's an order."

"Yes ma'am!" Dominque says, saluting Zya. Everybody laughs as they raise their glasses together.

"We're so proud of you. You are an amazing designer, mom, and friend. We love you. To much happiness—and success."

Amber steals a glance at Dominque. She can see the sullenness creep up at the thought of not being able to do anything more. She looks defeated. It shocks Amber seeing how hollow her eyes and cheekbones are and the pasty-gray look of her skin. She watches as Dominque pushes her salad around on her plate.

Dominque continues to sink in her chair as Zya exclaims, "I've ordered the entrees for everyone this evening. No picking at your food,"—looking over at Dominque—"or wrinkling up your noses at least until you've tasted it. I think we should all take a bite and then rotate the plates around the table, so we all get to try everything."

Two young waiters come out with steaming hot trays filled with meats, plates of pasta, and seafood. So many delicious aromas are filling their noses and making their mouths water—all except for Dominque, that is.

As they serve dessert, the maître d arrives with a package for Debra. The box, elegantly wrapped in Louis Vuitton's signature paper. Debra gasps as they hand the package to her.

"I bet I know who that is from," Amber teases.

"Who?" the others ask in unison.

Debra opens the package and finds the leopard scarf neatly folded inside the designer's signature tissue paper. As she pulls the scarf from the packaging, a note falls out. Debra can only assume Roberto has sent this expensive and lovely gift. However, she is even more shocked to find two tickets to see Gioachino Rossini's L'occasione fa il ladro at the Teatro Alla Scala Opera Theater for the next evening. The note reads:

Signora Debra, I wish to thank you
for a most enjoyable afternoon.
I hope it is okay I gift you the scarf
you like from the window.
I am too sending tickets to the opera
for you to enjoy.
I hope you choose me.
Ciao Mia Bella.

Debra looks up to find all eyes on her.

"Well, are you going to tell us?" Dominque asks.

"I can't accept this—it's too much. I knew we shouldn't have gone with him this afternoon," Debra says, folding the scarf neatly in the tissue paper with the note and the tickets.

"Debra," Amber starts.

Debra looks up at her with tears in her eyes.

"It's okay."

Zya, sitting next to her, puts her hand on Debra's arm as Amber continues, "You are a beautiful, vibrant woman. Why can't a pleasant and romantic man buy you something nice and take you to the opera?"

"George has only been gone for a short time. I'm not interested in seeing anyone romantically yet. It's too soon. I miss him so much," Debra cries into her hands.

Zya smooths Debra's hair. "Feels good to cry, doesn't it?"

Debra nods in agreement.

"Honey, you shouldn't feel guilty over enjoying the company of a gentleman. George would want you to have fun and get on with your life. If you want my advice, I know you didn't ask for it, but I'm going to give it to you anyway."

Debra looks up with a slight smile.

"You should take the box to him personally and explain how you feel. You had a wonderful afternoon with him, right?"

Debra nods as she wipes her eyes.

"Then go talk to him. He knows you're pregnant; maybe he just enjoys your company."

Debra looks at Zya sarcastically, as if to say, 'You don't think that for a second.'

"All Zya is saying is go talk to the man. He truly is a gentleman, and I'm sure he'll understand. It's the least you can do." Amber adds.

"Okay, okay, I'll take it to him tomorrow morning," Debra says, defeated as she grabs the last bit of wine in Dominque's glass. "It's okay. Doc said I could have a glass of wine from time to time."

Debra exits the dining room in a hurry with Amber trailing quickly behind her.

Debra waits for Roberto outside the spa where he's expected for his first appointment.

As Roberto approaches, he has a big smile on his face, and his eyes sparkle.

Debra's heart skips a beat—he's so handsome and he has such a kind face. She shakes herself out of her trance as he approaches and reaches for her hand, kissing it softly.

"Mia Bella, what a nice surprise."

Debra's face twists as she tries to find the right words. Pulling her hand gently from his, she says, "Roberto, thank you so very much for the beautiful scarf and the tickets to the opera, however,"—pulling the box from behind her, Roberto's smile fades—"I cannot accept this." She hands them to him, which he reluctantly accepts.

His shoulders slump, and the sparkle vanishes from his eyes. He looks directly at the floor as he apologizes for bothering her.

Debra's heart goes out to him, sensing he's taking it personally. "Roberto, please don't be upset." Debra reaches out and touches his shoulder, causing him to look up into her deep blue eyes. "It's not you—really. You're sweet and kind, and very generous. You know I am pregnant, but you haven't asked if there is anyone special in my life."

"Signora Debra, you not wear ring on finger. I do not think you married. I try to be your friend and see what happens. Again, I am sorry if I did not understand properly."

"I should apologize. I 'm not married—I'm a widow."

Roberto's eyebrows go up in surprise. He can see the pain in her eyes, as she explains. "My husband, George, died unexpectedly about two months ago. He was the love of my life."

She shifts her gaze out a nearby window as her eyes pool. "I'm not ready for this—I still miss him terribly."

Roberto gently puts his arm around her shoulders and motions his approval for her to use his shoulder.

Without a thought, she lowers her head as the sobs and tears wrack her body.

Roberto puts both arms around her without saying a word. He holds her gently and allows her to cry. As guests pass them, he slowly turns her around to conceal her face.

Sensing she is regaining control, Roberto pulls back enough to remove a handkerchief from his pocket and offer it to her. As she dabs at her eyes apologizing, Roberto softly states, "Mia Bella, I understand your pain. My Theresa was taken from me six years ago."

Debra looks up and sees a familiar look of agony flit across his chiseled features.

"I will miss always, my Theresa. You will miss always, your George. Please, I wish you to keep my gift as friendship." Roberto hands Debra back the box. "I wish to be your friend only, okay?"

Debra smiles at him, nodding.

Kissing her lightly on the cheek, he says, "I have car here six o'clock tonight for opera. You take friend."

The words come out of her mouth before she realizes what she is saying. "You are my friend."

Roberto looks up at her, smiling. "Dinner too? Just friends?" he asks.

"Just friends," Debra confirms.

"Until tonight, Mia Bella, ciao." Roberto smiles and kisses her hand, then hurries away to his appointment.

Debra returns to the Royal Suite, as Amber steps out of the shower. "Did you not see him?" Amber asks, noticing the box in Debra's lap.

"I saw him. How can someone I just met seem to know me so completely?"

Wrapping the robe tightly around her, Amber joins Debra on the bed. "Tell me what happened."

Debra goes over the details, not only for Amber's benefit but also for herself. She needs to rehash what just happened.

"Well, sounds to me you two have a lot more in common then you thought. So, what's the plan?"

"He's picking me up for dinner and the opera tonight. We're going as friends—just friends," Debra replies.

At Dominque and Amber's persuasion, Debra meets Roberto in the lobby wearing the simple, yet elegant, cobalt blue sheath silk dress—George's favorite.

"Mia Bella, you the most beautiful woman in all of Milan," Robert says as he greets her and kisses her hand. "You take my breath."

Roberto takes the Louis Vuitton scarf from her arms and places it gently around her shoulders. He extends his elbow to her. "If you are ready?"

When they enter the restaurant, the maître d comes and hugs Roberto and begins chattering away in Italian.

"Your favorite table is ready."

"You come here often?" Debra asks.

"Before. My Theresa and I came here often. I still come from time to time, but always alone. Tonight the first time I bring date since…" Roberto trails off.

Debra reaches for Roberto's hand and squeezes it gently. "Thank you."

"For?"

"For making me feel comfortable; for being my friend."

Roberto smiles, and when the waiter arrives, orders a bottle of San Pellegrino and antipasto. Roberto is very much the gentleman as he orders dinner for both of them, then whisks her off to the opera.

Roberto sits back, watching as Debra gets swept away by the love and betrayal on stage. He watches her intently and thinks, *an American steal my heart.*

The phone rings as Amber buckles her strappy heel. "Your car is ready, Signoras," the voice states.

Giddy with excitement, Amber and Debra hurry to the lobby. "I feel like a little kid again," Amber states.

"Yeah, this is so much fun. How do you think Dominque feels right about now?" Debra asks.

"Probably scared to death—I bet she's a nervous wreck."

"I'm happy for her. She's been trying so hard to get a modeling contract. Still, all she seems to get called back for lately are cheesy videos. Not to mention the crackpot photographers who want to take her money, promising a wonderful portfolio. Did she tell you about the call she went on before we left? The one where the guy asked her to disrobe so he can see what he's getting?"

"No way!" Amber exclaims.

"Yep, turned out he was casting for an adult movie and he was looking for the next up-and-coming porno star. You know, Dominque said she hesitated at first, but thought about it, but thankfully left instead."

"She thought about it?" Amber asks, perplexed.

"She said maybe that's where she's going to make her big break. I told her she wasn't that desperate; there's more to life than modeling or becoming a star. Zya asking her to model the final gown in her show was the right thing at the right time for that girl. Not sure where her head would be right now."

"We need to keep an eye on her. Her self-esteem seems to be at an all-time low. You're right—Zya's show may be just the thing she needs. Are you going to tell me how your *friendly* evening with Roberto went last night?"

"He made it all okay. I didn't feel like I was cheating on George or guilty for being with him. He was the perfect gentleman, all the way up until he dropped me off in the lobby with a kiss on the cheek, thanking me for a lovely evening. I have to say, I was nervous he was going to kiss me goodnight, but he didn't. He just turned and left."

"Okay, now answer me honestly, did you want him to kiss you?"

"No. It was the perfect end to our evening. I'm not ready for anything like that."

"Okay. Are you going to see him again?"

"I'm so glad you reminded me, he wants to take us all out for a light dinner tomorrow night to celebrate Zya's show. I told him we were heading to St. Tropez on Monday, and he insisted on escorting us to the airport too. Don't let me forget to tell Zya and Dominque."

The limo pulls up in front of the Milano Moda Showroom, dropping the girls at the end of the carpet between the velvet ropes. People, cameras, and videos are everywhere. They make their way to the front row, finding three chairs reserved for them. Immediately a small-framed Italian girl comes over with a tray holding flutes of champagne.

After taking one each, Debra says, "I'm only having a sip."

Amber smiles, looks at her glass, and asks, "Tina?"

"I bet. Zya's probably running around crazy right now," Debra says as she takes a sip of her bubbly drink.

Seeing her friends have arrived and found their seats, Zya focuses on the finishing touches of her show. She stops at each workstation where the models are having the finishing touches of their wild, teased up hair and African style make-up, motioning for more height on one model and less yellow around the eyes of another.

Spotting Dominque at the end, she places her hands on her shoulders and asks, "Ready?"

Dominque nods.

Zya whispers to the make-up artist to put more foundation on her face and neck. Her skin looks too gray.

After she's approved the hair and make-up, she joins her assistant Stan, who's outfitting the first models. Thanks to Tine, everything is organized and well planned out.

The lights fade to black. The room goes quiet. We can only hear a few murmurs of anticipation from the crowd. Nearly a full minute goes by when suddenly, the lights come on full blast along as African drumbeats blast from the speakers. Smoke fills the stage from the back, and the drumbeats quiet down then stop.

The announcer makes the introduction, "The exotic and mysterious look of *Label Zya*."

The attendees clap as the first model emerges from the smoke as the drums beat again; the djembe sending out a piercing high-pitched, slapping sound. One exotic, sexy, and colorful design after another floats down the runway. *Label Zya*'s winter collection is bright and vibrant. Although the models are wearing many of the necklines extremely low, their super-long legs make the dresses appear much shorter than reality.

The lights dim again, and the drumbeats quiet down to a steady pulse.

Dominque emerges in the final gown of the show. She seems to float in a cream-colored natural silk cloud with intricate entredeux lace patterns embroidered along the bottom edge and the square neckline. The sleeves are mid length with a flash of deep purple silk showing beneath the embroidered cutouts.

As she moves down the runway, flashes of tomato red, cobalt blue, and golden yellow, are seen beneath the skirt. With each step, a new color emerges. The gown seems to be casual yet elegant at the same time. Traditional, yet modern…a contradiction in terms. This is the gown all the brides will order next June.

Zya walks onto the beach to join the gals in a flowing cotton gown, the same honey color as her skin covering her legs, arms, and even a little hoodie over her hair. Big sunglasses complete her comfortable look.

"Wow, look at you," Amber says as she approaches. "I love that dress; didn't I see that on the runway?"

"Yes, you did. I designed it for myself and Stan loved it so much, he insisted I put it in the show. He messaged me yesterday...the orders are pouring in for it in every color. Who would have thought this simple one-piece number would be such a big hit?"

"Where's Tina?" Dominque asks as she pulls off her cotton gauze long-sleeved top.

The girls do not respond; their jaws hang open, looking at the bones sticking out all over Dominque's body. She continues to pull off the matching slacks and turns around, wondering why nobody has answered her.

"What? You all look like you've seen a ghost or something."

"Dominque," Amber says in a whisper. "I love you so much, and I can't tell you how much my heart is breaking right now seeing you so thin. I'm sorry, honey, but you look sick."

Dominque looks down at herself, pinching the sagging skin on her thighs. Looking at her ribs, she pulls her hands in around her waist. "You think if I get this lower rib removed, my waist would smaller?"

Zya says, in a slightly angry tone, "Don't you dare! If I had known you'd taken this weight issue this far, I would never have allowed you to take part in my show."

Dominque looks up in shock at Zya. "What do you mean?"

"Many other designers and I refuse to allow this unhealthy anorexic look on the runway. Had you worn anything other than that gown, I would have seen just how far you've taken this. Girls have died dieting like this."

"But I only want to look better than the other girls. How will I ever get chosen to work if I'm not thinner or prettier than them?"

Amber pipes up, "I should have asked you about this sooner. Your beautiful red hair looks so weak and frizzy—the sheen has gone. Your crystal blue eyes don't sparkle like they used to."

"And can you see how pale and your skin is?" Zya asks.

Dominque looks closely at both arms, then down her body. With tears in her eyes, she looks up and says, "I just want to be chosen. I want someone to want me."

Amber quickly comes over and puts her arm around a very bony and frail Dominque.

As Amber consoles her, Zya motions for a waiter to come over. "Can you please send us over four of your signature lobster dishes?" Looking directly at Dominque, she chides, "You're eating two!"

Dominque smiles and wipes her eyes.

As the girls finish up their delicious food, a string of models parade around the beach, showing the wares of the beach shop within the hotel.

Zya watches the handsome, chiseled men in their linen shirts, holding the arms of gorgeous and sexy women wearing swimsuits and sarongs while carrying stylish beach bags. She's been waging war between inside her mind, between her religion, and her morality, regarding her feelings for Tina. She has been so patient, so gentle and so caring. Does she love her? Is she a friend? Or is she more? She hasn't been following the

Muslim faith for some time now. There's nothing wrong with being gay, right? As the battle in her head continues, Tina comes out and joins them.

"Sorry it's taken me so long; I was on the phone with Stacey. She was telling me all about this boy she's crushing on. She met him at the homeschooled function last night. Oh, young love."

She looks out in the distance.

Zya watches Tina intently. *Why is my heart beating so fast? Are these butterflies I feel in my stomach?*

Tina, knowing Zya is watching, slowly takes off her sundress, stretching her arms up high over her head, intentionally delaying the process of removal. Looking directly into her eyes, she reaches around behind her and unfastens her suit top.

Zya gasps silently, feeling a warm sensation between her legs.

Tina slowly lowers herself into the chair across from Zya. Opening the bottle of sunscreen, she applies it first over her legs, slowly stroking from the top of her feet up to her thigh. She can see Zya watching intently from the corner of her eye. She moves to her arms, taking the time to make sure she covers every inch of her skin. Sitting back in the chair, she puts the lotion in both hands and starts from her neck, slowly brings her hands down her chest and over her large, firm breasts.

The nerve endings dance on her hard nipples as she slowly circles each breast, brushing the hard buds with each swirl. Her hands lower down to her abdomen while her eyes remain locked on Zya. She parts her lips slightly as she runs her fingers under the top of her suit bottoms. She parts her legs, hoping Zya notices the wetness.

Zya jumps up from her chair quickly. "Oh my gosh, I almost forgot. I have to call Stan about the samples from the show." She takes two steps then turns around. "Tina, I know you just got here, but would you mind helping me out for a few minutes?"

Tina smirks and quickly grabs her sundress, pulling it over her head as she runs up to join Zya.

Dominque turns over to Amber. "I hate to leave you alone, but all that food, I'm not feeling too well. I think I need to go lay down. Don't worry, I'm not going to throw it up. I'm just not used to eating that much. By the way, where is Debra?"

"Roberto drove down early this morning. He wanted to take her on a traditional French picnic over at Colline du Château—as friends."

As Amber watches Dominque make her way back through the beach chairs, a Frisbee hits her shin. "Ouch," she yells and pulls her leg up.

A tan young man runs over apologizing profusely, "*Mademoiselle, Je suis désolé.*" Sitting on the end of her chair, he quickly grabs her calf and examines the mark left by his Frisbee.

"I don't speak French," Amber responds.

"Pardon, I'm very sorry. Does it hurt?" he asks.

Amber imagines he's going to lean over and kiss her boo-boo—he seems so young. He can't be any older than eighteen. He has sun-kissed hair and ice-blue eyes with a few cute freckles on his cheeks. He strokes the area of her shin now showing a red mark from the hit. Amber watches his six-pack abs tighten up as he leans over and gently kisses it.

"Feel better? I am Christoph," he says, extending his hand.

Chapter Eight

"Hi, you probably don't remember me..." Stewart's voice trails off as the woman on the phone says, "I remember you. You're my heavy breather." She says the last two words in a seductive, breathless voice.

He gulps while his excitement grows, making his jeans snug. Not sure if it's the husky, sexy voice or her boldness. Whatever it is, this woman is like none he's ever met.

"Are you a boxers kind of guy so everything can hang free and clear, or do you wear *tighty-whities*, feeling himself grow hard against his abdomen right now?"

Stewart's cheeks flush by this woman's sexual prowess. *Did she just go right there*, he asks himself? "I prefer to go commando," he cleverly replies.

"Now, that's an image. Are you swinging free right now?"

"Are we having phone sex? I hardly even know you." He chuckles. "Well, if you must know, why don't you come on over and find out for yourself."

"Tempting, but I think playing on the phone adds more excitement and mystery, don't you? Luckily for you, I was just getting out of the shower. Should I drip dry?"

"Huh—okay. How about I come over and dry you myself? But then again, that would just make you wetter."

"Oh, I like you. Do you like to be spanked? I do!" Stewart can hear her making a slapping noise in the background.

He decides he wants to see where this leads. He's never had phone sex before; he's always had all the bodies he can handle. Unsure of himself, he asks, "Did you just spank yourself?"

"No, silly, that was you. Want me to do it again on the other side?"

"Yes, but please be sure to rub it real good afterward. I want to see a perfect red handprint on those luscious firm cheeks." He unconsciously begins rubbing himself through his jeans as he visualizes his hands on her.

"My you've got big hands—is it true?" she asks, breathing heavy.

"Big hands, big feet, and my—big tool. Too bad for you, you can't see it for yourself."

"Oh, don't you worry—I have a mental image. Is this going to be one-sided, or are you going to join me?"

Stewart drops his jeans and his *tighty-whities,* he lied, pulling his T-shirt over his head as he heads outside to the spa. Good thing he has this headset; this is going to be a two-han-der.

"Did I hear a splash? Where are you?"

"I jumped into my hot tub. I figured if you were here, this is where we would be."

"And tell me, what would you be doing to me?"

Stewart closes his eyes and imagines they're together and not on the phone. He instructs her how to move her hands as if they were his. He likes to tease, so he instructs her to do just that; hoping she's paying attention and doing as she's told. Maybe she'll need another spanking.

Stewart can hear her breath catch slightly on the phone—she is doing exactly as she's told.

It takes a moment before Stewart realizes she is giving him instructions back and without thinking about it, he is obliging. They spoke no other words. Moans, deep breathing, and from his end, lots of splashing, are the only sounds.

The sounds from her end subside as he's getting into the groove. She asks if she can wrap her lips around him—that's all it takes for him to surrender into oblivion.

After what seems like a silent eternity on the phone, she says, "Well, that was fun, hope you enjoyed it."

"I did, thank you. I have to share something with you. This is the first time I've had phone sex with anyone. It's nice, but I think I still prefer the actual process."

"I couldn't agree more. However, there is something about the mystery. Call me anytime you need a little—release."

"Good morning Debra," Brian says as he greets her for her weekly session. "You're looking wonderful. Italy must have agreed with you."

"Oh, it did, and my morning sickness is finally gone."

"Glad to hear doing better. So, want to tell me about your trip?"

Smiling as her cheeks blush slightly, she answers, "There isn't much to tell—well, maybe there is. I know I should feel guilty, but I'm not."

Brian sits up in his chair; she has his full attention.

"I met someone while I was there."

"Really?" Brian asks as he feels a flush inside.

"He was so sweet and nice. He lost his fiancé six years ago. He knew exactly how I was feeling."

Before he can stop himself, he asks, "Anything, in particular, happen with…"

"Roberto, his name is Roberto, and no, nothing happened. He was a perfect gentleman and said we would just be friends."

Brian breathes a sigh of relief. "So, why do you think you should feel guilty?"

"Well, although nothing happened, he is a man, and we did go on what felt like a few dates. I know it's silly, I go out with my girlfriends all the time, so it shouldn't be any different just because he's a man, but it feels different."

"Were you attracted to him?" Brian asks, feeling jealous.

As she thinks about her answer, she begins to fidget in her seat. "I don't think so. I don't know…maybe. I'm not allowed to feel that yet, with anybody."

"Says who? Who told you you're not allowed to be happy—to want a relationship or companionship?"

"Well, no one, I guess…society? It's too soon. I loved, *love* George so much, how could I possibly be interested in another man so soon?"

"Debra, maybe you just want male company, like a companion. You're a healthy, beautiful woman; you have needs. You shouldn't feel ashamed."

Debra cheeks flush a deeper red as she looks down at her fumbling hands in her lap. "Maybe I should learn to do it for myself." Her head jerks up as she gasps, not able to believe she just said that.

"It's okay, Debra. Masturbation is perfectly normal for both men and women; it's nothing to be ashamed of." Brian feels a different flush rise through his body as he utters these words. An image, a rather graphic one of Debra naked, flashes in his mind.

"The girls all say I should have asked George for more. Oh, don't get me wrong, we had a great sex life. I just never really let him pleasure me," Debra says, ending in a whisper.

Feeling uncomfortable, Brian says, "Debra, we don't need to talk about this if you're uncomfortable." He prays, she changes the subject.

"No, for some odd reason I feel I can talk to you about this. If George has taught me anything, it's you only live once—no regrets."

"Okay, what do you think might happen if you felt some-thing for someone closer to home? Roberto is in Italy, so maybe you figured he was safe because he's so far away?"

Smiling again, Debra says, "Roberto drove over to St. Tropez and took me to this wonderful park that used to be ruins for a lovely picnic. He wants to come here and visit. I would love to see him again, but he can't stay with me. I don't think I'm ready for that yet, but if he comes all this way here, isn't he expecting it?"

Finding himself becoming more jealous and agitated, Brian answers, "That seems a bit high-school, don't you think." His response is more curt than he intends. He wishes he could take it back. "What I mean is, if he's truly a gentleman like you say, he won't expect anything but to get to know you better. You just have to ask yourself if you're ready for male friendship or companionship."

"Oh, you're right. What was I thinking? I'm not ready for this. I guess I'll break down and buy my own Buzz." Blushing, she gets up to leave. "Well, thanks for your time and helping me get my head on straight."

She comes around the desk and gives him a gentle hug goodbye.

He breathes in her sweet perfume and holds her a second longer than he should.

She pulls back, slightly shaking her head, before she leaves. *What was that?*

"Hey, I just wanted to call and say thank you. You should know, I've made an appointment at the hospital; I'm going to get through this. I love you, and I wanted you to know how grateful I am to you and Zya for being so brutally"—chuckling— "honest with me. Love you. Bye."

Amber sits down in the chair next to her answering machine, breathing a sigh of relief. She's been so worried about Dominque, hoping she could break out of this funk she's been in. She's definitely on the right track.

The phone rings. "Hey Zya, I was just thinking about you. Dominque has an appointment over at the hospital to help her deal with her eating issues and hopefully, help with her lack of self-esteem."

"That's great news, I've been thinking about her," Zya says, relieved.

"Yeah, me too. I'm happy we got through to her before it got any worse," Amber responds.

"Can it get any worse?" Zya asks, remembering how bad Dominque looked.

"I'm sure. Just glad we didn't have to go down that road. How's Tina?" Amber asks.

Zya was wondering when Amber would ask her about her rather complicated friendship. "She's doing great. And it seems like Stacey and Ashanti are emailing and texting each other every hour," Zya responds a bit hastily.

"Would I be prying if I asked you to tell me more about Tina?" Amber asks.

"You wouldn't be my dear friend, if you didn't ask," Zya responds, laughing. "Tina is great. She's funny and witty yet knows when and how to be serious. She's brilliant, but has this knack for making me feel like I'm the smarter one—I know I'm not. She's strong, yet gentle at the same time. It's hard to explain, but I feel so safe and alive when I'm with her. It's like she knows what I'm feeling, and I don't even have to say anything."

"Are you in love with her?" Amber asks.

Zya's response is slightly defensive. "What? What do you mean, in love with her? Like a girlfriend?"

"Zya, it's perfectly okay to have feelings for her. I can hear it in your voice. You're in love with Tina."

"Oh, Amber, I'm so confused." Her shoulders slump as she puts her forehead in her hand. "I *do* love her, but I can't—I'm not gay. I'm Muslim. I'm not allowed to be with another woman."

"Being deeply in love with someone isn't just about physical attraction, you know that. It's about being safe. Feeling complete; wanting and needing to be with that person. They compliment you. Whether or not that person has a penis is irrelevant. It's how they make you feel that's important," Amber says, trying to calm Zya's nerves.

"I know you're right, but what will people think?" Answering herself, "I know, since when do I care what other people think? What about Ashanti?"

"What's right for you is not necessarily the same for anybody else, and vice versa. You can't live your life on what others think. Ashanti will be okay if you let her in. Share this with her—tell her how you feel. You know, she may surprise you. Besides, isn't this a valuable lesson you could teach her?"

"You're right, but people can be cruel. It seems as soon as they find out you're different, you become an alien or worse, a plague to them. I've seen people go out of their way to hurt others because they don't think or act as they do. Don't get me wrong, I love my country; I'm just ashamed sometimes of who we have become."

"I'm sorry for anyone who would be mean or say cruel things to you because you've found happiness and true love with another woman. Zya, you deserve to be happy. If Tina does that for you, embrace it and hope for the best. Anyone who would think otherwise doesn't deserve to be in your life or give you advice on how you should live it."

"I wish it was that easy. I have a business that's getting lots and lots of exposure and PR right now. I've been vocal about my religion because of Ashanti, but I'm still struggling with the reasons I became Muslim. Did I do it because I believe in Islam? Or did I do it foolishly because I thought it would keep Doug around? I love so many parts about it, but now I'm even more conflicted. Can I stay Muslim and love a woman? I also have a young daughter whose opinion matters very much. I just don't know if my happiness is worth the price I might have to pay. I know you say I should talk to her, but I'm afraid of what she might think."

"First off, you're in the fashion industry. Girlfriend, have you looked at your competitors lately? I'm not sure if many of them are straight! And as far as regarding Ashanti, that little girl is a lot stronger and smarter than you're giving her credit for. You should talk to her."

"Yeah, I guess you're right, I should talk to her—but there's more. This is strange for me to talk about, but I'm not sure how to be physical with Tina. I don't think they publish *Lesbians for Dummies* books, and I'm too embarrassed to ask."

"Is she pressuring you?"

"Oh gosh, no, she's been wonderful."

"Can I ask…just how far you've taken things?"

Zya, blushing and pausing, unsure what the right words are. "Hmm, she's, well, she's satisfied me. She likes to hug, and we've kissed a few times. I might have used my tongue."

Amber, sensing Zya's discomfort, says, "Zya, if she's not pressuring you, why not just go along for the ride and see what happens? Tina seems like a patient and willing teacher if you let her."

"When I go to bed at night, I wish she were beside me; us holding each other. Somehow, I feel so much stronger when we're together. Maybe you're right. I'll see if I have the guts to talk to Ashanti tonight. I'll let you know how it goes."

"Good luck, and hey, call me anytime. You don't need to be embarrassed. I love you just the way you are. And you being happy, makes me ecstatic."

Finishing folding a load of laundry, Debra hurries and answers the phone after five rings. "Mia Bella, it is so good to hear your voice. I was afraid you not home."

Hearing Roberto's accent and husky voice, Debra feels butterflies in her stomach. "Roberto, I'm sorry, I was doing laundry. How are you?"

"Me? Well, thank you. Better when I can see you?"

"Please don't take this the wrong way, but I don't think I'm ready for this yet. You are sweet and kind…it's not you, it's me. It's too soon; I just can't do this yet, I'm sorry."

"Very well, Signora Debra, it is as you like. No problem, I understand. You phone me when you want to talk. When you need friend, okay?"

Debra can sense she's hurt Roberto's feelings. "Roberto, I will call you, I promise. I *do* want to see you, but not now—not yet."

"Okay, call me. Ciao Bella."

"Ciao."

Debra slides down the wall, confused. She wants to see him —badly, but it's just not right. It's disrespectful to George's memory. Yet her heart beats rapidly, remembering their time together in Milan.

Roberto hangs up the courtesy phone and turns back to the Departures, looking for the next flight back home.

The doorbell startles Debra and brings her back to reality. She just needs to get through this day—why did Roberto have to call her today? Answering the door and wiping her eyes, Debra's heart skips a beat as two dozen sterling silver roses, and a

148

deliveryman greets her.

"Someone really loves you, ma'am. These are some beautiful roses. Please sign here."

The tears flow down her cheeks. "There must be a mistake."

"Are you Debra Harris?"

She nods.

"Then there's no mistake. These were ordered months ago. These are very hard to come by."

Debra absently signs and takes the bouquet from the deliveryman.

"Have a nice day, ma'am."

Without saying a word, she walks over to the table and puts the vase down. She looks at the card for what seems like an eternity before finding the courage to read it.

> *My dearest darling, how do I love thee?*
> *Let me count the ways. How much time do you have?*
> *I don't know how I got so lucky to have found you, but I want you to know, I cherish every day we're together. You have made me so happy; I hope I've returned that back to you—ten fold.*
> *The best gift you've given me, is your heart.*
> *I love you honey-bunny.*
> *Happy Anniversary.*

Putting her head on her crossed arms, Debra balls for a short eternity. Once she's cried out, she looks up at the beautiful and scented roses. George had found them by accident one day.

It was their first anniversary, and he was unsure of what to send her. After wandering around the flower shop, he overheard a manager yelling at a worker. "You told him we would refund his money? Do you know how much these cost? These are very rare and expensive; I have to order these way in advance; and I can only get two dozen at a time. What am I supposed to do with them now? Take them to the cooler and hope they get bought. If not, it is coming out of your check."

George walked to the front of the store and saw the worker with his head hung low walking to the cooler with these beautiful purple-gray roses. "Excuse me, but what are those?"

"Sterling silver roses, sir; very rare, and expensive too."

"I'll take them!"

Looking up, the worker says, "Really? Are you sure? I haven't even told you how much."

"That's okay; they're perfect."

Debra remembers the first time she ever saw a sterling silver rose. Actually, she smelled them before she saw them. George came home with a big grin on his face and asked her to close her eyes. She did but couldn't help herself as an incredibly sweet aroma passed by her. She opened her eyes to see the most beautiful roses she'd ever seen. George teased her every year about not following instructions and peeking before she was allowed. He told her they were very rare but still not as special as she was.

Eyes tearing again, she can't help but think how deep their love was. Rereading the card, the words, *the best gift you have given me is your heart.* Wiping her eyes, she rushes to her purse to find Roberto's phone number. *George is watching over me. He wants me to be happy.*

Roberto's phone rings eight times before his machine picks

up.

She hangs up without leaving a message.

CHAPTER NINE

"Hi, how are you?" Amber asks.

"You're calling me to find out how my appointment went today, aren't you?"

"Well, that, and to say hello."

Chuckling, Dominque says, "It went well; better than I thought it would. I was nervous about going, and I didn't want anyone coming down on me, telling me how stupid I've been —I already know that. Anyway, my social worker, Maggie, couldn't have been any nicer. She sat me down in front of a mirror and asked what I saw. You know me, I went straight for the belly that could be a little flatter, the arms that could be a little more toned, and don't even get me started about the flesh that hangs under my neck.

"After that little exercise, she showed me pictures of models like me, and asked me to do the same. It took about eight of them before I realized I was comparing myself to every single one of them; what I loved and how I wish I could look like them. She told me their answers to the first exercise we went through. I couldn't believe these women didn't think they were perfect. I guess you could say it was my *ah-ha* moment.

"So, tonight's homework is for me to look at myself in the

mirror before I change into my nighty and find three things I love about myself—I'm not allowed to go to bed until I find them."

"I can name at least five off the top of my head, and I can't even see you! You have the most beautiful crystal blue eyes, and your red hair is so thick and shiny. Not many women can pull it off, but on you, it's super sexy. You have high chiseled cheekbones that many women would die for; you have super long legs that go up to your armpits. And your lips make Angelina Jolie jealous."

"You said nothing about my body, other than my legs."

"That's because you are way too thin. Before you went on this diet craze, I always thought you had a great figure. Your breasts were perky and high. You had the perfect hourglass shape. Your hips and butt—oh my gosh, you drove all the guys crazy at the gym every time you walked by them. They literally fell all over themselves watching you sashay past. I still think you're beautiful—inside and out, I just want the healthy version of you back."

"Me too, I'm forcing myself to look at the bones sticking out everywhere. I look in the mirror and try to imagine it's someone else's reflection, and what I think of it. You're right; I'm way too skinny, I look sick. Thanks again for caring. You, Debra, and Zya, are my family. I'm so grateful to have all of you."

As she says good night and hangs up, Amber can't help but think how strong yet fragile Dominque is. Brought up in and out of foster homes until she was sixteen, she had the potential of turning into a train wreck; instead, she chose the high road, took responsibility for herself, and changed her name from

Matilda. Her self-esteem problems stem back to never feeling like she belonged anywhere; never feeling wanted, or worthy of being loved. One day she'll find true love and happiness. She has so much to offer…so much to give.

Amber vows to be there every step of the way while Dominque struggles through this—no matter what!

"Hello?" Amber grabbed the phone on the sixth ring with her arms full of groceries. She is expecting a call from Dominque; she's surprised to hear Zya's voice.

"Amber, I'm really stuck. I don't know what to do."

Hearing the exasperation in her friend's voice, Amber realizes Zya has to be upset to call in the middle of the afternoon when she should have her nose to the grind.

Before Amber can respond, Zya continues, "Ashanti doesn't want me to see Tina. In fact, she's having a hard time believing I'm interested in pursuing a relationship with a woman. I think the fact that it's Stacey's mom doesn't help either. She said if I continue to see Tina, she go live with her dad. I know she's being melodramatic, and Tina said it's not uncommon for kids to react like this when their parents come out. Am I coming out? I never imagined this was what it's like. Tina thinks I should put my foot down and tell Ashanti I have a right to be happy, but Ashanti is so hurt."

"Does Stacey know about you two?"

"I'm not sure. I didn't ask Tina, should I?"

"That might be a start. At least Ashanti will feel she has someone to talk to about this." *Beep. Beep.* Call waiting, Dominque is calling in. "Maybe you should let her calm down a bit and then suggest she talk to Stacey."

"She's not even talking to me right now. My daughter comes first, right? Before my own happiness?"

Beep. Beep. Amber promised to be there for Dominque no matter what, but she didn't think she would have to pick between her and Zya.

"Zya, honey, I hate to do this to you, but can you hold just a second? Dominque's calling…"

Without waiting for a response, Amber clicks over to the other call. "Hey, Dom."

"I didn't think you were home." Without giving Amber a chance to respond. "I have to go get all these tests done. I filled out a questionnaire the other day, and since I don't know anything about my birth parents, I have to see a doctor. And if that's not enough, I got a notice in the mail today—I'm being audited!" Dominque sounds scared and worried.

"Are you home?" asks Amber.

"Yes," Dominque replies in a tiny voice.

"I'm on my way. Don't move a muscle."

Amber clicks back. "Zya, I'm back," she says as she grabs her keys and heads out the door.

"Is everything okay with Dom?"

"Yes, she has to get some tests done—no family history, so she's a little scared. I'm heading over there now."

"Should I come too?"

"I think you have your own crisis to deal with at home, but you're always welcome, you know that."

"I'll pass. I think I need to have a heart to heart with Ashanti. And you're right; I'll wait until after she cools down."

As Amber maneuvers her phone, purse, and keys, a familiar sports car pulls up behind her in the parking lot, blocking her way—it's Patrick.

He bounces out of his car and comes up to her. "Just hear me out, please. All I ask is that you give me ten minutes, please."

Zya hears his voice in the background. "Who's that?"

"Um—it's Patrick," she says to Zya. Then tells him, "I can't talk right now. Now is not a good time."

Realizing she's on the phone, he says, "I'll wait. Take your time." He leans up against the side of his car with his arms folded in front of him.

"What does he want?" Zya asks.

"To talk. The timing!"

"Go talk to the man, and I'll call you later."

"Are you sure? You know I'll blow him off. You are much more important to me," Amber says loud enough for him to hear.

Hearing the edge in Amber's voice, Patrick wonders if this was such a good idea. He can't go back now. This is his chance —his last one. He looks up, and Amber is staring at him with her hand on her hip.

"Please move your car and get out of my way. I have to go somewhere—it's important."

"I'll go, I promise, just please hear me out first. I thought she was you. I turned the lights down low and ended up putting that napkin over my face after I took my shorts off. I was embarrassed for being so bold—unsure how you'd react. I was nervous about making love to you too…I wasn't thinking. I thought she was you, and when I realized she wasn't, you were

157

leaving and wouldn't let me explain."

"What? Who was she?" Amber asks, confused.

"I don't know. I think she's one of Stewart's girls. She must have seen the note on the door. I heard the bushes rustling, and I couldn't look. I knew if I did, I would lose my nerve—and probably my erection. Please believe me, I really thought she was you."

"Well, then, how was I?" Amber asks, chuckling. She can't believe *Mr. Always in Control* is stuttering and so uncomfortable.

Seeing Amber smile, Patrick pleads, "Please give me another chance? I want to see you...dinner? You pick the time and the place."

"Okay, but just dinner." Shaking her head and still chuckling, Amber says, "Now, do you mind? I really have to be somewhere important."

"Oh, so you'll call me? With a day and a location?"

"Yes, now move—please."

With his palms sweating, he quickly pulls out of the driveway with a smile on his face.

"Okay, now tell me what Maggie said today, all of it?" Amber asks.

"They had me fill out a medical questionnaire. I put in a question mark in all the spaces about family history. She asked me about it today, and I told her I didn't know who my family was, so I couldn't answer those. She seemed a little concerned, but she hid it well. She told me since I was thirty-five, the first thing I had to do was get a baseline mammogram along with some blood work. She made an appointment for me with the Breast Center at the hospital. She also told me she would have to refer me to a psychiatrist in case my eating problem was the symptom of another, possibly deeper, problem. She didn't want to alarm me, but she asked me to please go the following day to speak with this doctor. She wants to be cautious and make sure we check everything. And I always thought never getting sick was a good thing."

"I'm sure it's nothing. She's just covering all the bases."

"Yeah, probably, then I get home and get this." Dominque throws down an opened letter stating there were some questions about her deductions, and an auditor will contact her to set up an appointment. "I don't have any records; you know I'm not good at keeping things organized."

"Can you call someone and try to get copies?"

"I'm going to look in my desk at work tomorrow first and see if maybe I stuffed them somewhere. When it rains, it pours."

Dominque lifts a glass of the wine from a bottle Amber has opened while they were talking.

Amber lifts hers to Dominque's. "Here's to sunshine—less rain."

Stewart enters the dining room, where Patrick is reading through tomorrow's cases. Stewart looks pale and shaken.

"What's up?" Patrick asks.

"Isabel called me. She's pregnant—she says it's mine!"

"What? Wait a minute—who's Isabel?" Patrick asks.

"You know, my late night, last resort booty call. I swear I've always used condoms with her. I always protect myself!"

Patrick goes to the fridge and brings Stewart a cold beer. "Here, it looks like you need this. How does she know it's yours? Isn't she the one you call a nymph? Who knows how many guys she's slept with. I bet it's a trap."

"That's what I thought too, but she swears it happened the night she surprised me in the hot tub, and I wasn't wearing any protection."

Patrick's face turns ghost white.

"I've wracked my brain and I swear, I don't remember. I must have been really drunk."

Patrick grabs Stewart's beer and drains it in one long gulp. "I thought it was Amber. I turned the lights practically off and put a napkin over my face because I didn't want to chicken out. I didn't realize it wasn't her until it was too late. I just wanted to get our first intimate encounter over with. I was stressing so much over it, I didn't even think about protection." Patrick continues, "Oh my God, I could have picked up something from her! I have to get tested. What if it is my baby? Oh, I'm fucked!"

Stewart goes to the fridge and gets the last two beers, opens one and puts it in front of Patrick. "Thank God! At least this time, you're the one with the drama."

Patrick looks up as if to say, *really?*

"Sorry man, it's going to be okay. First off, I'm sure you're not the father. She sleeps around with all the eligible men in South Florida—that girl can never get enough. But, she always insists I wear a condom... You mean to tell me you didn't think about using one with Amber? I know it's been a while for you but come on man, you're smarter than that."

"I know, you're right, I was nervous about making love to her—I didn't think it through. Where do I go to get tested? What if she has AIDS?"

"There's a clinic downtown that'll do the testing anony- mously—for AIDS that is. If you want to get tested for any other STD, you should see a urologist."

Patrick looks up at Stewart, surprised.

"Yes, I do know way too much about this, which is exactly why I always use a condom. Now, as far as Isabel goes, let me deal with her, okay?"

"Sorry man, you definitely want to get tested.

CHAPTER TEN

"I think I blew it. Roberto called, I told him I wasn't ready," Debra states in her appointment with Brian.

Brian hears the disappointment in her voice, but doesn't share it—he's glad.

"I called him back about an hour later, but he didn't answer. It was almost midnight there so I'm sure he was home he just didn't want to talk to me. I hurt him. I left a message but I haven't heard from him."

"Have you decided now you *want* to be with him?" Brian asks.

Debra tells Brian about the roses George sent her for their anniversary. At first, it was painful, but then she felt it was a sign; it was George telling her to be happy.

As she explains, he notices the sparkle in her deep blue eyes. His eyes lock onto her full lips, moving so fast as she talks about how wonderful George was, and how he always knew how to say the right thing at the right time. Brian tries to imagine how sweet her lips would be. Can *he* make her this happy? He catches himself and realizes he has to get her to another doctor; he can't see her anymore. But how? Does he tell her how he feels? Will she feel embarrassed, violated, or even worse, threatened?

"Debra, you've come a long way in a very short time. I have to say, I'm impressed. I think it might be time to go to the next step in your life, inviting companionship, and I happen to know the perfect therapist who can help you with this. She's a woman, so it might be easier for you to open up and discuss these things with her."

Unsure why the sudden need to change, Debra says, "Really? You don't want to be my therapist anymore? I'm comfortable with you. Did I say, or do, something?"

"No, no—no, you didn't do or say anything wrong. I just think you might be more comfortable discussing these things with another woman."

"I have my friends, and they're great, but I feel as if I can say things to you I can't tell them. If you think it would be best for me to change therapists, I will. But I'd prefer to keep seeing you."

"As long as you are comfortable, then yes, I would be happy to continue seeing you…as your therapist. The offer is always on the table in case you change your mind."

Brian's fidgeting makes her nervous. She's never seen him like this and can't imagine what she might have said to make him behave this way. "Okay, well, I have to pick up Tracey. I'll see you next week."

Debra leaves his office a bit confused and unsure. He's always been so attentive and helpful. If she's honest with herself, it's felt a few times like he wasn't listening. His eyes were looking at her, but he wasn't seeing her. And a few times when she's talked about Roberto, he's become anxious—not able to sit in his seat. She wonders if Brian is jealous but dismisses the thought since that would be unethical. He can't be interested in his clients. Or maybe, that's why he wants her to see another therapist… Could it be?

"So, how did your blood test and mammogram come out?" Amber asks Dominque on the phone.

"Blood tests came out good. My blood sugar was a little high, so we're going to monitor it. I haven't had my mammogram yet. The insurance company says I'm too young to have one, so Maggie is fighting them. I have to get a pap smear, and they'll do a manual breast exam on me, for now."

"You don't get regular pap smears?" Amber asks, alarmed.

"No, I guess it's been about six years since my last one. I never liked going to the doctor, so I guess I kept putting it off. Maggie made me an appointment with a female, so that should help."

Knowing how sexually active she is, Amber is shocked to hear Dominque's laid-back attitude. She can't believe she hasn't been getting her regular screening done. Deciding to brush it aside, for now, she says, "Well, tell me how you're feeling overall."

"Pretty good—I'm making myself see my bony ribs and shoulders, and I am seeing some changes. I've gained three pounds this past week. I'm up to ninety-four now."

Amber cringes as she hears how little Dominque weighs. Tears roll down her cheek as she imagines how close she came to hurting herself beyond repair. "That's great honey, I'm glad to hear you're doing so well," Amber says, sniffling quietly.

"Are you crying?"

"Out of joy—just glad to know you're getting better."

"I have to share," Dominque continues. "I'm doing even better. You know, the *Is it the Uniform* article you're writing for the magazine?"

"Yes," Amber replies.

"Well, this sexy hot cop came into the office today looking for you. Did I mention he was hot?"

Amber chuckles as Dominque continues.

"Anyway, I told him you were out and asked if I could help. He immediately goes into his *hubba-hubba can you ever help me* routine. I used to fall for that crap just wanting the chance to be with this hot guy. This time, I didn't bite. I gave him the cold shoulder, and he immediately did some fast back-pedaling, apologizing for coming on so strong, of which I agree —he did. He asked me for my phone number, and I told him, *no, thank you* and to have a nice day."

"I'm proud of you. That's a big step. I don't mean to sound insensitive, but you do have a history of getting down and dirty too quickly with the hotties."

"No, you're right. Anyway, late this afternoon, I got a sweet flower arrangement from him. Apologizing again, along with his number."

"What are you going to do?" Amber asks.

"I'm going to send him a note to the station thanking him and I accept his apology, but I still won't go out with him."

Amber, laughing on the phone, asks, "Really? You're not going to call him?"

"No, I think it's good for me to say no. I think I need to be more selective."

"Wow, what's gotten into you?"

"I don't know. I guess I have to take control of something in my life. First, my health, then my self-esteem, and finally this damn auditing crap."

"Oh yeah, how's that going?"

"Well, I found some of my receipts. They're not in the best of shape, but I have them. The auditor called me; he's coming by tonight."

Dominque's doorbell rings.

"Speak of the devil, and I mean the devil—gotta go. I'll call you later if I survive."

"You better call me," Amber says, fading away as Dominque quickly hangs up and rushes to the door.

On the other side, she finds a typical accounting nerd nervously fixing his hair. His dark gray suit, crisp white shirt, and dark maroon tie are very generic. His light brown hair parted over way too far to the side needs a cut. His wire-rim glasses seem too big for his face as he pushes them up.

He quickly shifts his black leather briefcase into his other hand, extending the now empty one. "Matilda Patterson?" he asks.

Refusing his hand, she responds, "I'd prefer it if you call me Dominque; I had it legally changed."

"I'm sorry, Miss Patterson. I'm Tad Johnson."

Trying desperately from laughing out loud, she turns her face to the side as she invites him in. She bets he has a tad of a johnson, and can't help but let out a little chuckle.

"Something funny?" he asks.

"No, I apologize. Just got off the phone with a friend, remembered a joke she told me."

"Good, for a moment there I thought maybe you're laughing at my name."

Dominque bursts out, laughing. "I'm sorry."

"It's okay. You're not laughing at me; we're laughing together. My parents have a sense of humor."

"Well, that certainly broke the ice," Dominque says, breathing a sigh of relief.

"Miss Patterson, I don't want to take up too much of your time. You can't find any of the receipts or documentation for the year 2012, is that correct?"

Dominque motions to the dining room table for Tad to have a seat. "I've found a few," she says as she hands him a stack of wrinkled, wet-stained documents.

"Miss Patterson, if you're unable to provide back-up for these deductions, I'm afraid I'm going to have to collect a check for $7,639.27. Just over five thousand of that is the amount of the deductions you took, the rest being penalties and interest."

"I don't have that kind of money. How much time do I have to get it to you?" Her bottom lids now pooling as she bites her lower lip.

Tad puffs up his chest, he's used to this part of the job. This is when he puts on his cold shoulder—I'm not buying your sad story routine. "Miss Patterson, I'm sorry about this. However, this is serious. Do you realize you can go to jail for tax evasion?"

Eyes wide and lower lip quivering, Dominque asks, "Jail?"

"Yes, ma'am, you can. I'm not saying that's what's going to happen. However, you need to get this taken care of as quickly as possible. You're being charged a substantial penalty and in-terest every day it's left unpaid."

Pleading, Dominque asks, "Do I have any alternatives at all? Can I make payments?"

"Miss Patterson, we can set up a payment schedule for you for say, one year? We will still charge you with penalties and interest. I can calculate roughly how much your monthly pay-ment will be." He removes a calculator from his case, his bony fingers flying across the numbers. Jotting figures down on a notepad, he finally looks up. "Your payments will be roughly $850.00 a month."

"I can't afford that. I'm barely getting by as it is now. I live paycheck to paycheck."

"Do you have any credit cards to get a cash advance?"

Dominque shakes her head.

"Any property you can borrow against?"

Again, she shakes her head. The tears spill over as she drops her face into her hands. Just when she thought she was getting a grip on her life, someone pulls the rug out from under her.

Tad keeps his cool, not letting her emotions sway him. He's seen every *pretty girl* routine out there. He could probably write a book on it. "Now, now, Miss Patterson, let's dry up the tears; they won't make this go away."

Jumping up from the table, her hair askew, through gritted teeth, she says, "You think this is easy for me? You think these tears are for you, you—you—you cold fish." Dominque screams at him, "Don't pat yourself on the back, Mr. account-ing nerd."

Tad, stunned by the rage and emotion spewing from her.

She's not acting—those are actual tears. "I'm sorry Miss Patterson, I don't mean to be so cold. I see this all the time. I wish it could make a difference but it doesn't. My hands are tied."

Grabbing a tissue, she wipes her eyes on the way to the refrigerator. She pulls out two beers putting one in front of Tad.

"Oh, thank you, but I can't. I'm still on the job."

"Oh, give it a break, will you? Just when I thought I was getting my life back together, you come in here all smug and rip it back apart. The least you can do is have a drink with me," Dominque demands.

Tad opens the beer and takes a sip without saying a word.

"Not that you would care, but they tossed me around between several foster homes as a kid. It seems no one wanted me—I was too much to handle." Putting her fingers up and making quotes signs as she says the last few words. "It's taken me over twenty years to get to the point in my life where I like myself and I'm in control of my life. They recently diagnosed me with anorexia. I'm on the road to recovery; and I've gained five pounds in the last ten days. I even turned down this hot cop today at the office. Before, I would jump at the chance to get into his pants. But today, I was turning my life around. Today was the first day of the rest of my life. Then you come in here telling me I have to pay you eight hundred and fifty dollars a month for the next year because I lost my receipts. Well, sorry if I seem a little upset. I'm a little tired of being kicked down every time I pick myself up." The anger surpasses as Dominque looks down at her hands with tears streaming down her face.

Tad, feeling ashamed, says, "Miss Patterson—Dominque, maybe I can give you some time to get those receipts together…let's say a month? Will that help you out?"

"It will just prolong the inevitable. I don't have them. I'm not the most organized person if you haven't already figured that out." She picks up and waves the document to prove her point.

Looking over his notes. "Well, let's see, you claimed gas, mileage, and some clothing expenses here."

"I'm a model; I was told I could deduct those things when I needed to go on calls."

"That is correct, you can. You have several hundreds of dollars for make-up, hair, nails…"

Dominque cuts him off. "All things I needed. The revenue that year was for the few jobs I got. Other than that, I didn't have any income."

"Since I'm having a beer with you, can we say I'm off the clock?"

Not sure where he's going with this, however, she decides, there's no way she's going to sleep with this geek.

"You're a lovely woman…"

Here we go!

"I'm sure you can go back to the gas stations, hair salons and department stores and try to get copies of those receipts. For the mileage, I just need a form filled out with the beginning and ending mileage on your odometer from your car. You can download the form from our website."

"You think those people are going to have receipts from three years ago?"

"You're a smart girl; you'll figure it out."

Tad puts everything away in his briefcase. Taking a sheet of paper off his notepad, he scribbles something on it and hands it to her. "Here's my cell number; call me if you have any questions. In the meantime, I'll put a thirty-day hold on your audit. I'll be back to see you next month. Keep up the good work, everybody deserves a break sometime and today seems to be your lucky day. All I ask is that you keep this friendly get-together between us. I want to help, but if my boss finds out, I could lose my job. And unfortunately, you'll still owe the money." Tad shakes her hand. "Good luck, I'll see myself out."

Dominque's jaw drops. She's stunned at the quick turn of events. Unable to say anything, she watches him leave, closing the front door gently behind him.

Patrick's assistant beeps him to announce a call from Amber.

"Can you please tell her I'm on a call and take a message?"

"I'll be happy to, but you know this is the third time she's called. She probably won't call back again."

"I'll take it."

"Amber, hi, how are you?"

"Good, I thought maybe you were avoiding me."

"What do you mean?"

"I've called you two times; didn't you get my messages?"

"No, I didn't. I'm so sorry. The office has been crazy these past two weeks. I'm sure they're here in this massive pile of phone messages on my desk," Patrick says as he looks at the two pink slips bearing her name sitting on his desk.

"Well, I'm glad I called back then—I almost didn't. I thought about what happened, and although it goes against my better judgment, I'm gonna give you a chance to make it up to me."

Patrick panics inside. He has yet to receive the results from his AIDS test. They told him it would only take 48-hours, but that was six days ago.

With no comment from Patrick and sensing his uneasiness, she adds, "That is if you still want one?"

"What? Huh? Oh yes, I'm sorry—have my head wrapped around this important case." Patrick picks up a file on his desk, a standard *Last Will and Testament*.

A bit exasperated, Amber continues, "Why don't you give me a call when and if you want to see me again."

Before she can hang up, he says, "Amber, I'm very sorry. Yes, I really want to see you again. Please, name the time and the place, and thank you for giving me a second chance."

A little calmer, she says, "How about tomorrow night? Johnny V's at eight? I think maybe we should start over."

"Eight o'clock, I'll be there. Better yet, I'll be there at seven-thirty."

Amber chuckles. "Okay, I'll see you then. Now get back to work."

Amber set him up for a test, and he passed. A player would already have plans for Saturday night—date night. Maybe he was telling the truth.

Debra uses the time when she's doing menial work, such as laundry, to think things through. To set some goals and make plans. At least until the next time she can think straight. Her bouts of depression are coming less frequently, but she still has them. Her last appointment with Brian is playing in a loop. She can't make heads or tails of it. *Maybe he's uncomfortable talking about sex and relationships? That can't be, he's a therapist. Surely he's used to hearing a lot more vivid and detailed stories.*

Debra pictures Brian in her mind as her body leans up against the corner of the washing machine. She's abruptly taken back to reality as the machine goes into its spin cycle. Thoughts of needing a new washer quickly leave her mind as her body reacts to the advantage of having an old one that bounces around and vibrates uncontrollably. Instead of fighting it, she goes along for the ride.

Slightly embarrassed, yet in need of release, she lets her mind wander as she hopes and prays for a long spin cycle. She fantasizes about Roberto. She quickly changes that image and visualizes George. His hands are slow and gentle—his caresses are so sweet. His shoulders are broad, and when he wraps his arms around her, they seem to go on forever, cradling her, making her safe. Her hair keeps changing to dark brown. Her brows furrow as she forces herself to think of dirty blonde instead. She cannot see his face, but she imagines his kisses on her neck, on her chest.

Without realizing it, she undulates her hips towards the corner of the washer imaging them connected—making love. Losing control the image turns into Roberto thrusting faster and deeper; her hips matching the rhythm.

Within minutes, Debra explodes into ecstasy and releases the pent-up tension and stress from the previous three months. She opens her eyes and thinks she may have to do laundry more often. Closing her eyes, she lets out a deep breath as the dark-haired man to trying to push out of her mind, reappears. He pulls his head back to look into her eyes, and his head goes into the light. His hair isn't as dark as she thought; it's more light brown...and he has hazel eyes.

Throwing her eyes open, she gasps. Her hand goes immediately to her mouth as she realizes her fantasy man isn't Roberto or George—it's Brian!

Patrick arrives at seven-thirty, on the dot, as promised.

Amber walks through the door at eight-fifteen. She's usually prompt, but tonight, she wants him to be uncomfortable—maybe even think she won't show. Although she's giving him a chance, the pain still exists.

Patrick sees her from the bar and immediately smiles wide and greets her.

"Sorry I'm late, I wasn't able to get out of the office when I had hoped."

"That's okay, I deserve it. And may I say..."—he looks her up and down—"totally worth the wait."

Walking to the table behind her, he can't help but watch her hips sway from side to side in her knit skirt.

Amber smiles as she drops her head to look at the menu. She wants to be here, but she's so nervous. No one's ever made her feel insecure, yet this man makes her knees go weak and her heart go pitter-patter. They've been off to a rocky start since almost the beginning. Something keeps pulling her back to him, but she must protect her heart. "I'll have the rack of lamb, please—medium," she says as the waiter arrives at the table.

"Would you care for a drink to start the evening, Madame?"

Embarrassed, she jumped to the main meal before ordering cocktails, she nods and orders a glass of house merlot.

"Wow, you must be hungry."

"Famished actually, no time for lunch. I'm working on this article, *Is it the Uniform,* and my deadline to go to editing is tomorrow."

"So?" he asks.

"So…what?"

"Is it the uniform?"

Chuckling, she replies, "Actually, it's not. It's the attitude—the pride, when he's wearing it." Amber gets right into the details of her article and her research, telling Patrick all about the test sessions she set up. "I interviewed these men with and without their uniforms. It's amazing how many, not all, were so much more secure—more masculine than when they were in uniform. It's like it's some armor of testosterone."

"Not all of them changed?" Patrick asks, intrigued.

"No, it's funny, but most of the older ones seemed comfortable in their skin regardless of what they had on. It was amazing to ask the same questions and get similar answers, but the body language was so different. I enjoyed doing this project. So, is your suit your uniform?" Amber asks.

Cheeks changing color, Patrick says, "Maybe. We've proven I sometimes have a hard time being in nothing but my skin." He takes Amber's hands in his. "I'm sorry about what happened. It was so stupid of me; I never imagined what happened, could actually—happen."

"It's hard, but I understand how it all played out. We're

starting over again, remember?" Amber lifts her glass and toasts, "To new beginnings."

"To new beginnings!"

"So, tell me about this tough case you're working on?"

Almost choking on his wine. "It's boring—you wouldn't be interested."

"Try me. I might surprise you," Amber says.

"That you already do." Patrick looks into her eyes. "You are beautiful, smart, strong, and extremely sexy. How is a total package like you, still single?"

"Smooth way to change the subject. Thank you for the compliments…let's just say I refuse to settle. I want someone who will complement my life, not complicate it. I'm perfectly happy on my own. I have a great job, great friends, I love to paint…"

He interrupts her, "Paint? Really? What do you like to paint?"

"I'm an animal lover so I like to draw and paint them. Wild animals, domestic ones, even fish and imaginary creatures of the deep."

"Wow, you surprise me. You don't seem to be the artsy, bohemian type."

"I'll take that as another compliment, I think. It relaxes me. My biggest problem is I don't know when to stop. So, I won't start one until Friday night after work. That way, I can paint through the weekend and hope that at some point on Sunday, I can put my brush down and leave it alone until the next weekend. Sometimes I can't resist and I touch it up here and there during the week."

"Isn't that the number one problem most artists have?

Knowing when it's done?"

"Yeah, I guess. There is such a thing as overdoing it. Some potential masterpieces were ruined because they kept messing with it." After an uncomfortable pause, she adds, "I've never done people yet, but I want to try. You want to pose for me sometime."

"I would love to; just tell me when and what to wear and I'll be there."

"What to wear? That's easy—your birthday suit."

Patrick's eyes dart around the room as he gulps down his water.

Amber, noticing the reaction, chuckles as dinner arrives. She's enjoying the effect she has on him, so she takes it to the next level; this feeling of being in control with a man she typically feels like she's in high-school. She promised herself she wouldn't sleep with him tonight; but it feels right. Deciding to take the heat up a notch, she replicates a famous dance movie scene by slowly sucking the meat off one of her chops. Looking directly into his eyes, she licks the juices from her lips.

Pressing his fist against his thigh, *breathe—breathe*—he has to remind himself.

She turns her head slightly. With their eyes locked, she tilts her head back slightly, putting the entire chop in her mouth. "Mmm, this is good—so hot and juicy."

Patrick shifts in his seat and bunches up the napkin so no one can see the tent forming in his lap.

She sucks on the chop a few times before devouring the meat. She licks her lips again—hoping get gets the hint.

Entranced, he reaches over and touches her face.

She turns, capturing his finger between her lips, deciding to give it the same treatment she did to the chop.

He is oblivious to everything around him. The noise from the other diners, their silverware clinking against their plates, the servers weaving in and out between the tables, and the delicious aromas coming from the kitchen, all fade away. He sees nothing but this beautiful creature—her face aglow by candlelight, teasing him. He grabs his cell phone from his pocket and looks at the screen.

"Am I boring you?" she asks, the trance broken by his action.

"Oh no, are you kidding? I'm waiting for an important text. I was hoping it would come tonight."

Amber pulls out the knife and fork and finishes her meal quickly—embarrassed at herself for being so forward. *Any man who would pull out his phone while being seduced is not the one for me.* She pushes her plate away from her with half the meal left and motions the waiter over. "Check, please."

"Wait, I haven't even taken a bite of my meal. Wait?"

Amber gets up from the table as the waiter comes over.

She looks at the check and drops $150 on the table. "Keep the change." She walks out of the restaurant.

Patrick's phone chimes with the text he was waiting for from Stewart. *It's negative. You're good to go, bro.* Hoping tonight would be the night, he asked his roommate to pretend to be him when they called with the results of his AIDS test.

Debra is excited and anxious, like a little girl at Christmas waiting to open her presents. His flight got delayed enough to get her heart racing and for her to doubt herself. She can't send him back now—she asked him to come. She needs to move ahead with her feelings and see where they lead.

Out of the corner of her eye, she sees a person exit the terminal—it's him. Her heart skips a beat as he comes towards her with a smile so big, it makes her knees buckled. He's so handsome in a white cotton button-down shirt and relaxed blue jeans.

He picks her up and twirls her around. Before she can say anything, his lips are on hers. She doesn't have time to think; her head is in the clouds. Being lifted with her feet dangling is partially to blame.

"Mia Bella, I have missed you."

The kiss flusters Debra. She needs to gain her composure. As she looks into his handsome face, she grabs the sides of his head and kisses him slowly. Passion takes over as her kisses become more passionate. "Where are you staying?"

"Marriott on beach," Roberto replies in his thick accent.

"Come on, let's go." She grabs his arm and heads towards the door.

Laughing, he says, "Debra, Mia Bella, I must get my case, no?"

Blushing, she slows down, realizing how this must look. "Wow, I'm so sorry. I can only imagine what you must think of me right now."

He stops, twirls her around, and cups her chin in his hand. "I think you are most beautiful woman my eyes have seen. You have very good heart. Mia Bella, I think I love you."

He kisses her gently, and this time, her knees go weak, but he catches her. He hugs her and whispers, "I love you."

"I wanted to fill you in on my talk with Ashanti; she's finally talking to me. It's a start. I think she's confused more than anything. She promised she won't call her dad or do anything stupid, but she asked me to please be sure, one hundred percent positive this is what I really want. She can't talk to Stacey about it. In fact, she's not sure she wants to stay friends with her. When I asked her why, she said she didn't want to turn gay."

"Oh my! You told her she can't become gay if it's not in her DNA, right? Wait a minute—it might be in her DNA," Amber replies teasing.

"Thanks, Amber, you're a big help. I told her I never imagined in my wildest dreams I would have this conversation with her. If I hadn't met Tina, I would still be straight or at least not know I was gay, or bi…I'm so confused."

"Take a deep breath; I really wish you drank because now would be a great time for a glass of wine. Let's simplify this, shall we?"

"Oh, please do," Zya states.

"Tell me what the ideal mate for you would be. Just blurt out their qualities, starting with the most important one. Don't think about what you're going to say, and don't worry, I'm going to write them down, okay?"

"Okay here goes, makes me feel safe, is the strong one from time to time, smart, funny, cares about what I want, unselfish, loving, giving, honest, creative, my best friend…"

"Shall I read them back to you?"

"No, I get it. I didn't list any physical attributes, did I?"

"No, you didn't."

"Tina fits every single one of those, doesn't she?"

"I don't know, you tell me…does she?" Amber asks.

"Yes, she completes me. Oh, that sounds so corny." Zya chuckles. "Thank you, Amber. Maybe I was making it all so difficult. Now, if only I can get my wonderful daughter to accept it. She wants me to be happy; I know she does. She also asked me if that's why I turned down Doug's proposal."

"What? Doug proposed to you? When?"

"A few months ago. I didn't know she knew, but she said she overhead our phone conversation."

"You never told me. I'm proud of you for turning him down. I know how much you love him."

"I think it was more habit than love. It's funny, I think about Tina, and I have everything I ever wanted right here. Then I think about Doug and our time together…I spent sixteen years of my life trying to mold him into what I wanted and then myself into what he wanted. I guess even if it doesn't work out with Tina, she's taught me a lot. Now I know how it feels to be loved unconditionally."

"So, Ashanti is okay with you turning down her dad?"

"Absolutely not. In fact, she still has it in her mind that maybe this thing with Tina is just a fling, and it will help me find my way back to Doug. I know I need to help her through this; I wish she would call Stacey and talk to her."

"Have you mentioned this to Tina?"

"Yeah, we talked earlier tonight. She said it's my decision—it's my life. She wants me to choose a certain way, but she said no matter what, meeting and loving me, was one of the greatest things to have ever happened to her. She doesn't regret a thing."

"Wow, I think I'm in love with her," Amber says, laughing.

"Yeah, she's pretty special." She quickly changes the subject. "Ashanti went to the homecoming game at school. She really loves it—even if she is a lowly freshman."

The front door bursts open by a distraught Ashanti with a ripped and blood-stained shirt and her hair sticking out in all directions.

"Oh, my God!" Zya drops the phone, forgetting all about Amber.

"Zya! Zya! What's wrong?" screams Amber through the receiver.

Zya meets Ashanti as she runs into her mom's arms, crying hysterically. "Oh, baby girl, what's wrong? What happened to you?"

Ashanti holds on tight. Her cries sound like that of an injured animal. Not cries—screams.

Zya smooths her daughter's hair as tears pool in her lower lids. "It's okay, honey, whatever it is, it's okay. Want to tell me about it?"

Ashanti shakes her head.

"Okay," Zya responds as the first helpless tear falls. Zya sits on the couch with Ashanti curled into a ball, wailing nonstop. Zya rocks her back and forth and starts singing one of her favorite childhood songs. "Hush little darling, don't you cry…"

After about ten minutes of hard sobbing, Ashanti's tears dry up. Taking a tissue from the cocktail table, Zya wipes her eyes and nose for her. "Now, can you tell me what happened?"

"They're so mean, mommy. How can they be so mean to

me? I didn't do anything to them! I don't even know them!" Ashanti buries her face into her mom's lap again. The never-ending waterworks flowing full force.

"Baby, who was mean to you?"

Between sobs, she says, "The kids...those nasty mean kids."

"What did they do to you, and why do you have blood on your blouse?"

Pulling back, Ashanti looks down at her blouse then pulls it away, revealing a minor cut in her side.

"What happened?" Her eyes wide, Zya says as she moves her into the kitchen for better light. And to see if she will need stitches. It's like someone punched her in the gut, seeing her child hurt like this.

"They had a knife, mommy. They said we didn't need any more of my kind here and they were going to make me suffer."

"I don't understand—because you're black?"

"No, because I'm Muslim."

Without knocking, Amber rushes into Zya's house. She finds her in the living room rocking Ashanti, who's sound asleep, back and forth. The wet trails on her face, displaying the grief in her heart. "Is she okay? Oh my God, Zya, is she okay?"

Zya shakes her head.

Ashanti wakes up and looks up at Amber.

Amber's heart breaks as she can see the hurt and pain in their hearts.

"Come on, honey. Why don't I help you get cleaned up and to bed? Don't worry about your homework tonight, I'll talk to your teachers tomorrow," Zya says. Exhausted and defeated, Zya helps her upstairs, leaving Amber at the dining room table.

Zya comes down about ten minutes later. The tears replaced with glaring eyes, fists, and a vein bulging on her forehead—if looks could kill!

"Please tell me what happened. Is she all right?" Amber pleads.

Zya says nothing as she gets a mug and fills it with boiling water. After putting in a tea bag and honey, she rests her hands on the counter, dropping her head. "I'm not sure if she is okay —I don't think I'm okay!" Zya hits her fist hard against the kitchen bar top, making everything on it jump.

Amber jumps at the same time. She's never seen Zya so mad.

Zya takes a deep drink from her mug, the liquid scorching all the way day her throat. "Ashanti got beat up tonight at the game."

"What? Why? Because you might be gay?" Amber asks.

"No, because we're Muslim," Zya answers through gritted teeth.

Amber feels the wind knocked out of her from the venom in Zya's words.

"I guess this resolves my relationship with Tina."

"What do you mean?"

"I'm moving back to Africa with Ashanti. I don't want her raised in this toxic environment."

"Wait a minute, is that the right thing to do? Aren't you giving them exactly what they want? What about your business?"

"I don't care if I am giving them what they want—they win! They pulled a knife on her, Amber," she says as fresh hot tears stream down Zya's cheeks.

Amber walks over and hugs her. "I'm sorry. I'm so very, very sorry. I wish I had a magic wand, and I could make the mean, hating people in the world just go away."

Zya smiles a little, then drinks the last of her hot tea. "I'll say extra prayers tomorrow. I need something stronger." Walking to her kitchen, she pulls out a bottle of scotch and pours an inch into the bottom of her cup. In one gulp, it's gone. "That's better."

"Zya, please think twice about leaving. Really, is that the lesson you want to teach Ashanti?"

"They cut her! They could have killed her! What if I stay and they succeed next time? She won't be around for me to teach her any lessons. She loved going to school; she felt safe there. Now what do I do?"

"How about going to the school and talking to her teachers? Or the principal? Have you thought about talking to the cops?" Amber asks.

"I suggested that, but Ashanti asked me to let her handle it."

"Zya, you have a vast enterprise here. Think about all the people who work for you."

"I started this business on my own, and I can start another one. I know I'd be putting all those people out of work, but Ashanti is my number one priority; I can't pick my staff over her. I could have set up manufacturing overseas like most of the other designers, but I wanted to print, *Made in the USA*, proudly on my label. My workers are like family—Ashanti *is* family."

Thinking about Ashanti, her face softens. "I remember September eleven like it was yesterday. I had just finished my morning prayers, thinking about one day teaching Ashanti the Koran. I was full of so much love. Then I looked up and watched the towers fall. Why? Why would anyone want to hurt so many innocent people? Would I dare to raise a Muslim child when these radicals were so full of hatred and vile? Islam is a loving religion, one of forgiveness and peace, and caring for one another. I couldn't believe someone could warp our religion into a terrorist act, and now this...funny how everything comes full circle," Zya states.

"Feel better?" Amber asks.

"No, but thanks for listening. I hear about this all the time on the TV and the radio, but I never think it's going to happen here. We're good people; helping wherever we can. Even suffering ourselves, so others don't go without."

"Zya, you are one of the warmest, kindest, most generous person I know. I wish it weren't true, but bad things happen to good people—I just really wish it wasn't happening to you."

"Funny, two days ago we were sitting around this dining room table enjoying Thanksgiving together, saying how thankful we were for so many things. Remember what I was most thankful for?"

Amber nods her head.

"Yeah, that's right, I'm thankful for the opportunities this country has given me. Becoming a citizen was one of the best days of my life."

"Right behind giving birth to Ashanti?" Amber asks.

That was enough to help calm Zya down and cause her to take a deep breath. "You're right, right behind having my baby girl. I know it's not most people I'm mad at. I just wish the authorities and people with at least half a brain would start doing something about it."

Amber gives Zya a big hug. "It's all going to work out, you'll see."

"I'm going to count on that little Miss Optimistic."

"Yep, that's me! Better than the alternative."

CHAPTER ELEVEN

Debra helps Tracey pack her weekend bag a little too hastily.

"Mommy, those don't match! Those are my school clothes! Can I pack my bag myself?"

"Okay," Debra replies.

Debra painfully stands by and watches as her neat and organized little girl slowly and diligently, picks and matches her outfits before she packs them away for her weekend with Grandma. Debra is so glad her mom agreed to take her on such short notice.

"Ooh," Debra says as she feels something swim across her abdomen.

"Is it the baby? Is it the baby?" Tracey squeals.

"Either that or a powerful gas pang."

"Oh, Mommy." Tracey giggles and runs over and puts her hands on Debra's belly. "I feel it! I feel it! It's my little sister. She wants to come out and play."

Glowing, Debra corrects her, "It could be your little brother, you know, and you have plenty of time before he or she can come out to play. Now let's hurry and get you packed. Grandma is waiting in the living room."

Debra goes out of Tracey's room and stops to lean up

against the wall. Holding her belly with one hand, she looks up at the ceiling, kissing her other hand and blowing a kiss, *thank you* she whispers.

While Tracey is with her grandmother, Debra and Roberto spend most of their time in his hotel room. However, tonight they enjoy a meal at a popular restaurant on the Intracoastal.

Waiting for their table, Debra is excited when she spots Brian leaving the restaurant. As he notices her and smiles, she immediately becomes uncomfortable. "Oh, Brian, It's so good to see you."

"You too, Debra," Brian replies. His smile drops as soon as the Italian standing beside her turns around with a scowl on his face.

"Brian, I'd like to introduce you to Roberto."

"Hello, I've heard so much about you," Brian says as he extends his hand with a strained smile.

"I cannot say the same," Roberto replies with a slight growl and one eyebrow raised.

"No, you don't understand, this is Brian Phelps, Dr. Brian Phelps—my therapist."

Relaxing his shoulders, Roberto says, "Oh, yes, Debra has talked of you." He shakes Brian's hand with both of his.

"Are you coming in for dinner?" Debra asks.

"No, actually, I've just eaten and now heading home to a pile of paperwork."

"Bet your wife will be glad to have you home," Debra unconsciously adds. *Why would I care?*

"No little woman waiting for me—that would be so cliché. Nice to meet you; have a good evening," he says, shaking hands with Roberto. He leaves without meeting Debra's gaze.

"He likes you," Roberto states.

"What? Oh no, he can't, he's not allowed. It's against the law, or code of ethics, or something like that. No fraternizing with the patients," Debra says too quickly.

Roberto looks at her, scratching his chin.

"He doesn't like me," she states.

"He likes you, I can see it," Roberto states, then turns, denying her the chance to respond.

The hostess escorts them to a romantic corner table on the dock. Debra's glow from their afternoon of slow, passionate lovemaking, now replaced with tension as she bites her lower lip and twirls her hair. Roberto has told her in all the dialects he knows, including body language, how much he loves her. She can't say it back—it's too soon, but she cares so deeply for him. Now she's completely confused. Why did her stomach do flips when she saw Brian? Why would she want to know if he's married?

Roberto, sensing Debra's mind is far away, gently takes her hand into his to regain her attention. "You like him too?" Roberto asks, a little hurt in his eyes.

"Oh no, please, you are so wrong, Roberto. He's just my therapist."

"Mia Bella, no one understands the look of love better than us Italians, no? I will have to work harder to win your heart." He brings her hand to his lips and kisses it gently.

"Roberto, I'm so glad we met. You've been so patient and understand with me, I wouldn't do anything to jeopardize that, I promise. I would like to see how it goes with us. I still need time—I miss my husband desperately, but being with you, especially this weekend, has been heaven. You make me happy."

"They why you no say you love me? You love him instead."

George was not the jealous type. When other men appreci- ated her, it made him feel lucky. They trusted each other com- pletely. This green monster she feels from Roberto is some- thing she's never dealt with before. Although he may be right —there is something that happens to her when Brian is around, she pushes it down; she's with Roberto now.

"No, I don't—I love you."

Amber rushes out the door to catch her cab to the airport as her cell phone rings. Dominque is calling.

"Hello."

"Hey, you busy?"

"Well—actually, I'm on my way to the airport."

"You are? Where you going?"

"I'm on assignment to do some research on women and the stock market. I thought I'd take a weekend trip to the Big Apple. They're lighting the tree in Rockefeller Center. I've never seen it before, so I'll finally get my chance."

"Wow, that sounds great. Going alone?"

"Yes, alone. Who would I take with me?"

"Patrick?"

"He's history The dreams are over—he's over! What was I thinking!"

"Well, have a good time, and let's get together when you get back."

"Hang on a sec." Amber tells the taxi driver, "Airport please, *US Airways.*" Now speaking to Dominque again she says, "Sorry, don't want to miss my flight. So, what's up? You called me, remember?"

"Oh yeah, it can wait until you get back."

"Spill it," Amber demands.

"I got a CD in the mail today from the President of my Fan Club. It's nice jazzy stuff. The card said this music reminded him of my flowing red silky locks. He hopes it relaxes me and puts my mind at ease."

"Who is sending these gifts to you?"

"I wish I knew; it's getting fun, the mystery and all."

"Still think it's the cop?"

"I don't know, maybe. I ran into him the other day at Star-buck's. I waved to him, but he didn't wave back. It was a bit uncomfortable."

"Enjoy this while you can, my dear. One day the fantasy may turn out to be better than reality."

"Ouch, is that a bit of pessimism from Miss Optimistic?"

"Maybe, just a bit…shame on me. I refuse to let Patrick, or any other man, have control over my feelings. I'm sorry, I hope he's as perfect in real life. Not to change the subject, but how is everything else going?"

"You meant to change the subject, and everything is great. Maggie is a dream to work with; she's like the mother I always wish I had. She gave me her cell phone number and told me to call her anytime."

"How about your gyno appointment?" Amber asks.

"That was a piece of cake. Her office was empty—it was lunchtime, so I was in and out in no time flat. She said her office would call me if anything came back from my pap smear. So far, no news is good news."

"Any luck getting those other receipts yet?"

"Working on it; my gal at Sherman's is going back into the archives to see if she can find them. If she succeeds, I promised her you would come and spruce up your wardrobe with her."

"Thanks a lot!"

"You said you'd do whatever you could to help me. Sherman's is way better priced than NM, anyway."

Amber laughs. "Well, then, I guess lucky for you, I will require some new items in January. I'm going to lift weights at the gym. I may need some clothes for my soon-to-be toned arms and legs. My saleslady at NM will not be happy."

"Really? Can I tag along? I could probably use some meat on my bones."

"You should come with me. We'll get together when I get back, and I'll introduce you to my trainer. Maybe he'll give us a two-for-one deal?"

"Hey, one more question before you go, do you know anything about this mileage form? Tad told me I could download it from their site."

"Sorry, can't help you with that one. He gave you his phone number, call him. I'm sure he'd be than happy to help."

"Yeah, maybe. Okay. Have a great trip and take lots of pictures."

Dominque quickly dials the number written in front of her after she hangs up from Amber. "Hey, it's me, Dominque. I'm sorry, but it looks like you'll have to fly to New York if you want to see her. She's on her way to the airport now; won't be back until Monday."

❧

Zya makes sure Ashanti is okay in the morning before she calls Tina to fill her in. The cut on her side ended up being just a scratch—no stitches.

When Zya tries to persuade her not to go to the nursing home where she frequently volunteers, Ashanti replies, "If I stay home, Mommy, and don't live my life, they win. They tried to scare me—I can't let them."

"Are you sure? Want me to come with you? I can help too."

"Thanks, Mom." Ashanti kisses her on the cheek. "Let's forget about it for now. I promise I'll handle it; I'll be ready for them next time." Ashanti opens her book bag, showing her mom the pepper spray she gave her a few years back. Thank God she's never had to use it. Hopefully, she still won't. Ashanti refuses a ride; she wants to keep life as normal as possible. It's important to continue as usual and not to give them power over her.

Thinking about what a strong young woman she has raised, Zya sits down drinking a hot cup of tea, much slower this time, her mouth still burned from last night. Maybe it's Ashanti who has taught her the lesson instead.

Ding. Dong.

Zya opens her front door to see Tina and Stacey, their faces pale with trebling lips. She didn't expect them to drive over; they must have left immediately.

Tina rushes in the room, hugging Zya, tears in a constant stream.

Zya looks over at Stacey and can see her eyes are all red; they both must have cried the entire three-hour trip up.

"Where is she? Is she all right?" Tina asks.

"She wanted to do her volunteer work today. I asked her to stay home, but she thought that wasn't the right message to send. I'm a nervous wreck. She took her cell phone with her and promised she would call when she got there and throughout the day. If things were hectic, she would at least send a text." On cue, Zya's phone beeps with a text message.

Ashanti: im ok. luv u

Zya exhales—it's only been a little over an hour since her last text, but it seems like an eternity.

Tina's arms go around Zya at the sight of the pools filling in her lower lids. "It's okay; we're here for both of you. Whatever you need—for however long."

"What about school for Stacey?" Zya asks, feeling relieved to have Tina with her.

"Didn't I tell you? She's homeschooled. Best decision we ever made."

"Yeah, the school system was slowing me down way too much. I could only go as fast as the slowest kid," proudly states Stacey.

Zya admires her for her mature attitude. Although Stacey is only two years older than Ashanti—she's so much wiser. No wonder Ashanti likes her so much. Not sure if it was the right thing to do or not, Zya tells both Tina and Stacey about her last conversation with Ashanti and their relationship.

"Stacey would love to talk to Ashanti for you, wouldn't

you, honey?"

Stacey's eyes dart around the room, then back at her hands, clutching each other. "Yeah, but I'm not sure it'll do any good."

"What? Why not?" they both ask.

"I understand how she feels. Although mom you've always been a lesbian, it's an awkward conversation when kids ask me about my dad."

"You never told me this before. How do you respond?"

"I tell them my dad was killed when I was very young, I don't know him. I'm not comfortable telling them I had two moms."

Taking Stacey into her arms and hugging her. "Oh, honey, I really wish you would have told me. You're the most important person in my universe. How can I be happy if you're not?"

Smiling, Stacey looks up at her mother, returning the affection. "I'm no unhappy mom—it's just awkward. I don't want the other kids to think I'm a lesbian too. Another advantage of being homeschooled."

Zya's eyes water as she watches this interaction, wondering if Ashanti feels the same way. Wiping them, she says, "I'd like to find out how Ashanti feels. Let's have some lunch and discuss this more. I hope you like Mexican food. There's this cute little cantina down the street from the nursing home."

Amber loves the city—she could live here. She handled her interviews yesterday when she landed so she has the weekend to enjoy the sites. Walking down Times Square in a tweed coat and scarf, she misses not having seasons in Florida. *Another day in paradise* has always been her mantra back home, but maybe she's missing something.

She heads over to Rockefeller Center, where she sees the massive tree in the center. She can't wait to see them light it up, wondering how much energy they waste every year on this beauty. As she turns away to do more damage in the stores, she glimpses a handsome man in a business suit crossing the street in her direction. He looks very familiar. *Come closer…I know you from somewhere.* In an instant, she realizes who he is as he flags down a taxi. His voice gives him away.

She turns in the opposite direction, melding into the morning crowd. Looking back, she's confident he didn't see her. "Phew!" she says out loud. "What in the world is Patrick doing in New York?"

Rushing back to her hotel, she curses her misfortune. I was hoping to get away from him and drive him out of my mind, and here he is. Deep in thought, as she walks to the elevators, she's unaware of the man leaning up against the wall as she passes him.

He quickly gets into step right behind her and slides in quietly beside her in the elevator.

She pushes fourteen on the wall.

Once the elevator reaches between the tenth and eleventh floors, he reaches over and hits the emergency stop button.

Her eyes go wide as she realizes the fog she's been.

He reaches for her hand and gently pushes her up against the corner of the elevator.

Afraid for her life, she beats him on his chest, but his powerful body holds her firmly in place.

He puts his finger up against her lips. "Shh," he instructs and pulls off his sunglasses.

"Christoph? Do you want to give me a heart attack? What are you doing here?"

"Seeing you, mon cheri." His hand grasps her breast as his mouth passionately covers hers.

Instantly, she's feverish. He learned what buttons to push during their romantic fling while she was in St. Tropez.

His hand moves quickly, pulling up her skirt. His thigh goes between her legs, pushing them apart.

Their kiss deepens as their tongues dance, remembering the steps from not so long ago.

She fumbles with his zipper, her hands trembling with urgency. Gasping, she puts her arm on his chest, pushing him away. "We can't do this here! We're in an elevator, and you know how serious I am about protection."

"Yes, I do," he replies with a smirk. He puts her hand inside his zipper, motioning her to push the condom the rest of the way.

Amber smiles then wraps her arms around his neck once again, letting their tongues dance.

He grabs her ass and pulls her up as she wraps her long legs around him. He pulls her thong to one side, then in one smooth thrust—he buries himself deep inside. She's so wet; he just slips right in.

Amber's moans and gasping make it impossible to kiss her. So, his lips find her hard nipple, pushing against the fabric of her blouse. With each thrust, he sinks deeper and increases his tempo. Within moments he joins her, riding the crescendo of cymbals crashing.

"Hello, excuse me, is everything okay in there?"

They look at each other and giggle. Neither of them realized there was a speaker in the elevator.

"Just fine—sorry, must have hit the stop button by mistake."

Turning to Christoph as he tucks in her shirt. "Where are you staying?" Amber asks.

"Nowhere…yet."

They barely get the door open when he pushes her up against the wall, his thigh again between her legs, rubbing her swollen clit while his teeth playfully nip at her lower lip.

She barely gets the door to her room open when he playfully chases her inside, thoughts of the tree lighting, forgotten.

"Mom, I'm home," shouts Ashanti once inside the door.

Stacey comes running from around the corner and nearly plows her down, hugging her, asking her, "Are you okay? I mean, are you really okay?"

Ashanti laughs out loud. "Yes, I'm okay. What are you doing here?" she asks, looking confused.

"Your mom called my mom this morning before you got up. She told us what happened. Let me see?"

Looking for the cut along her side, Ashanti reassures her. "I'm okay. It's just a scratch. I think they were trying to scare me more than anything."

Zya comes around the corner and gives Ashanti a big hug.

While reassuring her mom she's okay, she sees Tina standing behind her with tear-stained cheeks.

Tina walks over and joins the group hug. "I'm so glad you're okay. We were so scared."

"They drove right over as soon as I got off the phone with them; they've been here all afternoon. I'm so glad they came. They've helped keep me sane and distracted. Did you see any of the kids from last night?"

They all walk into the dining room. "Yeah, I saw two of them right after lunch. They tried to act like they were going to come after me, but I knew they wouldn't while I was at the nursing home, so I kept my cool and acted like they weren't even there."

"You did? Wow, I don't think I could have done that," a stunned Stacey replies.

"They scared me to death. I was shaking like a leaf, but you couldn't see it on the outside. How long are you guys staying?"

Zya jumps in, "However long you want them here. Ashanti, we talked about the circumstances today at lunch. We've decided to just be friends. Tina's going to stay in the guest room, and Stacey can sleep on the other bed in your room."

"Or on the couch, if you prefer," interjects Stacey.

"In my room! We can play Monopoly until the wee hours! Yippee!"

"Don't you go taking advantage of this now, you hear me," states Zya to Ashanti. "You still have to be in bed by ten, with or without a guest. Got it?"

"Yes, ma'am." Ashanti grabs her books and her guest's arm. "Let's go to my room."

"Are you sure you're okay with this? It's not just about Ashanti and me, it's about you and Stacey too," Zya says.

"Being here with you as a friend is better than not being

able to be with you at all. I'll take you any way I can for now."

Zya grabs Tina's hand across the table. "Thank you. Thank you for being so wonderful and patient."

Tad told her to call if she had any questions or needed help with anything. It still didn't make it any easier picking up the phone. Not really wanting his help, she had no other choice.

"Tad, it's Dominque. Uh, I mean Matilda Patterson."

"Oh yes, hi, what can I do for you?"

"I'm sorry to bother you, but I can't seem to find the mileage form. Can you point me in the right direction?"

"Grab a piece of paper and write this down. Publication 589, table two, the *Daily Business Mileage and Expense Log*. You can go to the website and download a copy. Did you get that?" Tad asks coldly.

Sensing the agitation in his voice, she says, "Yes, thanks."

"No problem, I'm glad I could help Miss. Patterson. Bye."

Dominque now doubts he meant it when he said to call and help her.

"Tad, this is your last warning, if you don't have what it takes to be an auditor, then I'll have to let you go. I want to make sure this is perfectly clear; the next time you give an extension to someone without getting proper approval first, you're fired, *capisce*?"

"Yes, sir, I understand."

"Now get out of my office." His boss mumbles as Tad leaves, "The audacity, taking a call when he's being reprimanded. Wish he had balls that big when he's out in the field."

☯

"Did you take care of Isabel for me? Is it my kid?" Patrick asks.

"No worries my man, it's all taken care of. I told her you were shooting blanks," Stewart says, chuckling.

"What? You told her what?"

"Calm down, she'll never know the truth."

"That's a lie; did she believe you?"

"Yeah, she said, 'Okay,' and hung up."

"Is she pregnant?"

"She says she is."

"And it could be my kid?" Patrick asks, panicking.

"Yeah, unless you *are* shooting blanks. I guess it could be yours. Do you really want to go there?"

"I don't know. I should do the right thing, right? If it's mine, shouldn't I do the responsible thing and take care of it?"

"Man, you are all screwed up. Chances are very slim Isabel can remember who she slept with last night, let alone a few months ago. Let it go. It's probably not yours, anyway." Intentionally changing the subject, he asks, "So what's going on with you lately? I saw your suitcase by the door. Finally, get back on track with Amber?"

"No, and that will never happen. I blew it twice. I'm sure I won't get another chance with her. Too bad—she was perfect."

"So where are you?" Stewart asks.

"I'm in New York finalizing the last will for a client. My client pays for it, so why not? They're lighting the tree this weekend, so I thought I'd stay for a few days and get some shopping in while I'm here."

"Rumor has it your little firefly is there this weekend."

"What are you talking about? How do you know this?"

"I was at NeoQuest this morning and overheard Dominque on the phone with her."

"Why were you at NeoQuest?"

"If you must know, your article, '*The Ethical Attorney,*' Amber wrote about you, impresses the ladies."

"How does my article help you get lucky?" Patrick asks, afraid of the answer.

"Well, I tell them I live with you and all the other ways you are sickeningly moral and ethical, not only in business but in your everyday life. You're like my puppy dog; only I don't have to pick up after you."

"There's a compliment in there somewhere—I think. New York is a big city. I'm sure I won't be running into her while I'm here. In fact, if she sees me, she'll run the other way."

The Hotel housekeeper has been trying to get in to clean Amber's room all day. The housekeeper's boss doesn't tolerate any excuses for not getting the job done. Even honeymooners have to leave their room sometime.

Frustrated and scared, she calls her boss to explain the situation. "I cannot clean room 1407. The *Do Not Disturb* sign up has not moved all day—they do not leave. I have tried to call, but no one answer. Please, I have tried everything I can, but I cannot clean."

The manager walks with her to the room and knocks loudly. So loud, it wakes them from a deep sleep; a nice long Sunday afternoon nap.

"Madame Fiore, is everything okay? We have tried to clean your room for you, ma'am, but no one answers. I have a master key to allow me entrance into your room. So please, if you are there, would you let me know?"

Amber bolts out of bed and runs around the room, looking for her clothes—something to put on. "Wait one minute, please."

Christoph throws her a robe as he runs into the bathroom closing the door behind him.

Amber gets the belt tied as the door to her room opens. "Pardon me, ma'am, we are concerned as you do not come out of your room or answer your phone. Is everything okay?"

Seeing the housekeeper behind the manager, Amber knows they get upset if they can't do their job. They could get fired for it, or worse—deported.

"Everything's fine. Please give me about ten minutes, and I'll go out and get a late lunch."

The manager and housekeeper walk out the door in time to reveal Patrick entering his room across the hall. He turns and sees her as she's closing the door.

"Amber?" he calls out.

Without responding, Amber's door closes.

It's their last evening together, Debra can't believe how fast these last three days have gone. They're strolling together along the beach, the last walk before they must leave. Roberto has a flight to catch this evening.

"The sun, it is beautiful, yes?"

"You should see the sunrise. The sun fills the morning sky with these daggers of peach streaks, which gradually turn into bright orange and red. It's like God takes out his paintbrush and throws these beautiful colors along the horizon. I guess we've slept in so you didn't get a chance to see it."

"Mia Bella, this time with you has been special. I am feeling for you like I have not in long time. Please." He takes Debra's hand in his and gets down on one knee in front of her.

Unsure of his intentions, her palms sweat.

He pulls a leather pouch from his shirt pocket. Inside is a large round cut diamond ring set in an antique, Italian yellow gold setting. "This, it was my momma's, she told me to give it to the woman who has my heart. If you do not mind, my Theresa wore it, but now I give to you." He takes her hand and slips the ring onto her finger.

She quickly yanks her hand back. "Wait, Roberto. I can't do this. It's way too fast for me. Please."

"You do not like the ring? I should have it put into a different gold piece, yes?"

"Oh, Roberto, the ring is beautiful, and I'm honored you would even consider giving it to me. It's just too soon."

Initially feeling like she punched him in the stomach, Robert quickly recovers. "Marry me, who say anything about marrying? I only wish to express my love. I give you this ring as a token of how much I care."

"Thank you so very much, Roberto. This weekend has been extraordinary, and I hope we have many, many more just like it. Please, I cannot accept this lavish gift from you, but I hope you will try again later, once we've had more time together. In this country, a ring like this is a sign of intending marriage. Maybe someday, just not today, okay?"

"Okay, but can I see it fits?"

She nods as he slips the ring on her…it slides easily over her knuckle. It fits perfectly.

The last rays of sunlight glisten off the facets. The deep warm glow from the setting orb enhances the beautiful yellow stone. Smiling, she holds her hand out away from her. Looking at it, she thinks, *maybe one day.*

Dominque, going through Amber's mail, finds an envelope addressed to her. It's a fine, high-quality paper with elegant handwriting on the outside with no return address. She opens the seal on the back too quickly, cutting her finger on the flap. *Damn,* she mumbles.

She puts her finger in her mouth to help stop the bleeding. Eager to know what's inside, she quickly wraps a napkin around her finger. The paper is too beautiful to ruin.

The notecard is hand-painted with various species of butter-flies. Inside is the same elegant handwriting it reads:

To new beginnings…Your biggest fan

The envelope still feels heavy, so she looks inside and finds a gift card for Red Door Spa. It's for a full day spa package.

"How did he know this was the spa I go to?" she says out loud. She looks up and around as if he might be right here in this very office. Seeing no one looking her way, she sits back down, running her fingers over the beautiful artwork. She opens it back up, her heart bursting as she rereads the message when she gets an idea. She dials the number from memory.

"Red Door Spa, how may I help you?"

"This might seem a little strange, but I received this generous gift card for your spa, but it doesn't say who sent it. Can you look it up for me so I can thank my most generous giver?"

"Sure, give me the number on the back."

Dominque reads the number to the girl on the phone two different times. "I'm sorry, but that card wasn't purchased here. They must have purchased it somewhere else or maybe even over the internet."

"Thanks anyway."

"No problem, would you like to book your appointment now?"

"Not just yet, I'll call you back."

Dominque sits back and looks off into space, wondering who this wonderful man could be. *Maybe it is the cop,* she thinks, it says, *To New Beginnings.*

Reluctantly, Amber and Christoph leave room 1407 for the last time. With suitcases in hand, Christoph cannot resist the opportunity for one last adventure. He pushes Amber up against the wall outside their room, forcing his leg between hers. He drops his case to the ground and pulls her head back with one hand while the other gropes her breast— his tongue searches inside her lips.

She struggles at first; they shouldn't be doing this in the

hallway. Then she gets swept up in the combustion between her legs.

He lets go of the back of her head and pushes his hand between her legs.

She lets out a sigh, oblivious to everything around her until she hears her name…

"Amber? Are you all right?"

Both Christoph and Amber look towards the source and see Patrick with his case in hand, leaving his room.

Embarrassed, Amber quickly gathers her composure and replies, "Oh, yes, sorry, were we too loud?"

Patrick's cheeks flush bright red as he realizes she wasn't in trouble at all.

Trying to hide the effect this minor scene has on him, Patrick says, "Carry on."

As he stomps to the elevator, he thinks, *I didn't know Amber was the loose type.*

Christoph will not take no for an answer. He wants to make love to her in a public place; that look as she tries to remain quiet and composed as she climaxes. He continues what they started in the hallway. He pulls her panties off, smelling them, then pushes them into a front pocket of his carryon. "My souvenir; something to remember you by on my long flight home." With a wicked grin on his face, he pushes her up against the wall. He bends down just enough to push the tip of his erection inside, causing a long, low moan to escape her lips.

Her hands quickly go to her mouth as her eyes grow wide.

With his hands under her arms, he picks her up then lowers her the rest of the way on him.

She wraps her arms around his neck and says, "Okay, but you've got to be quick."

"Yes ma'am," he says as he leans her against the wall and pumps his hips quickly. The thought of being caught is so exciting for them both, it's only a matter of minutes before they explode, covering the other's mouth to muffle their cries to heaven.

When he places her on the ground she says, "Oh my—that's one hell of a sendoff. Can I have my panties back though, I'm going to be cold."

"You are on fire; the cold will do you good, so no, they're mine. As the cool air rushes between your legs, you're going to remember me." He kisses her gently on the lips. "I could wake up to that your face every morning. Be careful, mon cheri, I might just move myself to the States for you." He grabs both of the suitcases and heads for the elevator. He looks so together. Especially for someone who just climaxed.

Their hallway escapade, along with afternoon traffic, makes them late for the airport.

She runs up to the gate and yells, "Please wait for me; I'm coming."

The airline attendant hears her and holds the door until she arrives. "We almost left you behind."

"I'm glad you didn't. Thank you."

"We have a full flight. Put your bag under your seat if you can. I'm sure all the overhead space is taken."

Amber counts the rows back until she finally reaches sixteen. Turning to her left, she sees the only empty seat on the plane—hers, right next to Patrick.

CHAPTER TWELVE

Seeing Amber stop in her tracks, he gets out of his seat and takes her case from her. Opening the overhead compartment, he puts her case in it without saying a word.

"After you." He motions for her to take the middle seat. "Sure is a small world, isn't it?"

The stewardess comes down the aisle, and Amber asks if she could please have a scotch and soda. "Once we are in the air, dear, I'll be happy to bring you one. We're getting ready to take off now so it won't be long," the stewardess replies with a bright, cheerful smile.

Amber wishes her seat would open up and swallow her.

Patrick reaches into his duffle bag under the seat and pulls out three different bottles of liquor—he raided the minibar. "Which one will hold you over?"

Amber looks up at him and grabs one blindly. Opening it, she gulps down its contents without stopping. She gasps and gags and then looks at the label—Jack Daniels. Trying desperately not to show weakness, she whispers, "Thank you, that hit the spot."

They continue in silence until the plane levels off, and an

attendant makes the announcement they are free to move about the cabin.

Quickly, Amber jumps up to hit the lavatory. She can smell Christoph all over her. She feels as if she's been unfaithful and got caught. After freshening up, she decides she's being silly. He had his chance—he blew it*! So what if he can smell sex all over me. Let him stew and think about what he's missing.*

As she walks back to her seat, she sees the stewardess standing over Patrick, giggling and flirting.

As Patrick senses her approach, he lays it on thick. "So Marie, do you get any playtime when you get to Fort Lauderdale?"

Amber is waiting to get into her seat, foot-tapping, and blowing puffs of air with each breath.

Patrick gets up but holds onto the flight attendant's arm to keep her from leaving as Amber takes her seat. As he rubs her arm, his knuckles intentionally stroke the side of her breast, making her nipples stand up in attention. He leans in close and says, "Here's my card…let's play later tonight. We can go somewhere private, like my house, or somewhere public." He glances over at Amber, then looks back at the attendant. "Your choice." He winks at her and then takes his seat.

Cheeks aglow, the flight attendant backs away, waving his card to him and says, "I'll call you later."

"That didn't take you long," Amber states annoyed.

"Longer than it took you." Looking down at the magazine in his lap, he pretends to read an article. He can't focus—he's angry and hurt.

Amber, seething inside, turns away, crossing her arms in a huff. About forty-five minutes later, she opens her eyes and realizes she must have fallen asleep.

"Rough weekend?" he asks, with his face still in the magazine.

"Not that I care what you think, the gentleman you saw me with is someone I've been seeing for about two months now."

Patrick snaps his head towards her. "Really? You didn't strike me as the sleep around kind of gal."

"I don't! I met him when we went to France after Zya's show. We've kept in contact, but it's nothing serious; just a fling."

"Wow, that's one hot fling. I guess that's what keeps you going?"

"You have no right to judge me, especially after what you did to me."

"Fair enough, truce?"

"Whatever."

"So, have a drink with me at the airport when we land."

"Are you kidding me? What about your little rendezvous with Marie? Oh, and whoever texts you during your dates?"

"That was bad, wasn't it?"

Amber nods and says, "You betcha!"

"Yeah, I know how that must have looked. Let me tell you how it was. I was waiting for a text from my roommate, giving me the results from the test I took, to make sure I didn't catch anything from the hot tub slut, so, I could go home and make sweet love to the woman who was doing one hell of a job seducing me."

Amber's eyes open up wide in surprise. "Why didn't you tell me?"

"You didn't exactly give me a chance, remember? You

called for the check, wolfed down two more lamb chops, and got cash out of your wallet to pay the bill, all while getting up and walking out of the restaurant. When could I have explained?"

"Maybe we're not meant to be together?"

"Maybe, or it's possible, we're trying to find out how badly we want it." Patrick reaches over and grabs Amber's seat belt and fastens it for her. "So, about that drink?"

"Marie?"

"Marie, who?"

Amber smiles as they hear the announcement to prepare for landing. They arrive into the Fort Lauderdale International Airport in twenty minutes.

Dominque is seething, waiting for Tad to arrive. He's the enemy; she can't wait till the moment he leaves. Thinking she has ten more minutes, she heads for the bathroom for last-minute touch-ups when the doorbell rings. "Oh, hi, you're early."

"I hope you don't mind. I can wait in my car if you prefer?"

Her tight smile and crossed arms indicate that he should do that forever, as far as she's concerned. "Oh, don't be silly, come in."

As Tad walks in, he sees a beautiful arrangement of red, pink, and white roses made into a holiday assortment. "Wow, those are gorgeous flowers. Someone must love you."

"They are, aren't they? I've never seen any like them before. I wish I knew who they were from."

"What? A secret admirer?"

"Yep, I guess it doesn't only happen in the movies."

"That is so exciting!"

"Yes, it is, thank you," she says, still tight-lipped.

"Should we get down to business? Were you able to get the copies of your receipts?"

Her face changes to a proud grin as Dominque hands him a folder containing copies of most of the missing receipts. "I even put them in order with similar types together, grouped by month." Dominque is very proud of herself.

Smiling back at her, Tad takes the folder from her and moves over to her kitchen table. Pulling out her file from his briefcase, he makes comparisons and then starts punching in a serious of numbers on his calculator, and jotting notes.

"Well, everything is here except you're missing $398.00 from your clothing deductions. It looks like you owe $156.94."

"That's it?" she asks, stunned.

"Yep, that's it."

"I can swing that." Dominque anxiously grabs her checkbook and writes the check quickly before he changes his mind. "Well, I guess that's that."

"Yes, Dominque, your audit troubles are over—for now."

"Let's hope forever!"

Tad laughs and puts the paperwork back into his case, along with the check. "Well, I'll be getting out of your hair now." Extending his hand to hers. "It was a real pleasure meeting you."

"Likewise, are you done for the night?"

"Yeah, you were my last appointment."

"Can you take your auditor hat off and stay and have a beer with me? I think I need to do a little celebrating."

"Sure." He looks over at the flowers. "Am I going to make someone jealous?"

She shrugs her shoulders and says, "I don't know, maybe."

He laughs along with Dominque. "Well, in that case, I would love to stay and celebrate with you." Tad takes off his jacket, removes his tie, and unbuttons the top button of his shirt.

Dominque turns around and pauses briefly at his relaxed appearance.

Taking the beer from her, he says, "I have to apologize to you for the other day."

"First, a toast to new beginnings," Dominque says.

Tad takes his beer and clinks hers. "When you called me the other day to ask about that form, I was in my boss's office. I'm sorry if I seemed short with you."

"Why on earth would you take my call if you were in your boss's office?"

"I can't stand the guy. Hearing your voice was a pleasant change after listening to him rant for over an hour."

Cheeks flushing, Dominque's cast down, and says, "Why, thank you."

"I have to tell you, you look great." Suddenly nervous seeing her eyes narrow, he backpedals. "You told me you were getting through some health problems when I was here last— you look great. I mean, you looked great when I met you, but you look even better now."

Dominque laughs as he tries to explain himself. "I understand what you're saying and thank you. It's been a rough road, but one I'm thrilled I finally got on."

Tad wanted to know all about her recovery. He told her he

had a sister that was always having weight issues.

Dominque told him all about her childhood, lack of respect for her body, and her determination to get on track and take control of her life. It was so easy to talk to him. She had never had a guy friend before. Looking at Tad, she smiles thinking, *I guess he's my first one.*

Dominque looks down at her watch, wondering where three hours went. "Oh my, it's almost nine o'clock. I can't believe it's this late already."

Tad thanked her for the beer and for being so open and honest about her experience. As he prepares to leave, he turns to her. "Good luck, I hope you get everything in life you want." He kisses her on the cheek. "Thanks again."

"Tad."

He stops and turns towards her.

She steps up and getting on her tippy toes and kisses him back on the cheek.

The last thing Zya wants to do is pressure Ashanti. And she doesn't want her to see how nervous she is every day when she leaves for school. Today, however, she can't stand it anymore. "Hi honey, how was school?"

"Okay. I'm going to head up to my room and do my homework. What time is dinner?"

"Wait a minute—can you sit down with me for a minute?"

Ashanti sits down and looks at her mother with her beautiful and innocent face. "Yesssss," she draws it out.

"You haven't said anything more about the incident. I want to make sure you aren't having any more problems."

Ashanti looks at her mother, wondering if she should tell her the truth or not. Deciding it might be best to keep out some details, she says, "The kids still call me terrorist and traitor from time to time, but other than that, it's been pretty normal."

"Are you sure there's nothing else you're not telling me?" Zya asks, concerned.

"I'm sure. Can I go now?"

"Yeah, yeah, go do your homework, and I'm going to check it when you're finished."

"Since when do you know how to do pre-calculus or anything about physics?"

"Smart-aleck—go to your room." Ashanti is too smart for her own good. One day she may find a cure for cancer. What a tribute to her grandmother that would be to find a cure for the very disease that took her, just as they were getting to know one another.

Stacey: how did it go today?

Ashanti: fine. normal.

Stacey: have you told your mom yet?

Ashanti: no and not going 2

Stacey: you should

Ashanti: maybe. not living her life because of me. wish she wouldn't

Stacey: about her and?

Ashanti: yes. want her happy. maybe she'll try again

Stacey: should I have mom call her?

Ashanti: k. but don't say I said

Stacey: mention dinner. bye

Brian's eyes appear blank—he's not there, as Debra comes in for her weekly session. She was looking forward to seeing him, but now she's wondering why. His crossed arms and rigid body make him appear guarded and unapproachable. Not the kind, welcoming man she's used to seeing.

"Good afternoon Debra, how are things? Anything new to tell me about?" he asks flatly.

"Actually yes, there is...Roberto asked me to marry him. Well, he tried to give me a diamond ring, says it was just to show he loved me, but it was definitely an engagement ring," Debra blurts out.

Brian's eyes dart to her hand.

Debra notices the color drain from his face. "No, I didn't take it. I wouldn't dream of it! I mean, we had a great weekend. I can't believe how close I feel to him after only knowing him a short time. Are these feelings real, or am I looking for a replacement for George? I don't want to hurt anybody, but I'm so confused."

Brian's shoulders relax as he leans forward. "Debra, you need to live your life exactly the way you want; whatever makes you the happiest. Maybe now that he's gone back to Italy, it'll give you a chance to see how you really feel. Yes, you're still mourning George, and missing Roberto might be easier for you to deal with. Only you can know for sure. Stop being so hard on yourself. It's okay to feel love again. No matter how long it lasts with Roberto, if he makes you happy, why would you do anything to change that?"

"Well, that's not all of it; I don't know how to say this...a few times, when I've been with him, you know…I've gotten so caught up in the moment, I forget who I'm with. I'm shocked when I open my eyes."

"Who have you been imagining, George?"

"No—you?"

Brian's cheek flush as he locks eyes with her. He takes a deep breath and says, "Debra, I'm your therapist. It's not uncommon for you to think about me in that way. Many women who are going through trauma like you have become attached to their therapist. It doesn't mean anything."

She looks at him dumbfounded, absorbing his words. It makes sense…he is the one who's helped her through this troublesome time. But, it's so much more than that. She decides he's right. "I'm sorry and embarrassed."

"Don't be—it's okay. I'm flattered, really I am. Roberto is a lucky guy." He walks around his desk to open the door for her. His eyes are downcast as he shakes his head. A weak smile tries to form. He looks up at her and then quickly away as he says, "I'll see you next week. Take care."

She pauses to give him a brief kiss on the cheek, as has been the usual friendly gesture, but he pulls back and extends his hand.

"Yeah, next week," she blurts as she bolts out the door. Her heart is pounding as suddenly her upper body feels like it's on fire. She can't get out of there quick enough. As she fumbles for her keys, she thinks, *Why do I feel like he just broke up with me?*

Annoyed and wondering how she could be so stupid, Debra drives home, hitting her steering wheel, berating herself. It was clear from Brian's reaction she was overstepping the line.

She could tell by the shock on his face at her confession, he doesn't feel the same way. She must have been imagining it. *I'm such an idiot! He's right—how can I have feelings for two men? My husband just died!* She feels something roll around inside her. Her hand goes to her abdomen; smiling—in love with this little one already. When she was pregnant with Tracey, George was always putting his hands on her belly, telling her how she was glowing and the most beautiful pregnant woman in the world. Roberto laughed the few times he could felt the baby move. He doesn't see her as a pregnant woman, but rather a woman who's pregnant.

She sits out in her car, looking through the front window. Tracey is laughing as her Aunt Megan tickles her. It makes her laugh. *I need to take care of my family—they should be my priority. Love can wait.*

It's as if his hands are still on her. Her body is on fire, burning everywhere he touched.

He can't wait any longer—the anticipation has gotten the best of him. With their tongues entwined, he yanks her thong off and positions himself between her legs. He's still fully dressed in his suit and tie—she's still wearing her coat.

In one swift motion, his zipper is down, and he buries his full erection deep inside. He goes slowly at first, enjoying that first thrust. His hips don't move as his tongue searches; their kiss deepening while they both enjoy the sensation. Slowly he thrusts—in and out—savoring every stroke.

She breaks the kiss, panting, and puts her head on his shoulder as she wraps her legs around him.

He grabs her hips, working them in sync with his, pulling out almost to the tip, then buries himself as deep as possible, in smooth strokes.

Her head rolls back as the tingling in her toes work its way up her legs. Deep within, the fire explodes—stars imploding in her mind.

Beep. Beep. Beep.

"No! Not again!"

"No—not again." Patrick takes his phone with the alarm he had set for ten o'clock blaring, and throws it in the front seat.

Amber smiles as she realizes this isn't a dream and surrenders herself to him.

He falls right back into rhythm as her body writhes beneath him. She screams out his name. The sound so beautiful, his heart and body explode together.

He opens his eyes, only to drown in her lustful brown orbs. Her pouty lips begging for him to kiss them. "Well, I'm sure glad we finally got that out of the way."

She giggles and kisses him. "So much tension and pressure. I'm glad you had a condom with you." Her smile fades as she playfully slaps him on the shoulder. "Hey, why did you have one with you? Were you hoping to score with Marie?"

"Not a chance—you know that's not me. I was just trying to get back at you. It really hurt me seeing you with that guy. I really care about you."

She hugs him. "I'm sorry, I never meant to hurt you. What are the odds you would be in New York?"

"Fair enough." He sits up, pulling her up and into his arms. "I think we've got some making up to do. My place or yours?"

CHAPTER THIRTEEN

"**I** know that look, that glow, who is he?" Amber asks.

"I wish I knew." Dominque giggles like a schoolgirl.

"Your secret admirer again?"

"I went for my *Ultimate Indulgence* spa treatment on Saturday...hot stone massage, olive oil manicure, pedicure, and spa lunch—it was truly heaven."

"Wow, sounds like it. I wish I had someone send me a gift like that."

"I can talk to Patrick for you if you like." Dominque teases.

Amber blushes and quickly changes the subject. "I noticed a message from your doctor on your desk, everything all right?"

"Yeah, my pap came back slightly atypical. She's not worried about it, but asked me to come in for a repeat in three months."

"Three months? That long?"

"She said it's common; these tests are hyper-sensitive., and not to worry about it. We'll check it out early next year."

"Are you okay with that?"

"Yeah, I'm fine. I'm not worried if she's not."

"Okay. Let me just say for the record, I'm not okay with you waiting, but I'll relinquish to your doctor. What's going on with your new BFF Tad?"

"He's so cute. Why have I never had a guy friend before? We go to the movies, out to dinner, he even went shopping with me the other day. He must be gay though, this hot chick came out of the fitting room in this super-tight, short leather dress, and he didn't even give her a second look. It's cool—I'm so comfortable around him. I can talk to him about anything. And it's sweet how much he cares about his sister. He said she's not ready to talk to anybody about it yet, but sharing my experience has been a big help to her. Too bad he's not straight, dark, and handsome. He has the tall part though."

"Be careful; sometimes, you fall for the ones you least expect."

"Unless I turn into a man, we don't have to worry about that."

"Not to change the subject, but has your biggest fan mentioned the day and time he's going to reveal himself to you?"

"No, not yet, but I found a single red rose on my car this morning. The card said, *Patience is a virtue*. It's driving me crazy. He's so romantic and mysterious—it's making me nuts."

Dominque jumps up from the chair in Amber's office and hurries to answer her phone on her desk. "Miss Fiore's office. Hi Patrick, let me tell her you're on the line."

Blushing, Amber walks over and shuts her door. She can see the look of bewilderment on Dominque's face through the glass.

"Am I interrupting you?"

"Yep, but it's a distraction I'll take any time."

"Hey, I can't promise a gourmet meal, but if you don't have any plans yet, I'd love to have you over for dinner tonight. I'll be cooking."

"I don't know. All my boyfriends are getting mad at you. You've been occupying my evenings every night now for the past two weeks."

"Well, please tell them for me, if I had my way, I'd be tying you up every night—and morning."

Dead silence. He can't believe he said that. Thinking quickly, he adds, "Would you prefer silk ties or ropes?"

A confused Amber says, "Well, I'll tell them at least one more night?"

"See you at seven," Patrick says as he hurries and hangs up.

Amber sits at her desk, thinking about what Patrick said. *Did he mean that, or was he just making a joke? I wouldn't mind waking up to him every morning too, but I better pretend he never said it—unless he repeats it.*

Zya didn't make it to the phone in time, so she let the machine pick up. It's old-fashioned and uses tape, but it still works. Trying to do everything she can for the environment for future generations, Zya was not one to throw something away just because it was old or obsolete. *Still does its job, keep it,* is her motto. Zya's heart does flip-flops as she hears Tina's voice on the machine. She grabs the phone. "Tina. Is that really you?"

"Hey girl, it's me."

"I haven't heard from you for a while. I thought maybe you didn't want to be friends anymore."

"Well, that's why I called. I've been offered a job in Seattle. It's a great opportunity. The pay is great and—my ex has been calling. She misses me and wants to try again."

Zya's eyes tear up. She drops into the chair with a thud; as her legs give out. "I don't know what to say. I guess I knew this was a possibility; I just didn't think about it."

"Tell me to stay," Tina screams, also crying. "Tell me we'll work this out—we're meant to be together. Tell me you love me as much as I love you, and we'll get through this."

Zya's eyes go wide, hearing the hurt and pain in Tina's voice. As strong as Zya is, Tina is even stronger—the one who can keep her emotions in check.

"Oh, Tina, I wish I could. I want to say those things to you, but I can't. Ashanti is my number one priority. I would go to the ends of the earth and back and even give up my life for that girl. I do care about you. I don't want you to move back to Seattle."

Ashanti, standing at the top of the stairs, hears her mom's side of the conversation. Running down the stairs, almost tripping at the bottom, Ashanti also has tears streaming down her cheeks. "No, mom! I don't want you to give up your happiness or your life for me. You have every right to be happy—you deserve it. I'll be fine! I'm stronger and more in control than you give me credit for. I need you to stop smothering me. Stop trying to control what happens in my life. It's not always going to be perfect, but that's how I'm going to learn through adversity. If you love Tina, don't let her go."

Catching her breath, allowing the anger to subside a bit, she walks over to her mom. "Mom, I love you so much, and I know you love me too. I want you to be happy. If that means Tina becomes part of our life, so be it."

Zya pulls Ashanti into her arms. This is all she's wanted; Ashanti to be okay with her lifestyle.

"Now stop all these tears and find out when Stacey is moving in so I know when to clean out my closet—and under my bed," Ashanti states. She kisses her mom on the top of the head, then turns on her heel, running back upstairs wearing a bittersweet smile.

Zya puts the phone back to her ear. "Tina?"

"I heard."

"So, when?"

"Does this mean I'm not going to Seattle?"

"I have it on good authority you wouldn't like the weather there, and as far as jobs go, I believe there is this up-and-coming designer who is looking for a production designer. Know anybody who might have those skills?"

Both crying silently now, Tina responds, "I love you."

"I love you too."

"Hello."

"I've been wondering if you were going to answer my calls ever again."

"I've been very busy lately; no time for fraternizing on the phone."

"I'd much rather fraternize in person..." he says, trailing off.

"And mess up this fantasy we've got going here. This is so

much fun," the sexy voice replies.

"Let me guess, I caught you coming out of the shower again?" Stewart asks.

"Not this time. I'm just about to step into the tub. You have good timing. Oops, it looks like my robe slipped right off my shoulders; it's a bit chilly in here."

"Are your nipples hard?"

"Like little rocks, baby."

Setting a new record, Stewart instantly has to rearrange himself. His jeans have gone from relaxed fit to skinny in under 60-seconds.

"So, would you like to join me in the tub, or on my silk sheets?"

Stewart strips down and lies on his bed. This is the fifth time they've had phone sex, and each time she brings him to new heights. The things she comes up with, he can't even imagine. Stewart is no stranger to adventurous women and knows all the *Kama Sutra* positions, but phone sex with this woman has been so intense—and hot, he can't believe someone is teaching him a thing or two. The kind of woman all men wish they had waiting at home for them.

"So, what will we play today, Doctor?" Stewart asks.

"Oh, that's so cliché. How about engineer—or a tunnel excavator?"

Stewart comes out of his bedroom running his fingers through his hair. A silly grin on his face—but he's parched. They played engineer, excavator, driller and carpenter. She had some very unique jobs for his tool. He just broke a record— four orgasms in an hour and a half. Usually after two, his appendage won't wake up. Just the sound of her voice brought him back to attention and fully alert in less than ten minutes.

"You okay?" Patrick asks. "I couldn't help but hear you. These walls are thick, but I'm sure I heard you call the big man himself quite a few times."

"This chick is making me nuts. Or rather, she's draining them completely."

Patrick laughs. "I think you may have met your match."

"Yeah—I think I have to. Oh, I used up all the sesame oil. I'll pick up some at the store tomorrow."

"This is driving me nuts!" yells Dominque.

"Maybe that's what he's trying to do," Tad replies.

"If he is, it's working!" Dominque takes a big bite from the cheese danish sitting in front of her.

"It's so nice to see you enjoy and devour that. One day I hope you and Karen can enjoy these together," Tad says.

"Oh Tad, me too. I'm sorry, I've been going on and on about my secret admirer, I haven't even asked how your sister is doing."

"I love to listen to you talk. So please, don't apologize. Karen is doing better every day, thanks to you."

"I can't explain to you how I was able to turn things around so quickly for myself," Dominque interjects.

"Maybe it took longer than you think. You were asking for help all along. It just took you hitting rock bottom before any-one heard."

"Maybe. You always know exactly what to say. You have a

gift, you know." Dominque looks down at her hands, blushing a little.

Tad feels his face flush, so he hides it by taking a drink of his coffee.

"How come you don't have anyone special in your life? Haven't found the right guy?"

Spitting his coffee across the table, he says, "What? Guy? Do you think I'm gay? I'm not gay; trust me, I'm very much into women!"

"I'm sorry, I didn't mean to offend you. It's just you don't seem interested in the women around you, and you don't talk about them either. I just assumed. I'm sorry, please forgive me?"

With his cheeks still red with embarrassment. "I don't think it's right to gawk or talk about other women when you're on a date. It's rude."

"Date? You think we've been out on dates? Oh, I'm so sorry for misleading you. I think you're a great guy, and honestly, you've become a great friend to me, but a friend only. We're not compatible. You're not my type. Oh my, and here I've been going on about my secret admirer. You must think I'm very shallow."

Tad swallows hard and lowers his head. "I don't think you're shallow—I think you're terrific." He doesn't want to be just friends. "Good luck," he says as he leaves the café.

Dominque sits dumbfounded, thinking over in her head the time they've spent together. She doesn't think she's led him on. He's always been so kind and sweet, but he's still dorky to her. She could never be with him. He does nothing for her physically. She imagines them naked together, trying to visualize him with a hard chest and washboard abs. *Nope! I just can't.*

At seven-thirty, Amber rings the bell at Patrick's. "I'm sorry I'm late, I got into something at home, and I couldn't get out fast enough."

"No problem, although I've already opened the wine and started without you. You'll have to catch up."

Amber walks into the kitchen and picks up Patrick's full wine glass. Looking him straight in the eyes, she drinks it down without stopping, "Fast enough for you? Mmm, that's fantastic," Amber says with a surprised look staring at the wine glass.

"It's an Opus One; meant to sip and savor—not gulp."

"You know me, I never obey rules." She locks him in a deep, passionate kiss. After pulling back, she pushes up his chin, closing his mouth, then asks, "What's for dinner?"

"Huh? What? Wow, you're full of surprises, aren't you?" He walks into the kitchen, discreetly rearranging himself. "I've made my special marinara sauce over whole-wheat al dente angel hair pasta. The chicken breasts are marinated and ready to broil. French bread and Caesar salad are already on the table."

He takes her hand, kisses it softly as he escorts her to the dining room, grabbing an empty wineglass and the bottle along the way. Also on the table are white taper candles lit in cut crystal holders, fine china plates, crystal glasses, and silverware place settings for two.

"Wow, mister, if I didn't know any better, I'd think you are trying to seduce me."

"Me—seduce you? After seeing what you can do, I wouldn't even try." He pulls her seat out for her and offers a napkin for her lap.

"At all the fine dining restaurants I've been to, the waiter usually places the napkin for you," she says.

He smiles and says, "Gladly." He places her napkin on her lap, creasing the center in between her legs. "In the right spot?"

Her lips part slightly as her eyes glaze over. "I think you've done this before."

Patrick, with a smirk on his face, sits down next to her and fills their wine glasses.

"You never told me what we're having for dessert."

"You're right…I didn't. I didn't tell you on purpose; it's a surprise."

They polish off one bottle and began a second as they eat their last bites.

"That was delicious! I know you said it's simple—but wow —talk about flavor! You can cook for me anytime. You're much better in the kitchen then me. I guess we've figured out who'll do the cooking."

Patrick looks at her and pauses a little too long. Not sure how to comment, he says, "Ready for dessert?"

Amber nods, her eyes wide like a deer caught in headlights.

"Okay, let me take these plates into the kitchen, and I'll be right out with it."

"Need any help?"

"Not yet, but I will in a moment."

A few minutes later, Patrick exits the kitchen naked with a silver tray filled with bowls of chocolate and strawberry sauces, chopped nuts, cherries, and a can of whipped cream.

"Banana split anyone?" he asks.

"Funny, I don't see any bananas."

"There's only one for you. Shall we go into the living room?"

"Momma always told me to eat my food at the table."

Amber drops to her knees in front of him while he is still holding the tray and takes him into her mouth. "Ah, here's my banana…"

Moaning, he says, "Didn't your momma also tell you not to talk with your mouth full?"

The holidays are here; Debra wishes they would just pass— it will be her first without George. Roberto is coming to town, flying in on Saturday, two days before Christmas and leaving Tuesday night. It's such a long flight, both ways, for just three days, but he insisted. He couldn't bear to be without her over the holidays. Sorry he can't stay through the New Year. Debra is giddy, feeling like a high school girl with a crush. But this is definitely not a crush. Every time Brian appears in her dreams, or her mind, she pushes him out. The more she tries to forget about him—the more it seems he shows up.

On laundry days, she daydreams about Roberto as she enjoys her date with the spin cycle. Every time his hair turns dirty blonde, she opens her eyes and looks at the photo of Roberto in her hand. She looks forward to her mounds of dirty clothes. She often does laundry two to three times a week now instead of just once.

Amber is late leaving the office this evening and in a rush to get over to Patrick's, when a voice calls out to her from behind as she's walking to her car.

"Psst, miss, miss, excuse me."

Nervous because it's pitch-black and there's no one else around, she picks up the pace. Footsteps fall behind her, causing her to run. She drops her case and moves as fast as she can in her heels. She's too slow. He catches up with her and grabs her arm. She spins around, ready to fight her attacker when she sees Christoph standing before her. "Oh my gosh, you nearly gave me a heart attack!"

"I seem to have that knack, don't I?"

Remembering running into him in the elevator in New York, her cheeks flush.

"Here, let me feel." He brings his hand up and cups her left breast, pretending to feel her heart. Before she can stop him, his mouth is on hers. His lips and tongue expertly make her forget everything around her.

Caught up in the moment, she doesn't realize he's opened the back door of her car and is slowly backing her until the back of her legs touch the wheel well.

He reaches down and pinches her gently between her thighs. Gasping silently and oblivious to anything but him, he lowers her into the back seat, kissing her deeper, his tongue hungry for hers. His hand works its way up her blouse, tugging on her buttons, while the other is pulling up her skirt.

The attack on her body has her tingling everywhere. She keeps her eyes—surrendering to every sensation.

He teases her gently with his fingers, touching all the right spots but only lightly. He whispers, "I have missed you. I think I love you."

Caught up in the emotions, she replies, "I love you too! I know I love you too!" She opens her eyes, intending to grab his face when she realizes her mind has been on Patrick. "Stop! Stop!" Amber yells.

"Are you okay? Am I hurting you?"

Pushing her skirt back down and trying to pull her blouse together, she sits up. "No, I'm fine, and you're not hurting me."

"Then why tell me to stop?"

"It's complicated."

"Love not complicated, mon cheri. I love you, and you love me. What's complicated about that?"

"I don't love you. I mean, I know I said it, but I didn't mean it. Oh, Christoph, I'm so sorry, I don't want to hurt you. I thought you were somebody else."

"You knew it was me. You said my name."

"Yes, yes, but you started kissing me, getting me aroused, and when I closed my eyes, you became somebody else."

"I don't understand. How could I be anybody else?"

"Oh, Christoph, I started seeing someone since we were together in New York. I'm sorry, but I can't do this with you. I can't do this to him. I don't sleep around."

"You are boyfriend and girlfriend?"

"Yes. No. I don't know. We haven't said it, but it's implied."

"It's never implied. Until a man says he's not dating anyone else, he is seeing other people. He has told you he loves you?"

"No."

"He is seeing other people."

"I can't believe that we spend just about every night together. He doesn't have time to see anybody else." Amber defends Patrick. He hasn't said he loves her or asked her not to see other people.

"Please don't be naïve. Do you see him every day for a little afternoon delight? Do you see him every night?"

"No. And don't tell me I'm naïve. I've been around the block a few times—I know men," Amber says, getting out of the back of the car fixing her clothes.

"Why not call and ask him? It is the least you can do for me since I have traveled so far to see you."

"Okay, I will," Amber says defiantly. Her stomach becomes queasy as she dials Patrick's number. *What if he's right? What if she's been playing the good little girlfriend all this time and she's just another notch on his belt?*

"Where are you, girl? Are you calling to tell me you're going to be late—again?"

"I was on my way, but I wanted to ask you something before I get there."

"Ask away."

"What am I to you? Are we boyfriend-girlfriend? Are you seeing anyone else?"

"Where did this come from? You really want to have this conversation...right now, on the phone?"

"Yes, I want to know—right now."

Patrick, being backed into a corner, panics. They've been having such a great time; why now? "I like you a lot. We have a lot of fun together. Can't we leave it at that for now and see what happens?"

"No, we can't. I guess you've given me my answer. I'm sorry I won't be coming over tonight. My lover from France has surprised me with a visit. You know the one you met in the hallway in New York? I'll be enjoying his company this evening. I just wanted to be sure I wasn't violating some un-spoken rule we might have. Glad I called," she hangs up before he responds.

After she hangs up, dazed—Patrick stands with his phone in his hand. "That little slut! How could I be so stupid? What in the hell is wrong with me? I'll be damned if I'm going to be one of her conquests," he says to the empty room. Patrick picks up the gift he had for her and throws it across the room. The thin glass of the expensive perfume bottle shatters, sprinkling perfume all around the kitchen.

Chapter Fourteen

Debra calls Brian's office to change her weekly appointment from Thursday to Wednesday.

Miss Sanders answers the phone and explains to Debra that Brian won't be seeing any clients for the rest of the year. He left a number for a colleague of his he thought Debra would like.

Debra takes the information and realizes as she hangs up, she's numb, knowing she won't see him anymore. She tries to convince herself, it's for the best, but she feels empty inside. As she thinks about Brian, the baby moves around. Feeling foolish, she vows again to worry about her children and nobody else. She's done with all this drama. Nobody and nothing else is more important. Debra picks up the phone to call Roberto, this will never work, and he's too far away. Better to end it now than before somebody gets hurt.

She sits down to dial Roberto's number. As she hits the first number, her eyes water. She shakes her head, willing herself to be strong. She fails...the tears flow. She drops her head on her arm, sobbing uncontrollably after dialing just four numbers.

"Amber, I'm going to meet him finally," Dominque squeals.

"Really? When?"

"I found eleven roses in a vase on my front doorstep when I got home today. He left a note saying he would bring the twelfth one in person on Christmas Day at 4 p.m."

"That's scary—creepy even," Amber states.

"What do you mean?"

"He knows where you work. He knows what kind of car you drive, and now he knows where you live. Wait, how does he know where you live?"

"I don't know, and I don't think it's creepy. I feel as if I already know this man, and somehow he knows a lot about me. I've never had someone pay so much attention to me; interested in me as a person and not just for sex. Where is little Miss Optimistic?"

"She just became Miss Realistic. Listen, I don't want to burst your bubble, please be careful."

"So, what should I do?"

"I think your girlfriends will have your back and be at your house at 3:45. If his intentions are good, he won't mind you having a support group there."

"What about your Christmas dinner plans?"

"We can have dinner over at your house as easily as we can at mine. I'll call Zya and Debra and tell them the place has changed. You know Tina and Stacey are joining us, right?"

"Wow, that's a lot of people in my tiny apartment. You sure you're going to be okay with having dinner here?"

"We're very close. If it's too small, we'll get even closer. It'll be okay. Plus, this will give Mr. Fan Club President a chance to meet the rest of the gang. Think he'll want to stay for dinner?" Amber asks.

"I guess that will be up to him and you're right, this is a great test. If he's half the man I think he is, he'll ask to carve the turkey."

"It still creeps me out he know's where you live. It better all make sense or else…"

"Else what?"

"He'll have three crazy women interrogating him. Have you heard of the Spanish Inquisition?"

"You gonna tell me what that big grin on your face is for?" Zya asks Ashanti.

"You know Mr. Henderson down the street?"

Zya scowls, "Yes."

"Well, I helped him today."

"You helped him? He *let* you help him?" Zya asks curiously.

"He was in his garden as I walked by. You know me, I always say hi even if he is a grumpy old man. He didn't grunt or do anything. It seemed odd, so I backed up and asked if he was okay. He didn't answer, so I went into his yard. When I got over to him, I could tell he was in trouble. It was so hot today, and he was probably out longer than he should have been. Anyway, he came to a little when I touched him. You would have thought my fingers were made of hot coals," she says while laughing. "He jumped when he realized it was me and yelled at me to get out of his yard, go home, and leave him alone. He didn't need any help from my kind.

"I put my hands on my hips and told him to stop being a jerk. If he wanted to die there in his front yard, I'd be on my way. But if he wanted me to get him some water or help get him inside, he was going to have to overlook the color of my skin."

Zya has her hand over her mouth, chuckling.

"Anyway, he looked away and gave me his elbow. I got him inside, then he tried to rush me off. I didn't listen to him, I went and got him a cold drink and a wet towel. When I brought them, he motioned for me to put them on the table—he wouldn't even look at me. I left the phone by him so he could call for help if he needed someone. As I left, I told him he didn't have to thank me. I didn't do it because I wanted anything from him; I did it because it was the right thing to do. That old man looked up at me, smiled, and said, 'You're not all colored, are you? Your skin's too light.'"

They both go into hysterics, holding their stomachs as the laughter goes on and on.

Zya hugging her says, "That's my baby. When did you grow up?"

"Want to know what I said back?"

"Oh, I can't wait to hear this."

"I told him yes, I have the best of both worlds in me," Ashanti proudly states.

"I am so proud of you, honey. Many people would have left the old crank in his yard, but not you. You really are a special girl. You know that?"

Zya hugs her so hard, she grunts in pain. "Honey, you okay?"

She's looking down, taking shallow breaths. "I'm fine. I fell down the steps the other night and hurt my side."

"Let me look." Zya lifts her shirt, revealing a sizable yellowish-blue bruise on her ribcage. "Why didn't you tell me about this? Are you okay? Should we get x-rays? You might have a cracked rib."

"No, Mom, I'm fine…this is exactly why I didn't tell you. If I thought it was serious enough, I would have said something. It's been almost a week now. It's okay—just me and my clumsy feet. Momma, I got to tell you, it felt great helping Mr. Henderson."

"You certainly handled him diplomatically. Maybe there's a calling for you in politics."

"No way! I don't have any desire to be a part of that lying, cheating, greedy group."

A shocked Zya replies, "Well, honey, I didn't know you felt so strongly about this."

"I know better than to generalize, but I can't stand to listen to them anymore. Sorry, I just get so mad about this. Not sure when we decided loyalty to a political party was more important than doing what's right for our country."

"I never knew this meant so much to you. You shouldn't get yourself so worked up over this."

"I know. I look at you and see all the wonderful things you do for everybody else, sacrificing to help others. Why can't more people be like you?"

"Thank you, honey, that's sweet of you, and I'm glad to see you take notice of how I treat others. There's lots of good people in this world; they just don't yell. You wait—things will turn around, you'll see."

"Really? You think so? One kid in my economics class today tried to convince us the CEO's deserve to get millions of dollars in salary and bonuses because they work hard. If the company does well—everybody wins. I asked him who everybody was, and he said, the shareholders. I told him about you and how instead of taking a huge salary and bonus every year, you give a chunk of the profits to your employees, besides their Christmas bonus. He got all cocky, saying you must not have a big business. You should've seen the shock on his face when I told him *Label Zya* would profit over three million dollars this year. His eyes got so big…I couldn't stop. I explained why you manufacture your designs in the states, because you want to put people to work even though it cost you more. How you felt it was your duty to help your fellow Americans."

"Now, this boy is going to think you're little *Miss Rich Girl.*"

"No, I told him that instead of things, you want to make a difference to other peoples lives. Your legacy is not what you own but the lives you touch."

"That's right, baby, and I think I'm looking at my legacy right here."

"Momma, I'm going to find a cure for cancer. I want to help other families avoid going through what we experienced when great grandma died."

"Early detection is much better now; fewer people are dying from breast cancer. Medicine in Africa is not the same as here. Your great grandmother at least got the chance to know you—if even for just a little while. Being here in the states with us, she was happy. I know she was content when she passed. If you want to do something as big as curing cancer, I think that's wonderful. I'll be proud of you no matter what you choose."

"Yeah—that's what I want to do. Which, speaking of breast cancer, I noticed you have an appointment next week." Ashanti asks.

"Just my annual mammogram, nothing to worry about."

Ashanti sits quietly for a moment with her head tilted, looking into space. "There was a poem you told me about that helped you when great grandma died. You said it helped give you some direction. What was the name of it?"

"The Dash; it was anonymous back then, but I believe someone's claimed credit for it now."

"Can I make a copy of it? I want to bring it to school."

"Let's do a Google search and see if we can buy you a copy."

Stewart senses a change in his phone-sex girl. She's available a lot more lately making him eager to get home every night so they can connect. She's been his *call* girl, three, sometimes four, times a week now.

After an unusually long session, before she hangs up, he says, "Wait, can we talk for a few minutes?"

"You want to talk? Don't ruin this for us by getting all sappy on me now."

"I want to get to know you a little better."

"Honey, no one knows me as you do," she purrs in her husky, sexy voice.

"And boy, have I enjoyed you letting me in—literally. I'd like to know more about you…other than sex."

"Okay, what do you want to know?"

"First off, what's your name?" Stewart asks.

"Oh, that I'll never tell; I want to remain a mystery."

"So, I guess what you do for a living is out of the question as well?"

"Let's just say, I'm great with my hands—among other things."

A rise in his pants makes him to pause. He thinks about work to will him back to reality. "Yes, that you are. How old are you?"

"Old enough; age is only a number. It shouldn't matter how old I am," she states.

"It would if you were say…seventy."

"Don't you think that would be great if I was seventy years old and able to knock you for a loop?"

"Please, I need to meet you. This is driving me crazy. You're not like any other woman I've met. You're such a turn on to me in every way, not just sexually."

"I believe I sense a little urgency there."

"Look, I'm thirty-nine years old and a confirmed bachelor. I've been with lots of women, and no one has come close to being someone I want to share time with—I want to be with you."

"Now, now, what if we were to meet and find out we're not physically attracted to each other?"

"I doubt that'll happen. The things we've shared already."

"You have a mental image in your mind of what you think I look like?"

"Yes, you're smoking hot."

"What if I'm not? I could be your average girl, overweight or have bad acne."

"You exude a sex-appeal of someone comfortable in her own skin. I'm confident you're one sexy lady."

"How do you know I'll be as willing to experiment in person as I am on the phone? This could be my protection."

"I thought about that. If you aren't, let's just say I'm willing to do whatever I can on my end to help you try. I can get into any role you like."

"I don't know. I think there's something sexy about the mystery. I'll think about it, but don't get your hopes up. I'm having a lot of fun, and I'm not so sure I'm ready to give it up."

After he hangs up, he beats his fists against his thighs. He sounded so desperate—she must think he's one of those love-sick, clingy men. Come to think of it, he sounded needy, like some gals he's been with over the years. They wanted so badly to make him want them. They tried way too hard; it was a big turnoff. He figures he's blown it by doing just that with her.

CHAPTER FIFTEEN

Christmas decorations everywhere reminding him the holidays are coming fast. Some radio stations are playing holiday music even though it's still over 20-days away. He had hoped he'd be spending the holidays with Amber this year. They never talked about being exclusive. He assumed it was a given.

Stewart comes out of his room, freshly showered, wearing just his jeans, no shirt, and wet hair.

"You spend an awful lot of time alone in your room, dude. I'm worried about you. Are you giving up all the other ladies for this one?" Patrick asks.

"I don't want anyone else, I just can't get through to her. She refuses to meet me."

"Really? Maybe she thinks you won't like what you see."

"That's what she said, but I don't care what she looks like —I can't get her out of my head."

"You care what she looks like. I've known you for how long now? I've seen you in action; if she's not smoking hot, you won't want her."

"That's where you're wrong. It's not just the sex...she's gotten under my skin. I've never wanted anyone the way I want her. Just thinking about her makes me crazy."

"I don't believe my eyes. Is Stewart Lewis, South Florida's most confirmed bachelor, in love?"

"I don't know—maybe."

Patrick's eyes glaze over, staring at a spot on the wall. Stewart says, "Earth to Patrick."

Patrick looks back, "Oh sorry, I was just thinking."

"About Amber, weren't you?"

"Yeah, I can't believe the luck with her. I almost screwed it up not once, but twice. Then, when I think everything is going along great, BAM! I get knocked down again."

"Just call her, will you?"

"Why should I? It's probably better we end it now, anyway. She's been seeing that Frenchman; it's for the best."

Stewart sticks his elbows out and makes clucking noises. "Dude, you're chicken! She was right to ask you if you were seeing anyone else. In fact, kudos to her; she's my new hero."

"Thanks a lot, friend," Patrick says sarcastically. "Kick a man when he's down; what are friends for?"

Stewart grabs a chair next to Patrick. "Look, you like her, right?"

Patrick nods.

"You weren't seeing anyone else, right?"

Patrick nods again.

"Call her. Tell her you don't want to be with anybody else."

"After she spent this weekend with Christoph, I don't think so."

"She likes the guy, right? Do you want her to spend another weekend with him?"

"No."

"Then call her already."

Stewart walks back into his room as Patrick picks up his cell phone.

She answers on the second ring. "Patrick," Amber says a little too quickly.

"Hi, did I catch you at a bad time?"

"No, I'm just reading through some notes on a new story I'm working on."

"What's this one called?"

"How important is communication?"

"Ouch, I guess I deserve that one, don't I?"

"What can I do for you?" Amber asks coldly.

"I wanted to call and apologize. I guess I didn't handle our last conversation right. You took me by surprise. I didn't have an answer for you because I hadn't thought about it. We were having such a great time, and things were going so well...I didn't see why we should mess it up."

"All you had to do was tell me was yes, we should talk about it. And no, you didn't want to see anybody else."

"I haven't seen anybody else since we've been together. I'm not like that—I don't date around. I'm the complete opposite of my roommate Stewart."

"The town slut?" Amber asks.

"I don't know if slut would be the right word to use."

"Why not? They call a loose woman who dates and sleeps around one. Is that what you think of me? Did you call me a slut?"

"The old double standard, huh?"

"Wait a minute, did you say your roommate's name is Stewart?"

251

"Yes."

"Tall, dirty blond hair, gray-colored eyes, and a six-pack even Heineken is jealous of?"

"Hey, hey, watch it, I'm going to get jealous myself."

"I think he may have had a rendezvous with my good friend Dominque."

"The girl that works in your office?"

"Yes."

"He said something about a gal with flaming red hair some months back; I didn't think it was her. He didn't hurt her or anything, did he?"

"Oh no, in fact, she could probably in her past life, match him booty call for booty call."

"In her past life?"

"Yeah, she's gone through some recent changes and not given her body out to every Tom, Dick, and Stewart she meets. She has this secret admirer that's got her head spinning. She's going to meet him finally on Christmas Day."

"That's the reason I called!"

"To tell me you're her secret admirer?"

"No, I wanted to know if you would have dinner with me on Christmas night? I'm sure you probably have plans already—with family, but I want to see if you were available; I have a little something for you."

"Really, a gift for me? After what happened a few days ago?"

"Let me clarify, I'm not seeing anyone. But if want to, let me know and I'll go on my merry way."

"Okay. No, I don't want to see anyone else. As far as Christmas Dinner though, we're eating at Dom's house. All of us girls are going over to meet mystery man. You're welcome to join us and then we can head out and spend the rest of the night together alone."

"Deal. Can I bring anything?"

"How about a few bottles of that Opus One?"

Patrick gulps as he calculates how much two bottles will set him back. Not wanting to seem cheap, he asks, "Sure, how many bottles?"

"Four should do it."

"Alrighty then, send me the address," Patrick says, trying to breathe.

"Brian, is that you?"

Debra is at her favorite produce market in Hollywood, picking up some things she needs for Christmas dinner.

"Hi Debra, funny running into you here," Brian replies.

Watching Brian fidget with his hands and unable to meet her eyes, she is cordial and quick to ease his discomfort. "Just picking up some fresh veggies; Merry Christmas." She turns and walks away, before he can see the puddles forming in her lower lids.

He mumbles, "Merry Christmas." Then he turns and walks in the opposite direction. He can't believe he ran into her, here of all places. He's tried so hard to stay away from her.

Debra quickly picks some sweet potatoes and a bushel of green beans and heads for the cashier, eager to get out of there. She can't think straight. Not sure she has everything she came for, she absentmindedly heads for the cashier. She doesn't notice Brian put his basket down and leave.

He puts the key in, starts the car, and is about to put the car in reverse when he sees her rushing out of the store.

Her cheeks are flushed red, and she's crying.

Without thinking, he gets out of the car and walks straight over to her. He reaches her as she's opening the driver's side door to get in. "Debra," he says. Taking her arm, he spins her around. The pain in her eyes makes his heart hurt. He tilts her head and kisses her delicately.

She's frozen with shock, but soon melts into his arms as passion takes over.

"I'm sorry. I couldn't see you anymore. I couldn't hear about Roberto. Every time you cried about George, the baby or Roberto, I wanted to jump across the desk and pull you tight against me, protecting you from everything and everyone."

The tears stream continuously down her cheeks as she looks up into his sparkling pools of blue. "I've missed you so much."

He hugs her tight. "I've missed you."

"Still think it's because you're my therapist?"

He shakes his head. "No—I'm sorry. I couldn't see you anymore. I could have my license taken away; I'm not allowed to fraternize with my patients. I've seen too many good doctor's ruined because they fell in love with their patients. Oh God, it's so good to see you," he says as he wraps her back in his arms, his lips hungry for hers.

"What do we do now?"

"Roberto still in the picture?"

"No—Yes, I don't know," she says in barely a whisper.

"Do you love him?"

"I have feelings for him but…Oh, this is such a mess."

Brian steps back but keeps his hands on her arms. "I don't want to interfere. It wouldn't be right. Especially with everything you've been through. Here's my cell," he says as he takes a card from his wallet and writes his number on it. "Call me if anything changes." He kisses her again, gentler this time, then steps away and to his car.

She gets into her car and watches him; her heart leaping from her chest. She wants to scream, 'No, come back. It's you I want.' Instead, she watches as he pulls out of the driveway.

The office Christmas party at NeoQuest has always been a hit. The guys put mistletoe up all around, hoping to catch the ladies underneath after a few cocktails. Dominque, in the past, had always been one of the party's gossip topics. Not this year…she's not drinking.

"You sure you won't have just one?" Amber asks.

"If I do, I'll end up having more. I'd rather keep my senses about me this year."

"Suit yourself, that leaves more for me. So tell me, what you are wearing tomorrow for the big meeting?" Amber inquires as she makes her way over to the drink station.

"I have this dark green sweater. I thought I would wear it with my beige silk pants."

"No short skirt—skimpy top?"

"This guy seems special; I don't want to give him the wrong impression…not at first."

Laughing, Amber hugs Dominque.

"What was that for?" Dominque asks.

"Just because I'm proud of you; you've come a long way, baby."

"Thanks, I appreciate you being there for me. Okay, just a little sip."

She pours about an inch of punch into a glass. "To my best friend, Merry Christmas."

"Merry Christmas, Dom. May all your wishes come true."

"I hope so. On that note, I'm going to head home." She turns to leave, but spins too quickly and gets dizzy. She grabs the table to prevent herself from falling.

"You okay? Need to sit down?"

"No, I'm fine, just moved too fast. See, all better; see you tomorrow."

Dominque leaves, letting out a big breath when she reaches her car. These dizzy spells are becoming a nuisance. She needs to remember to take her iron—she's just anemic.

"Roberto, what are you doing here?" Debra asks, surprised to see him at her front door.

"What do you mean? How come you not meet me at airport?"

"I left you a message on your machine at home."

"And what did it say?"

Motioning for Roberto to enter, she says, "Come in, come in."

"Mommy, who is this man?"

"Tracey darling, this is my friend from Italy. His name is Roberto."

"The beautiful Tracey, I meet you finally. Your mother say you gorgeous, but she not say this much."

Tracey squeals as Roberto picks her up and swings her around. He reaches out for her hand, kissing it on the back. "It is a pleasure to meet you, Miss Tracey."

"Go to your room for a bit Tracey. Mommy wants to talk to Roberto."

"Is he staying for Christmas with us?"

"We'll see, now go on up."

"We'll see? I don't like."

"Roberto, I left you a message asking you not to come. I need more time; time to mourn the death of my husband, be with Tracey, and the new baby. I need to clear my head."

"Mia Bella, I come here once, and you say don't come, so I leave. This time, we talk."

"You were here?" Debra asks, puzzled.

"Yes, but I take first plane back to Milan—no problem."

"I'm sorry, you must think I'm acting like a schoolgirl."

"Debra, you cannot be anything but who you are. No sorries—I love you. I love you as you are. I come here this trip to be with you always. We can be in Milan, Florida, your choice. I want to be with you."

"Oh, Roberto, I don't want to hurt your feelings, but I'm not ready for this. Please give me more time."

The doorbell chimes, and someone calls out, "Flowers for Mrs. Harris."

Debra opens the door to find a flower courier with a massive bouquet of mixed red and sterling silver roses. "Thank you." She takes them and puts them on the dining room table.

"Please read card," Roberto says, through gritted teeth.

"Not now, it's okay."

"Now!" he yells.

She's never seen him like this. His eyes bulge as his face darkens to a deep red. "Roberto, please don't make me read it in front of you."

"Who? You seeing someone else?"

"It just happened; I didn't plan it. They're from my therapist."

"The man I met at dinner? Yes, I told you he like you. You like him?"

"I don't know. I don't think I should like or want to be with anybody right now. My husband just died."

"Stop. Your husband gone now five-months, and already you have two men?"

Debra is nervous, watching him pace back and forth. She's never seen him angry. He's always been so gentle and sweet. Tracey is here, if he does anything…she's concerned about her daughter, and the baby she's carrying.

"I'm angry. I go to hotel to think. I ask you not to be with doctor right now. Talk tomorrow, okay?"

"Okay."

Debra just wants him out of her house. She doesn't feel safe with him anymore. His face softens, and his eyes turn sad as he takes her hands and kisses it gently. "Merry Christmas, Mia Bella."

Debra watches as he walks to the door and leaves. She cries uncontrollably, not unlike when she first lost George.

"Mommy, Mommy, what's wrong?"

Through her tears, she sees Tracey standing next to her, looking worried. "Nothing sweetheart, Mommy's fine; just thinking that's all."

"Where did the nice man go? I like him. I hope he's coming for dinner tomorrow."

"I hope you don't mind, I set up the guest bedroom for you —for now."

"No, I don't mind. Listen, I want you to know I'm here for you and Ashanti. We'll go as slow as you both need and just take it one day at a time."

Zya hugs Tina. "Thank you."

"No, *thank* you."

Tina pulls Zya close to her and kisses her gently on the lips. Zya tenses at first, but then loses herself in the gentleness of Tina's touch. The sound of someone clearing their throat pulls them apart.

"Excuse me," Stacey says. "Should I put my stuff in Ashanti's room or the guest room with my mother?"

Zya pulls away embarrassed, as Tina ushers Stacey out of the room. "Just put them in my room for now. We'll work it out when Ashanti gets home."

"Miss Monroe, for what it's worth, if that isn't love I feel, I don't know what is," Tina says teasingly.

"I'm so embarrassed."

"Don't be."

"I don't want to flaunt this in front of either of them. To be honest, I don't think I can in front of anybody."

"That's perfectly natural, it's okay. Stop apologizing already and tell me all about my new job at *Label Zya*."

"We can talk about that later. I feel I'm being selfish. You turned down that job and pushed away a woman you know loves you dearly. And I'm not sure about us—yet. I'll get there, I just need to process this."

"You didn't put a gun to my head; you gave me hope. I love you, Zya Monroe. You're worth the wait."

Patrick knocks on the door, juggling four bottles of expensive wine. He knew dinner doesn't start for at least another hour, however, he wanted to come early and see the big moment happen.

Zya opens the door. "You must be Patrick, I recognize you from the article Amber wrote about you earlier this year."

"And you must be Zya."

"Because I'm black?"

"No…because you are so stylish."

"Watch out, mister, compliments will get you everywhere around here."

Patrick steps in and reluctantly hands over the bag to Zya. "Please be careful with those."

"I will."

Not able to wait until the bag rests on the counter, she peeks and whistles. "Patrick, you have incredible taste. This is some excellent wine."

"How do you know so much about wine?" Amber asks from the kitchen. "You don't even drink."

Tina walks over and takes the bottle from her hand. "Oh yes, this man has class. You better watch out spoiling us like this—we'll get used to it." She laughs as she walks to Patrick and introduces herself.

Amber is whispering to Zya in the kitchen about the wine. "What's the big deal?"

Zya whispers the price per bottle into her ear. Amber's mouth drops open. Zya closes it.

"We had it one night, and it was so good. I asked him to bring four bottles. I can't believe he actually did!"

"That boy has it bad for you."

Dominque comes out of her room—glowing.

"Dominque, what a pleasure to see you again. You look gorgeous. Mr. Wonderful may end up being swept off his feet instead of the other way around," Patrick says, admiring how the green sweater plays off her flaming red hair.

"How did you know?" she asks, looking over at guilty Amber.

"A little birdie told me," Patrick replies as he winks at Amber. He kisses Dominque's hand before exiting towards the living room.

Amber watches Patrick as he heads towards the kids playing one of those motion-controlled video games. Ashanti and Stacey are sword fighting with Tracey cheering them on.

Patrick walks back to the kitchen.

"Is Debra here? I was hoping to chat with her," he asks.

"She'll be here later. She dropped Tracey off, then left to take care of some business of the heart."

"Of the heart? Her husband just passed away."

Amber's body goes rigid. She takes a deep breath to relax before she answers. "George passed away five months ago, and believe me, she's fighting her heart right now—tooth and nail."

"Oh, you'll fill me in later," Patrick states while kissing her on her neck, realizing he hit a nerve.

After his lips succeed, she responds in a low whisper, "You better believe it, buddy. Or maybe it will be you filling me."

Patrick walks away in a hurry.

Amber watches him rush into the family room again and joins in with Tracey's hooting and hollering. She laughs, thinking, for someone so calm, cool and collected, it's so easy for her to push his buttons.

"Dom, it's almost four—you ready?"

"As ready as I'll ever be. I don't want to see him until he walks through the door, okay?"

"Sure, can I at least describe him as he walks up?"

"Okay, but no specifics, just in case it is the cop; I want to be surprised."

Everybody stops dead in their tracks as they hear a car door shut.

Zya rushes to the window. "Well, it's not Debra."

Amber walks over to Dominque and gives her the rest of her wine. "Here, drink this, it'll help calm your nerves."

"Okay, now get over there and tell me if he's tall, dark, and handsome."

Zya is looking out the window from one side of the door and Amber out the other. Zya comments first, "He looks nervous; that's a good sign."

Amber looks over at Dominque and then looks back out the window.

"What? No, don't tell me. It's not what's on the outside that counts, right?" Dominque stutters to Amber.

"No honey, he's handsome. And I bet underneath that jacket and slacks, he probably has a nice body."

"Hey, hey," Patrick comes up and joins Amber at the window. "Hey, I know that guy."

"Shh, don't say a word."

"No, he's cool, super nice—he'd give you the shirt off his back if you need it."

Dominque glows, hearing Patrick's enthusiastic description.

"How do I look?" asks Dominque, smoothing down her hair.

Patrick answers first, "Absolutely gorgeous. You're gonna knock him dead."

"I don't want him dead!"

CHAPTER SIXTEEN

Debra asked Roberto to meet her at a café on the beach—one she knew would be crowded.

Five minutes early, as she knew he would be, Roberto walks up to her and takes, kissing it gently. "Mia Bella, it is good to see you."

"I feel terrible about this. I'm sorry, I didn't plan for any of this to happen—please believe me."

"Don't upset yourself; it's no good for baby. Everything's okay. I'm not mad. I was, but not now. I needed to think is all. I'm sorry if I upset you."

Debra relaxes instantly as the Roberto she was so familiar with is back. "You've come all this way, please at least let me pay for your plane ticket."

"Nonsense, I am glad I come. If you have feelings for me, as you say you do, I ask you one thing, give us both a chance. Let me win your heart for good—please."

"How do I do that? I can't be with two men at once—it's just not right."

"Mia Bella, I will win you without making love to you. Please the same with doctor, yes?"

"You're willing to travel overseas and not sleep together?"

"I love you—the woman. Making love to you is like icing on a cake. Will you give me chance?"

Debra thinks about it; it's crazy, but maybe this is a way to help her figure out her feelings.

"Okay, I can do that."

"Good. You were meeting him today, right?"

"Yes. I'm sorry, I am."

"Please, you call and have him join us, now?"

"Come here and join us?"

"Yes, Mia Bella. It is only fair for him to know me, and me him. I would like to know he agrees with plan."

Debra pulls out her phone to call Brian. She hesitates at first, but if he really likes her, he'll go along. Nervous, yet giddy at the same time at the prospect of having two men competing for her, she dials his number.

Dominque closes her eyes when the door opens as her biggest fan steps into the room. He smells good—very musky—a sexy, sweet smell. Slowly she opens her eyes. At first, she can't see his face because the sunlight is glowing behind him—shadowing the front.

He takes a few steps towards her.

She notices he's tall and good build. Her jaw drops when the shadow falls from his face. The man before her is not the man she's wanted, but maybe the one she's always needed.

"Dominque, I'm sorry for all the secrecy and mystery. I knew you wouldn't give a guy like me a chance without first getting to know me. You're so beautiful, and you've become so strong these last few months. I can take your pick of who you want to be with; I'm hoping you could learn to love someone like me. Not how I look on the outside, but what's inside and how I feel about you."

She stands with mouth open, unable to say anything.

"If you want me to leave, I'll understand. I had to try."

Hearing him say these words and the beautiful friendship they developed, she decides he's the most handsome man in the world. She steps forward, puts her arms around him, and kisses him passionately.

Everybody claps and laughs.

He dips her. "I guess this means I can stay?"

With tears in her eyes, she's nodding her head enthusiastically. "You can stay forever."

He kisses her again, then noticing all the people in the room, steps away with flushed cheeks. He extends his hand to Patrick, and says, "Good to see you again, man."

"You too, Tad."

Brian smiles when he sees Debra stand at the table overlooking the beach. The man sitting next to her also stands. He looks confused as he walks up to the table.

Roberto extends his hand out to Brian. "Nice to see you again."

Brian looks confused. "Yeah—okay—" He looks over at Debra, willing her to explain.

After a long pause, Roberto says, "Dr. Brian, first I need to tell you, Debra left message for me not to come, but I not receive. I come last night like planned. She told me she care about you. At first, I'm angry but thought last night. I love her and she loves me. She says she's confused, so I ask the chance to win her heart. I ask her to give us both that chance."

Debra shifts uncomfortably in her seat, fidgeting with her dress. She doesn't even know if Brian is that serious about her.

Brian's words interrupt her thoughts. "I accept! And if I may say, I respect your honesty—and honor, bringing me here to discuss this like men. I'd like to think I'm the best man for Debra, but then again, you've proven yourself a worthy opponent." Brian shakes Roberto's hand and says, "I think I need a drink now."

"Make that two," Roberto says.

"Make that three," Debra adds, sitting up in her chair.

Both men look at each other, confused. In unison, "You're pregnant."

"Oh yeah, for a minute there, I totally forgot. I'm sorry, I was busy grieving over my dead husband, and listening to two wonderful men challenge each other to what seems likes nothing more than a friendly game of chess."

Roberto kisses her hand. "One more thing I wish to add..."

Brian motions him to continue.

"The winner has her hand in marriage."

Lunging forward in her chair, Debra says, "Wait a minute! I'm not ready to get married again. I'm pregnant with another man's baby—remember?"

"Deal," Brian says, looking Roberto in the eye, ignoring Debra's reaction.

She watches as the two men shake hands.

The drinks arrive, and Debra grabs Brian's. It's the closest to her and gulps it down. "I'm in my second trimester, and my doctor says one drink with dinner is fine. So what if it's not dinner—yet; I needed that." Debra sits back watching and listening a as both men talk about Italy and Florida, psychiatry, and massage therapy. They're getting along like best buddies.

"Wait, I think I've heard of you. Are you the Roberto Paulucci?"

Roberto nods.

"Wow, this is an honor, and now I may have to take my game up a notch." Brian looks over at Debra. "Do you know who this man is? He's famous for his incredible hands."

Debra blushes and drops her gaze to her hands. Yes, she's well aware just how talented his hands are.

Brian doesn't notice Debra's flush. "I'd ask to make an appointment while you're here, but I'm afraid you might choke me—or worse."

"Nonsense, my work very serious."

"Okay, great. A neck and shoulder massage sounds good. I get so tense writing up reports and files, and sometimes just listening to clients." He looks over at Debra. "Not you. Well, maybe when you talked about this one," he adds, pointing his thumb at Roberto.

"I think you have advantage," Roberto states.

"Maybe a small one, I blocked out what she said about you because I needed to keep my feelings in check."

Debra, sitting between them at the table, turns her head from side to side, like at a tennis match as they talk. Hearing Brian share how he zoned out during some of their sessions, makes her feel all warm inside. Oh, she could easily fall for this man.

"She told me many wonderful things about you. I just

didn't want to hear you were such a wonderful man; so patient and loving. It was nice to know you lived far away."

Debra looks over at Roberto and remembers how wonderful and understanding he's been. *Maybe this is the man for me?* Confused and flustered, she grabs a flatbread from the center table and starts munching like a squirrel stuffing his cheeks, staring off into the distance.

"Everything all right?" Brian asks.

"Just peachy, thanks." As she grabs another flatbread with her other hand, she alternates, taking bites from each without swallowing the one before.

Brian, looking at Roberto, says, "You are joining us for dinner, right?"

"No, I not—intrude? I find restaurant here."

"Nonsense, one more shouldn't be a problem, right Debra?"

"Right. Right. That would be great," Debra says, wondering how she's going to explain this one. The two men fight over who pays for the check for the drinks.

Debra grabs it. "Here, let me."

"I wonder what's keeping her. Let me call her," Amber says.

"Hi, Amber," Debra says, sounding tired.

"Hey, Deb, everything all right?"

Still dazed, she replies, "Just peachy. Two more coming for dinner tonight, I hope that's all right."

"Um—sure, we have plenty."

"See you in a minute," Debra says, defeated.

Amber hangs up the phone, wondering who the third person is.

"Do you celebrate Christmas?" Stacey asks Ashanti. While waiting for Debra and Roberto to arrive, Stacey pulls her BFF aside.

"We put up that little tree you saw, and exchange one gift. My mom goes to the Angel Tree and picks ten kids, and we go shopping for them, so they have a Christmas. I love doing that. I look forward to it every year."

"And, all the food!"

"Yeah, we love the traditional turkey with stuffing and cranberry sauce," Ashanti adds.

"So, what was the one gift you got?"

"I wanted pants. My mom felt bad I don't want to wear skirts anymore, so she got me four pairs then wrapped them all together."

"So, why is it you aren't wearing dresses anymore? You love to look girly." Stacey says, teasing Ashanti.

"The kids in high school don't dress the same as junior high. All my skirts were too childish. Jeans and slacks are more grown-up."

"Is that the real reason? Have you told your mom yet?"

"No, and I'm not gonna; it's under control now. I have their routine down. Plus, they're picking on this nerdy kid now."

"I'm glad they're leaving you along, but that poor kid. That doesn't sound like a good trade-off."

"No, it's not, but if my mom knew, she'd march down there and just make matters worse. I feel bad for him. It's my fault they're picking on him."

"Nonsense, you know how bullies are. They pick on anyone smaller and weaker than them because they know they'll win. So sad—ever wonder what life must be like at home to stoop so low?"

"You mean never feeling like you measure up. Never good enough to get your parent's attention. It's this keeping up with the Jones's mentality. Both parents working long hours so they can upgrade to a fancier car or bigger house. They think they're doing the right thing by giving their kids what they didn't have, when all they're doing is sacrificing their kids' love and attention they need."

"You're so mature, Ashanti. I'm glad we're friends. I'm even more glad our moms are in love."

"Thanks, Stacey. I'm glad we met too. We're one big happy family." Ashanti gives Stacey a bear hug.

Laughing, Stacey pulls out a wrapped box. "I hope it's all right if you get two gifts this year."

"Really? For me? I wish you wouldn't have. I don't have anything for you."

"Christmas is about giving—not receiving."

"Yeah, I guess getting is cool too," Ashanti says as she rips into the box.

Looking inside, she's confused about its contents. "You're my best friend. I want to be sure you're protected from those bullies. At least this might help even the odds a little," she says, showing Ashanti the details of the protection she's gifted.

"Hey, can we eat yet? All this great-smelling food is really getting to me," Dominque yells from the living room.

"In a few minutes, Debra is on her way with another guest?" Amber answers more like a question.

Zya and Dominque look at Amber with a puzzled look on their faces.

"I hope it's that nice man that came to the house last night," Tracey says as she runs by the table and grabs a roll.

The confusion increases as they try to think who she's talking about. They all run to the window when they hear a car pull up in the driveway. With wide eyes and their jaws open, they recognize Roberto in the passenger seat. Their eyes bulge even more when they see Brian's car pull up behind Debra.

Brian opens Debra's door and helps her out, then he joins Roberto in animated conversation as they walk towards the door. Debra slowly makes her way behind them, her eyes cast down at the ground.

Amber greets them at the door. "Hi guys. Surprised to see you here."

"Merry Christmas, Brian says, kissing her on the cheek." He steps aside, as does Roberto, allowing Debra to enter first.

Amber hugs her and asks, "Should I ask?"

Debra shakes her head. "I'm not sure I have an answer."

After dinner on their way to Amber's apartment, Patrick says, "Well, I have to admit, that was one of the most unusual groups of people I've ever had the pleasure of dining with."

Hitting him playfully on the arm, Amber replies, "Hey, those are my friends you're talking about, buddy."

Laughing, he says, "They are great. But one woman with two dates, how does that happen?"

"It seems a bit strange, doesn't it? I'll call tomorrow and

get the scoop. Brian and Roberto seemed like old pals. And poor Debra looked like she wanted to vanish into thin air."

"Yeah, she seemed uncomfortable. She didn't tell you anything?"

"No, and the last thing I want to do is embarrass her. She seemed pretty stressed and confused. Poor thing—stress is the last thing she needs right now." Amber opens the front door to her apartment and invites Patrick inside. "You didn't happen to save one of those bottles of wine for us, did you?"

"Actually, I brought something even nicer." Patrick pulls out a bottle of *Cristal* from under his jacket. "Glasses, please."

"How did you keep that cold all this time?"

"Planning, my dear—lots of planning."

Smiling, she saunters to him and kisses him gently—yet deeply—stoking the fire. "You really are something, aren't you?"

Amber pulls back. Satisfied the embers are glowing, she fetches two crystal flutes. "That wasn't there when I left." She points to the small box on the island with the big red bow.

"Really? Are you sure? Someone must have left it for you."

"Well, actually I think whoever it was,"—Amber reaches into one of the kitchen cabinets and pulls out a wrapped box, also with a big red bow—"deserves one too. Look, matching bows."

"Open yours first."

"Okay." Amber slowly and carefully pulls the bow off. Then even more delicately, peels back the scotch tape attempting to not rip the paper.

"Oh, come on already!" Patrick grabs the side of the box and rips the paper.

"Hey, I save that, you know."

"No, you don't, you're just enjoying making me wait."

"You're right," she replies as she rips off the remaining paper. Inside is a ring box.

"Don't get all excited now. I'm not ready to marry you yet."

Amber thinks about his use of 'yet,' as she carefully opens the box. Inside is a gold Claddagh ring.

"Okay, maybe somewhat old-fashioned, but I want to give you something as a token proving we're a couple—not casually dating."

"Does this mean we're going steady?"

"Well, I couldn't find my high school jacket or class ring, so I hope this will do."

Amber reaches for him as her eyes turn glassy. She pulls him close, locking lips again—this time, not so gently.

His knees go weak, and his stomach does flips.

"I like you."

"I like you too."

Patrick never opened his gift that night—the wrapped one that is.

CHAPTER SEVENTEEN

Brian gave Debra and Roberto their space for the rest of the weekend. They agreed when Roberto was in town, he would have her exclusively. Brian got all the other time, which was definitely a benefit.

"Hi. Are you on your way back from the airport?"

"I just got home."

"So, what would you like to do tonight?"

"Brian, I need a break. This entire weekend, the two of you competing for me…this mess has taken its toll on me. I'm going to soak in a hot bath and relax."

"I'm sorry you think it's a mess. If you want me to pull back, just say the word. Oh, and make sure that water isn't too hot," Brian lectures.

Chuckling, Debra says, "You're a psychiatrist, not an obstetrician—remember doc?" She pauses for a moment, trying to gather the right words. "I don't want you to pull back—I care about you. Maybe mess wasn't the best choice of words. I'm not sure how this is all going to play out. I'm tired just thinking about it."

"In that case, maybe I should come over and join you. You sound tense—I have some ideas on how to help you relax."

"Remember the deal, no sex allowed."

"How could I forget! How about you call me when you get all settled in your tub, and I tell you what you're missing?"

"You mean phone sex?"

"That doesn't count, does it? Come on, I'm not touching you. That can't count."

Laughing hearing the playful side of Brian, one she had yet to see, she replies chuckling herself, "I think that counts and besides, I could never have phone sex. At least not with someone I know."

"You mean you would if I were a total stranger?"

"Well, you could call 1-800-HOT-BABE and ask for Muffy. That might be me."

"What?" Brian is speechless. "Really? I'll call right now!"

"I'm kidding, you crazy man."

"I knew you were, just wanted to see how far you'd go. Well, the offer is on the table. If you want to have a fantastic night's sleep, and dreams you've never dreamed before, you know how to reach me."

"Thanks for the offer, but I have my washing machine."

"What?" Brian asks, confused.

Debra's cheeks burn as she realizes what she's just revealed. "I have to go now, good night."

Brian slowly hangs up thinking, *washing machine?*

Debra smiles as she ends the call. As she fills her bathtub, she thinks about both men. Roberto is tall, dark and so sexy. And that accent.... He's been so patient and kind with her. *Except when he got here,* she thinks as her brows furrow. But he lives so far away. The corners of her mouth turn up as Brian's image flashes in her mind. Very handsome, intelligent, and funny—he makes her laugh. He's helped her through her grief more than anybody. *Of course he has. That shouldn't count.* She's been able to say anything to him. He's become her friend and confidant.

She shakes her head as she steps carefully into the luke-warm water. *They're both so great. How am I ever going to pick one?* She says out loud, "And I'm not marrying them."

☯

"Are you sure it's okay for you to take kickboxing classes in your condition?"

"Yeah, as long as I don't become the punching bag. I just have to take it slow, and if I get winded, take a break. I'm on a mission to get my body back as quickly as possible after George Junior is born."

"George Junior? It's going to be a boy?"

"Yes, I just found out at my ultrasound yesterday. I wanted to tell you in person. I used to tease George the world couldn't survive with two of him running around. Since he's gone, I think it's the right thing to do."

Hugging her, Amber replies, "I think it's sweet."

"What's sweet?" Zya asks.

Zya and Tina join them as they await the start of class. Amber tells the good news to the girls.

"I always hoped I would have more children. Guess it's a little too late for that," Tina mentions.

"You want more kids?" Zya asks.

"Yeah, if I can—I love children."

"Being gay, you knew what you were giving up, right?"

"Zya, you know you can have a baby if you're gay, right?" Dominque asks.

Zya turns to Tina to see her reaction.

"I've always been gay. Remind me to tell you how Stacey came to be."

"I—I just assumed," Zya stutters. "You really want more kids?"

"I wouldn't rule it out," Tina responds.

"How does that work? You need both parts to make a baby." Zya spurts out, looking down into her hands and fidgeting.

"Same-sex couples all over the world have children. Two men can adopt, or they find a single woman who will impregnate herself with either, or both of their sperm—a surrogate," Dominque responds.

"And two women can give birth to a baby using the sperm of a donor of their choice," Tina adds.

"Is that how you got pregnant with Stacey?"

"Yes, but there's a lot more to the story."

Zya looks at Tina, unsure how to respond, remains quiet.

Sensing Zya's discomfort, Amber changes the conversation. "I don't know who to ask first?" As she looks between Debra and Dominque.

"Ask her." Debra says, pointing at Dominque.

Zya looks up and nods at Dominque, giving her a weak smile.

"I still don't know what the heck is going on. He's wonderful. I'm comfortable with him. He really is my friend, and so much more. I can't believe I would have missed out on this because he didn't fit my physical requirements."

"And the sex?" Tina asks.

"I don't know yet. He said he wants to wait. Nothing would make him happier, and he wants me more than I'll ever know, but he wants us to get to know each other better before we let lust and passion into the mix."

"Wow, that's unbelievable," Amber says, amazed.

"Yes, he is. It's hard having him sleep next to me in bed. I've tried to seduce him, but he stops me. He'll make love to me if I really want to—but he'd rather wait. He pulls me tight up against him, and we spoon all night. He tells me at least fifty times every night how much he loves me.

"He confessed something to me this morning—he told me his sister isn't suffering with anorexia anymore. She's been in treatment for almost two years now and doing remarkably well. He loved hearing how it was for me because she kept to herself throughout it. She only shared with her social worker. By listening to me and how I coped, it gave him hope. He was always afraid she would go back to her old destructive behavior. At first, I was a little mad at him, but I understand. I guess it was a little white lie."

"You know, I didn't think I would ever see it in your eyes."

"See what?"

"Love—full-blown, head-over-heels, love."

"You think so? I don't know. I've never felt like this with anyone. I always started with sex, hoping it would lead to a relationship. You really think I could be in love with him?"

"Think? It's written all over your face, girl," Zya adds.

"When he tells you every night how he feels, you don't say it back?"

"No—maybe I should."

The doors open, signaling the beginning of their weekly, hour-long kickboxing class.

Amber points at Debra. "You don't get out of spilling. Later—I want details."

CHAPTER EIGHTEEN

Zya sketches her designs from home, having her assistant Stan over three times a week to search for fabric samples and embellishment supplies.

When it's time to put it all together, she works in her studio/atelier most days and nights until the line is ready. It's important for her designs to be followed precisely as planned; insuring the seams, cutting, materials, etc., are up to her standards. She wants to keep her prices low so her designs are affordable to most women—of all ages. But she doesn't want the quality to suffer. A delicate balance, she knows, which is why she spends so much time when her visions come to life.

On the last day of completion, her employees greet her with hugs and pats on the back. The respect is mutual. They have a great place to work, with excellent benefits—so long as they keep up their end of the bargain. Don't respect your work, or the product you're producing, and you'll be looking for a new job. It's rare she has to deal with firing someone, but she has, and everyone knows she'll do it again. She's tough and ruthless, but she's like a mother to them. They are family.

Today is sketch day, so she's working at the dining room table. Ashanti is leaving for school and hugs on her way out.

"Mom, don't forget your appointment today."

"My little worrywart," Zya says as she takes Ashanti's chin in her hand, shaking it gently.

"It's important; I don't want you to die like great grandma."

"I know it is, sweetheart. I won't forget. In fact, I'll put an alarm on my phone right now."

"Thanks mom…I don't know what I'd do if I lost you."

"Come here." She pulls Ashanti into her arms and squeezes tight. "I'm not going anywhere. They say only the good die young."

"Don't say that—you're as good as they get."

Tears form in the corners of her eyes as she watches her daughter—her reason for living—walk out the door. *Lord knows I did something right in this world.*

Debra opens the door to find a messenger with a small package for her. After signing, she opens it before the door has closed. Inside, she finds a single red rose and a note.

> *I request the pleasure of your company.*
> *Fish 7 p.m., RSVP unnecessary*
> *Denying me is unacceptable. Brian*

They both score big in the romance department, Debra thinks as she looks up at the *Capodimonte* ceramic basket with twelve beautifully formed roses, Roberto sent. The card read:

Roses that will never die, like my love for you.

This is going to be a lot tougher than she thought. She looks down at her watch and realizes it's already 11 a.m. She can't call her regular babysitter since tonight is a school night. Thinking, she dials Zya's phone.

Zya answers on the fourth ring. "Hey Deb."

Knowing she's busy, she asks, "I'm sorry to bother you. I won't take up too much of your time."

"It's okay, I'm trying to get over to the hospital, looks like I'm going to be late for my appointment."

"Anything I should be worried about?"

"No—no, just my annual mammogram. And thanks, but Ashanti has the worry department covered. If I miss my appointment, she'll freak out."

"I have a date with Brian tonight, and I can't call Peggy since it's a school night. Is Ashanti available? I promise I won't be late," Debra says, pleading.

"What time would you like me to drop her off?"

"Oh, thank you, you are such a dear. Would 6:30 be okay?"

"Sure. Is it okay if she brings Stacey? Those two have become inseparable."

"Stacey is always welcome in my home."

"See you then, and Deb..."

"Yes."

"wear something sexy. I know you're not sleeping with the man, but no one says he shouldn't at least imagine what it would be like—little preggo belly and all."

Debra laughs. "See you tonight, and thanks again."

"Hey, don't you have an appointment today?"

"Yeah, but I'm going to reschedule. I've got so much paperwork to go through here on my desk. I guess being in love has its drawbacks."

Amber walks out of her office and takes the papers out of Dominque's hands. She takes her purse out of her drawer and hands it to her.

"It will all be here when you get back—now go."

"Okay, okay. I guess I can make it if there's no traffic."

Dominque rushes through the door at the Breast Center. "I'm so sorry I'm late," she says as she approaches the check-in desk.

"Dom?" Zya asks, surprised to see her.

"Zya? What are you doing here?"

"Annual breasts squeeze. You?"

"Ouch, does it hurt?"

"First time?"

"Yeah, I have to get a baseline. Since we don't have any family medical history on me, my social worker thought it was a good idea."

"It's a great idea. Early detection saves us."

Although both are more than an hour late for their appointments, they are accommodated one, right after the other. They see each other in the back waiting room dressed in matching pink smocks ready for the squeeze.

"It hurts, doesn't it?" Dominque asks.

"It's uncomfortable. I usually take an Advil before I come.

I'm sure it was a man who came up with this contraption. They have a cartoon in one room with a man putting his penis into a mammogram machine called *The Manogram*."

Dominque laughs just as they call her name. They call Zya into the room next door.

Zya is done first and waits for Dominque in the outside waiting room.

After ten minutes, Dominque walks out, holding her boobs, not caring who sees her.

"That bad, huh?"

"I guess implants complicate things."

"I didn't know they weren't yours."

"Oh, they're mine all right, paid for by me."

Laughing, Zya adds, "Bought mine too."

Dominque looks at Zya with a smile. She grabs her arm as they leave. "I always knew we had a lot more in common than I thought."

"Wasn't my idea, Doug talked me into it—not sure it was worth it?"

Debra arrives on time for dinner and is escorted to a table in the corner with floor to ceiling white sheers around it. You can still see the other patrons, but it's more romantic and private. When she sits down, she sees a note sitting in front of her with the same handwriting as from earlier.

Tonight, I will wow you, woo you, win you.

Chuckling, she looks up to see Brian dressed in a white

linen shirt and pants—South Florida's staple casual attire. "I might be a little overdressed," she says as she looks down at her silky gray tunic and pants.

"Nonsense, my dear, you look beautiful in anything—and nothing."

"Oh, how do you know? You haven't seen me naked."

"Oh, but I have—a thousand times in my mind."

Debra chuckling, she says, "Think you might be laying it on a little too thick?"

"Too much? I'm assuming Roberto is very romantic competition! I hope you don't mind, I've asked the chef to prepare a special dinner for us." As he finishes his sentence, the waiter brings over a bottle of red grape juice. He shows it to Brian as if he were presenting a fine wine. After twisting off the top, he sets it on the table, then ceremoniously drapes a white linen napkin over his arm, placing his other behind his back.

Brian picks it up and, looking very serious, sniffs it as if it were a cork from an expensive bottle of wine.

Debra snorts and laughs as she watches Brian's antics.

Brian motions the waiter to pour a bit in his glass for a taste test. He picks up the wineglass, twirls it around and sniffs the air on top of the glass. "Oh, this is a good year and very full-bodied." He takes a sip and says, "Excellent choice." He then motions the waiter to fill both glasses.

The young man, trying desperately not to laugh, does as instructed, keeping up the charade.

After an incredible meal mixed with more anecdotes and comedy skits from Brian, Debra floats in her front door, thinking about the delicious calamari, shrimp, and scallop appetizer

Brian insisted on feeding her himself. Her entrée was a mouthwatering, thick halibut steak topped with shrimp in a tomato and pineapple sauce. Definitely, one of the most enjoyable evenings she has had. Brian just moved up a notch. Giddy, she comes into the house to find Stacey looking at Ashanti's back.

They jump when they hear the door open.

"What's up?" Debra asks.

"Nothing," Ashanti and Stacey both say in unison, looking guilty.

No need to see where Tracey is; it's way past her bedtime, so she's fast asleep.

"Come here, let me look." Debra was a nurse when she met George. She was working on her P.A. when they married. She often thought about getting back into it once the baby is born. Debra walks over to Ashanti and lifts the back of her shirt to see an infected, large scrape on her back.

"How did this happen?" Debra asks.

"I fell off my bike."

"You don't have a bike. What happened?" she asks again—sternly.

Stacey looks at Ashanti. "I'm sorry. Mrs. Harris, these kids are picking on Ashanti at school. They chased her home the other day, and she tripped. She already had hurt her ribs from a few weeks ago, so she twisted so she wouldn't hurt them again and hit her back instead."

"Does your mom know about this?" Debra asks as she reaches for peroxide and bandages.

"No, and please, don't tell her."

"Why won't you tell her?"

"She said she wanted to move back to Africa, leave the country, and everything behind to protect me. There will always be bullies, people doing bad things, no matter where we live. Please, I don't want to move—I love it here."

"You really think your mom would leave over this?" Debra asks as she continues to examine the nasty scrape on Ashanti's back.

Both girls nod their heads.

"Your mom is one of my best friends. Although it goes against my better judgement, I won't say anything on one condition."

Ashanti looks sheepishly at her.

"If these kids lay one hand on you again, you call the police immediately. They need to learn their lesson."

"I promise," Ashanti agrees.

After cleaning out her wound and bandaging her up, Debra says, "I'm going to call your mom to come and get you. I won't say a word for now. You should be on an antibiotic. I put some ointment on it—hopefully it's enough. If not, you let me know."

"Thank you, Mrs. Harris. I'm sorry to put you in this position."

"Let's hope it doesn't come back and bite me in the butt."

Dominque is getting used to Tad sleeping over every night. She's encouraged him to bring some things from his home, so he could go straight to work in the morning.

This evening, she comes out of the bathroom wearing a

sexy, short white cotton nighty. Not see-through, but when the light shines through it, the outline of her body is visible.

Although Tad is wide awake, with all his might, he pretends to be asleep.

She slips under the covers and pushes her body up against his—nothing. She runs her fingers along the side of his face, as if tucking imaginary hair behind his ear—nothing.

Zzzzzz, zzzzzz, Tad lets out two big snores and then turns rolls over to the other side of the bed.

Resigned, she turns over to go to sleep.

Tad opens his eyes, thinking, *When will it be the right time?* He drifts off to sleep with thoughts of them making love.

At some point, in the middle of the night, he wakes up, spooning her. Unsure what woke him, his throbbing erection quickly proves to be the culprit.

Deciding now might be the perfect opportunity—it sure feels right—his hand cups her breast. He rubs her nipple as his erection pushes against her lower back. He snuggles up as close to her as possible, almost becoming one. Pushing a lock of hair from her face, he plants delicate—butterfly kisses along her neck. His hand goes back to her breast, this time under her gown, caressing her. He traces circles slowly down the curves of her body when he realizes she's not wearing anything else.

She takes his hand and brings it back up to her breast without turning.

After the sun comes up, they're still wrapped in each other's arms. They took the rest of the night to explore each other's bodies—slowly.

She tried so many times to rush things, but he slowed her

down. He kissed every inch of her body, exploring certain parts more thoroughly. He took her to the brink of release, and as she was ready to explode, he stopped to explore other areas.

It was driving her crazy—maddening, even.

He never penetrated her, yet they both came to satisfying climaxes. She is very talented, doing things to him he never imagined. The few lovers he's had barely touched him, let alone wrap their lips around him, draining every drop of fluid he released. When Dominque pulled back, wiping her lips with that shit-eating grin, he thought he was going to cum again. His other lovers wouldn't let him pleasure them except for one. She taught him how to use his tongue, tickling and teasing her to oblivion. He's grateful for that education. Seeing how he made his beautiful ginger goddess squirm and squeal in delight was as satisfying as the two orgasms he had.

As they wake up, he turns her over and looks deeply into her eyes, wondering how did he get so lucky. He kisses her gently at first, but the kiss quickly becomes intense and hot. He can't hold back any longer. The entire night was the prequel.

Sensing his urgency, she wraps her legs around him and intensifies their kiss, pulling his hips towards hers. They become one instantly, but don't move.

After a few seconds, they slowly and rhythmically begin moving in sync.

Looking into her eyes, he never imagined he could ever feel this way for anyone. *I can't believe how much in love I am with this woman.*

He notices tears rolling down her cheeks. His first reaction is, he's hurting her.

She smiles and says, "I love you." Reassuring him, they are

tears of love.

His own eyes copy hers as he pulls her close to him one last time as they surrender and explode in ecstasy.

Chapter Nineteen

"**M**om, there's a message for you on the machine. It's from the Breast Center. That's not normal, is it?"

"Oh, you worry too much, I'm sure it's nothing," Zya says, walking over to the answering machine. She turns her back to her daughter as she listens to the message. She turns back, nodding a few times and smiling at Ashanti, trying desperately to keep calm on the outside while she's panicking inside.

It's close to five in the evening, so she isn't sure if she can reach anyone. She picks up her cell phone and walks into her office. "Hi, this is Zya Monroe. You called me."

"Oh, Miss Monroe, I'm glad you called me back today. Can you please hold for Dr. Fritz?"

Waiting only a few moments feels like an eternity. "Miss Monroe, my name is Dr. Fritz, head of radiology. My colleagues and I have been reviewing your films, and, given your family history, we would like you to come in for an ultrasound-guided biopsy. Are you able to come in this Friday?"

"Yeah, sure," Zya answers in a fog, trying to comprehend what she's hearing.

Ashanti is in her doorway, watching her every move.

She turns away and asks softly, "Should I be worried?"

"I know it's easier said than done, but I would advise you not to worry until we can determine if the mass is malignant or not."

"Excuse me?"

"Your mammogram is showing a solid mass of approximately four-centimeters in size. It *is* solid, so we need to do a biopsy to determine if it's calcification or something else."

Smiling becomes more difficult as she's falls apart inside. "Okay. If you have an opening on Friday, I'll come in and redo the mammogram, no problem."

"Miss Monroe, maybe you don't quite understand."

"Oh, I understand."

Holding her hand over the phone, she says to Ashanti, "See honey, I told you it was nothing to worry about."

Addressing the doctor, she says, "What time, eight? Wow, I didn't know you started that early in the morning. Sounds great, I'll see you then."

Zya is playing it cool, but Ashanti has a watchful eye on her. She tries to be chipper and upbeat, but she knows Ashanti can sense something is off.

Tina walks in the door as they are setting the table for dinner.

Ashanti asks, "Mom, are you sure everything is okay?"

"Really, honey, it's fine, just a big old inconvenience is what it is."

"What is?" Tina inquires.

"Mom got a call from the Breast Center today. They want her to go back on Friday morning to have another mammogram."

Tina looks at Zya, waiting for an explanation.

"It's no big deal. Sometimes the pictures aren't that clear and they need to redo them."

"But they got you an appointment this week. Didn't you always say you had to book your appointment at least two months in advance to get in," Ashanti asks suspiciously.

"Honey, they had a cancellation, so they held it for me. They feel bad about messing up my films, so they're trying to accommodate me. Really, that's all it is."

"Would you tell me if it wasn't?" Ashanti asks.

Zya hesitates a bit too long.

With tears rolling down her face, Ashanti says, "You promised me you would never lie to me about this. You said you would always be upfront and honest with me because it's something I might have to deal with in the future."

Zya reaches out for Ashanti. "Come here, honey." Hugging her tight, Zya looks up at Tina, who's eyes are huge and starting to water. Zya's eyes do the same. After forcing back the waterworks, she pulls away from Ashanti. Looking into her eyes, she says, "Honey, I know how nervous you get about this. I don't want you to worry, okay?"

"So tell me the truth."

Zya wonders how much she should say. On the one hand, she promised to tell her the truth. But on the other, getting her worked up, before they know what they're dealing with, won't help. Moms are supposed to protect their children, so she decides on something somewhere in between.

"They want me to come back and have a magnified mammogram done. There is an area that looks suspicious. It's most likely calcification, but they won't know for sure until they do some more testing. PLEASE, do not get yourself worked up over this. They don't know. The doctor said not to worry."

Ashanti is trying hard to keep her composure. "Mom, it runs in our family. You know that chances are high you could get it."

"Yes, that's true. I promise you, when this blows over, I'll go get the BRAC testing done, once and for all. But you have to promise, when it comes back negative, you'll stop worrying and nagging me about this, okay?"

Ashanti smiles. She'd been trying to get her mom to do the genetic testing since she first heard about it. Her mom kept brushing it off, worrying that if the test comes back positive, she and Ashanti would live their lives in fear, wondering if, or when, it would strike. A better strategy would be to be diligent about getting tested, doing their monthly self-examinations, and taking care of their bodies.

"And if it comes back positive?"

"One thing at a time—we'll deal with it that if the time comes." Zya hugs her daughter and says, "Now hurry and get the plates on the table. Dinner is getting cold."

Tina grabs Zya's hand—It's ice cold. She looks at Zya, her eyes doing the asking.

Zya squeezes Tina's hand. "It's okay," she whispers.

Tina squeezes Zya's hand in return and goes to the bathroom. They had agreed not to show their affection for each other in front of the kids. The urge to throw her arms around her soulmate and comfort her is too strong. She has to walk away.

Zya waits a minute, then heads down the hallway to find the door slightly ajar. She walks and finds Tina sitting on the floor with her hands over her eyes, sobbing. "That's not it," Tina musters between sobs. "I know you didn't tell her the truth. I know you. What aren't you saying?"

"Tina, I held back some details, and I promise once the kids are in bed, I'll tell you everything; I planned to anyway. For now, they don't know what it is, so I'm trying to stay positive."

Tina jumps up from the floor and throws her arms around Zya, squeezing her. "I just found you; I can't lose you. Please don't leave me!"

Zya, returning the affection, says, "It's all going to be okay —I promise. I'm not going anywhere."

Tina pulls back lovingly, gazing at Zya. Her eyes, red and swollen, and tear-stained cheeks.

"Look, red, white & blue," Zya says, pointing at Tina's eyes, trying to ease the tension.

Tina manages a weak smile.

"Now wipe your eyes and wash your pretty face, then get your butt out there. I made a delicious roast with potatoes, and it's getting cold." Zya taps Tina on the butt as she turns and walks back to the kitchen.

They say the things that don't kill you make you stronger, but what about allowing yourself to be weak? If she has cancer, she must keep it together and stay strong for everyone. Who will comfort her?

As she turns the corner to the dining room, she sees Stacey and Ashanti sitting at the table, silent and somber. "Oh no, this is not how it's gonna be," Zya states firmly. She dances over to the stereo and turns it on and up as loud as she dares before the neighbors complain. The song playing is perfect. It's an oldie but goodie and one that makes you want to boogie.

"Come on, get up now. Don't let this old lady dance by herself."

The girls briefly look at each, then join her dancing all around the room, laughing.

Tina walks out of the bathroom and stops at the end of the hall. She pleads, *God, please don't take her from me.*

The girls are fast asleep. Although Ashanti is still upset, she drifted off.

Zya notices Tina reading on her bed as she walks by, heading for her own room. She has to tell Tina the truth. Not sure how to get the words out, she throws herself across her bed and sobs into her pillow.

Within a few minutes, she feels Tina lie down beside her and put her arm around her. "Cry, baby, cry… let it all out. It's healing. You'll feel better, I promise."

Zya turns around towards Tina, intending to say she's all right. Instead, she buries her head into her shoulder as more sobs escape. "I'm so scared."

"Me too, but we're going to get through this together," Tina says in a soothing voice.

After what seems like an eternity, Zya's eyes dry out. Feeling safe, she stays wrapped in Tina's arms thinking how different this would be if she and Doug were still together. He probably would have left and gone out drinking, wondering how he's going to deal with all this. He was such a selfish bastard.

Tina brushes Zya's hair away from her eyes and dries her cheeks with her fingers. "Feel better?"

"A little."

"Want to tell me what's up now?"

Zya explains to Tina about the large mass and the needle biopsy she's having done on Friday morning.

"I'm going with you," Tina says matter-of-factly.

"Okay, but we can't go together. Ashanti will get suspicious. We'll have to take two cars or you take a taxi there, and we'll go to the warehouse together afterward."

"You think you're going to be able to work after that?"

"Probably not. I figured it would be best to have a distraction."

"I'll take a cab, but you're not going to work afterward. I think we are going to need to do some serious shopping or whatever you want, but no work."

Zya, feeling better and stronger, says, "Okay, no work. Thank you, Tina."

"For what?"

"For being here."

"There's nowhere else on earth I would rather be, you know that."

Zya looks up and without hesitation, kisses her. Zya's heart has never felt so full. The love between them is so right—and honest. She's exactly where she's supposed to be. As their affection turns more passionate, Zya decides to just go with it and explores Tina's body from head to toe.

"I thought you said you never did this before." Tina gasps as Zya touches her in the right spots.

"Well, I figured I know my way around my body; yours is probably pretty much the same."

Tina laughs for a moment but cuts off as Zya's finger enters her, finding just the right spot to make her nerve endings dance.

Within a matter of moments, Tina thrashes as she grabs the

cover beneath her with both hands. She's trying so hard to be quiet, but it's difficult.

"I guess I was wrong, I never climax that quickly," Zya says as she watches Tina's face soften in the afterglow.

Tina catches her breath. She then pushes Zya over on her back and says, "My turn."

CHAPTER TWENTY

"I thought I blew it with you insisting we meet."

"Life is complicated for me right now. I don't think we should continue our phone fun."

"But you didn't even give me a chance. How do you know I'm not the right one for you?"

"I guess I don't, and I'll probably never will. Things are crazy right now; I don't think it would be right to throw you in the mix too."

"Meet me," Stewart states sternly.

"No, I don't think so."

"Just for one drink. Meet me for one drink. Please, give me a chance."

"For a drink, one drink. Promise, after one drink, you'll leave me alone, and never call me again."

☯

"Where are you?"

"Caught me in the tub again," she says with a little giggle.

"Really? Hold on; I have to get a visual."

"Make sure that vision includes this huge round belly. One more month to go, not soon enough if you ask me."

"I envisioned you with that beautiful pregnant belly, and I was right next to you kissing it," Brian responds.

Debra's eyes tear up, cursing the hormones that have her crying all the time. "That's very sweet, I almost wish you were here."

"Almost?"

"Well, I know if you were, I would have made my decision and chose you over Roberto."

"I'll be right there!"

Debra giggles. "You're so funny. Please don't take this the wrong way, but I see a bit of George in you when you're play-ful like this."

"I'll take that as a compliment. I liked the guy a lot. Any comparison to him is an honor."

"You knew George?" she says, sitting up in the tub so quickly, the water sloshes back and forth.

"Yeah, I did. I probably should have told you this sooner, but just as an acquaintance. We played racquetball together once or twice a month."

Tears appear in the corners of her eyes. This time caused by hormones. "Why didn't you tell me you knew him when I first came to you?"

"I should have. I met you once at a charity dinner. I don't know if you remember, it was about two years ago at the Heart Ball. George was always bragging about his beautiful, sexy wife, always telling everyone how wonderful she was. He painted you like an angel. We used to give him such a hard time—no woman was that perfect. Then I met you. You were so gorgeous, and the two of you were deeply and madly in love —I was jealous. I remember saying to myself, that's one lucky bastard. If I could only be half as fortunate, I'd be a lucky man.

"I didn't know George was your husband when I agreed to see, and I didn't put two and two together until it was too late. I didn't recognize you at first; you were a wreck. It wasn't until our third session it clicked. You were so upset; my heart was breaking watching you from across my desk. I couldn't believe George, the love of your life, was gone. By the time the session was over, I didn't have the heart to reject you, and then when I tried to back away, Amber begged me not to turn you over to someone else. I thought I could stay professional and neutral. I thought it was the right thing to do—what George would have wanted." After a long pause, he asks, "Debra, are you there?"

In a tiny voice, she replies, "Yes."

Brian continues, "Everything was going along okay, and I thought I could do this, but then you met Roberto and you came alive. I was so damn jealous—I wanted to be the one to make you whole again. It just got too much for me, so I did what I thought was best and took a leave of absence. Roberto made you happy—he loved you. And from what I could tell, you were falling for him as well. I couldn't remain neutral anymore. I'm sorry."

"So, you've been attracted to me for a while now?" Debra asks.

"I'm ashamed to say, but I've loved you since the day I laid eyes on you two years ago. I would never, ever try to steal another man's wife and, knowing how much you two loved each other, I didn't think I would've been able to even if I had tried."

The tears fall steady in a stream. She's finding it difficult to keep her composure. "I have to go now."

"Please don't be mad at me. I'm sorry, I should have told you sooner. I don't want to hurt you—I love you."

Debra quietly hangs up. She thought she was close to deciding. It's been tough, but somehow Roberto was coming out on top. He's been matching Brian in every way, which is impressive given the enormous distance between them. While taking her bath, Debra decided she would call Roberto and find what the living arrangements will be like, once they became a couple. Would she have to move to Italy, or would he be willing to come here? But now, Brian has evened the score.

Dominque is slowly persuading Tad to bring more and more items over to her apartment. She's even given him a part of her closet and two drawers in her dresser. She moved her make-up and toiletries to one side of the sink so he can have the other. She enjoys having him around; everything is perfect.

"Honey?"

"Yes, dear," Tad responds playfully.

"I know it's only been a month, but you already have so much of your stuff here."

"So, what are you saying?"

"Why don't you move in?" Dominque asks cheerfully.

Tad jumps up from the couch where he was reading the newspaper. Because he's shirtless, Dominque notices his upper body tense up.

"I don't think that's a good idea. Not yet, at least."

"I don't want to rush things. I just thought since you're practically living here already, maybe it's time to make it official."

Tad scans the room for his T-shirt, finds it, and throws it over his head. "I have to go."

"Where are you going?"

"I have an errand to run. I'll be back."

Dominque watches him walk out the front door with his shoes in his hands. He couldn't get out of the door fast enough. Dominque looks up at the ceiling, praying she didn't just lose him.

That same morning, Tad sat up in bed watching Dominque sleep, wondering how he could have gotten so lucky. He had dreamed so many nights of being exactly where he is, waking up every morning to the most beautiful woman in the world. He's not ready to move in. It was something he saw coming, but being old-fashioned, he never thought he would be, *living in sin*. He was quick to scold others when they moved in together way too soon. Now, his beautiful Dominque was asking him to do just that.

Patrick's plan was never to fall in love with anyone—ever. Guess it's a good thing sometimes the best-laid plans don't work out. He feels as if he has two minds; one telling him how incredible Amber is, and how he almost lost her with his male-ego. And the other, reminding him about his father and willing him to get the suicide note and reread it.

At the drug store, he's hit with the vision of big red hearts everyone. Valentine's Day is around the corner, even though it's barely 2018. They are a couple now, so he should get her something special, but what?

He thinks through some options. He'll send flowers for sure —that's a given, and a nice dinner. Jewelry? No, that's too much too soon. Perfume? No, too personal. A day at the spa? Yeah, that's what he'll get her. He remembers her talking about the Day of Indulgence Dominque enjoyed. It's decided; he's heading to the mall tomorrow. Today, he'll pick out her card. *Nothing too mushy*, he thinks as he picks up the first card. 'I'll love you forever,' it says. The next one, 'You have stolen my heart,' with the red symbol behind bars. He leaves frustrated, not purchasing one as they all were too much about love. Something he's not ready to commit—or admit—to.

"So, you're going to meet her, finally?"

"Yep, tomorrow night, I can't believe it. I'm so nervous— Me! I never get nervous!"

"If I didn't know any better, I would say you're smitten," Patrick says, teasing him.

"This woman—and I mean *woman*, is one in a million. I've only been with girls, that's so obvious to me now. But this one is…humph."

"What if she's fat and ugly?" Patrick continues the teasing.

"We've had this conversation already; I'll still love her," Stewart says wistfully.

"Yeah, right! You and I both know you'll walk right past her," Patrick says, chuckling and shaking his head.

"She has to be sexy and very confident. No fat and ugly girl is going to have phone sex like we did. And yeah, I'd walk right past her."

"That's cold and shallow of you man."

"It is, isn't it? I can't help it. Never mind...she's hot and sexy—I just know it."

"How will you know who she is?"

"She said she'd be wearing a red silk dress."

"Like the *Woman in Red*?"

"I didn't think about that. I hope she's hot like Kelly Le-Brock. What are you doing tomorrow night? Out with Amber again?"

"No, actually, she's going out with her friends. She said she needed some female bonding time."

"Things are going good for you two, aren't they?"

"Almost too good if you ask me. We've had so many miscommunications and falters. I'm waiting for the other shoe to drop."

"Be careful what you wish for. It just might."

Stewart leaves for his daily run along AIA; the ocean's boulevard, while Patrick kicks back on the couch, thinking about Amber.

The two minds start at it again. On the one hand, he's waiting for the other shoe to drop. While the other preaches, negative thinking invites negative energy. Yet, when thinking how it's gone so far, there's bound to be something else coming. He should prepare himself. However, what if they are meant to be together, and he blows it expecting the worst?

Frustrated, he jumps up, grabs his keys, and runs some errands. First stop, Amber's gift from the mall.

The spa's entrance is outside, so one could come and go and never see the inside of the mall. He sits in his car with the spa certificate in his hand. After a few minutes, he goes into the mall in search of a card store.

Feeling hungry and not able to resist the buttery aroma, he heads over to *Auntie Anne's* for one of their famous pretzels.

Walking past the stores, paying attention only to the salty delicacy in his hand, he drops a sizeable chunk on the ground. He picks it up quickly, blows it off thinking, *five-second rule,* then pops it into his mouth. His eyes got from the pretzel to the jewelry store in front of him. There's a turntable in the window, and something flashes him as it spins in the light above. As he moves closer, he sees a beautiful diamond ring is the culprit. The center stone is square and full of fire. He's mesmerized by its brilliance and beauty.

"It's stunning, isn't it?" He turns towards the saleswoman standing next to him. "It's only been here for two days, but I'm shocked we still have it. It's one of the most beautiful rings I've seen in a long time. It looks much bigger than it is—a great cutting job. And the side stones really make a statement too."

"It looks like it's about three carats?" Patrick asks.

"You're right. It looks it, but it's just over two and a half. It isn't often you can get a diamond like this—one that looks bigger and more expensive than what it actually is. It's an Asscher cut. I think, one of the most elegant and feminine cuts—very regal and timeless. One exceptional lady is going to own it. Have good evening," she says as she walks into the store.

Exceptional, huh? He walks in the store and finds the saleswoman rearranging watches. "I'm curious, how much is that stunner?" He can't believe what he's doing. He swears he won't ask to see it.

"Let's find out, shall we?" She takes the ring from the case and places it on top of a black velvet pad, willing him mentally to pick it up. The diamond is still sparkling without a pin light pointing right at it. This woman is skilled; a natural salesperson. How can he not hold it in his hand and imagine it on Amber's finger?

"The center diamond is 2.63 carats, GIA certified F-color, and VS1 clarity. The side stones are trillions, each 0.75 carats, E-color, and VS1 clarity. They're set in palladium."

Patrick looks up at her, questioning the metal choice.

"Palladium has been around for ages; it's part of the platinum group. It's lighter and stronger than platinum and just as white and bright. It's also used for people allergic to most metals. Many designers are using today. The price is $54,500."

Patrick reaches out for the ring; his fingers itch to pick it up —it's perfect. If she says no, he can always bring it back. But he can't ask her to marry him yet—it's too soon. "And my price is?" Patrick asks.

"I wish I could discount it, but that's the final price. Because it faces up like a three-carat center stone, it's priced way below what it looks like it should. It's a beautiful ring."

"Well, thank you anyway, I appreciate you showing it to me," Patrick says as he hands the ring back to her.

"No problem, I love getting it out to look at it. Thank you for giving me the chance to see it again today. Have a good evening."

Patrick walks out of the jewelry shop with sweaty palms. *Phew, that was close.* But then again…he spins around and marches back into the store. The saleswoman is not facing him, but he asks anyway, "Do you accept American Express?"

It surprises Tad when he sees Patrick walk out of the jewelry store with a bag. *Nah, there's no way he would buy a ring, probably an early Valentine's Day gift.*

Tad has been driving around, thinking about what happened this morning. Yes, he wants to live with her. There were many reasons behind that decision, but in the end, it came down to the two simple facts. One, he loves her, and two, he can't imagine living without her.

He walks into the store to find the saleslady cleaning a showcase. He can't afford much, but he still wants to put something on her finger before he moves in.

"May I help you?"

"I'm looking for an engagement ring. I'm on a limited budget, but I want to get something of good quality."

"Too bad you weren't here a little earlier. I sold a stunner, and the price was a steal."

Tad thinks for a minute, then looks towards the doors Patrick exited earlier.

"Nah, can't be," Tad mumbles.

"Excuse me?"

"Oh, nothing, just thinking out loud."

Tad points to several styles he thinks Dominque will like. After about forty minutes of looking and haggling, he leaves with a bag like Patrick's, and a big smile.

When he returns, he finds Dominque in the kitchen, still in her nightgown. Her face is blotchy, eyes swollen and red, and her hair in disarray. He feels bad he's hurt her; he never wants to cause her pain. He walks in and pulls her up from the kitchen table and into his arms. "Don't cry." His heart is breaking to think he did this to her. "I'm sorry. I needed some time to think. I'd like to wait a little while before we decide this, okay?"

"Okay," she says as new tears stream down her cheeks. "I was so afraid I had lost you. I thought I'd pushed you too fast."

"Let's leave things exactly as they are for now, please?"

"Okay."

Holding her, he realizes, beyond the shadow of a doubt, that this is the woman for him, his soul mate, as he plans his proposal.

The doctor has been moving the ultrasound wand around and around for what seems like an eternity, with a perplexed look on his face.

"I'm afraid to ask," Zya says, nervously.

"It's strange. I can't find it; the mass that showed up on your mammogram. I know it's deep, but I should be able to see it," the doctor says, puzzled.

"Is that a good thing?"

"It's a bizarre thing. Let me check the other side and see if maybe they made a mistake with the labeling." After another few minutes, checking both breasts, he finds nothing. "Well, I've heard of it, but I've never experienced it. Your mass has disappeared."

"What? Really?"

"I'm going to have you take another mammogram, but I can't find anything of concern."

Zya's eyes tear up as she releases her fists, allowing the blood to flow back into her fingertips. She can't get dressed fast enough to tell Tina the great news.

The big smile on her face instantly wipes the frown from Tina's. "It's gone. They can't explain it, but it's gone." Holding her close, Tina joins in the waterworks.

The other women in the room watch as the drama unfolds, speculating if they're good friends or something more.

Tina goes to kiss Zya but stops to make sure Zya is ready for a public display of affection.

Without hesitation, Zya kisses her back. "I love you, Tina; I love you so much. I can't believe I'm saying this but, yes, I'm gay."

After spending the day shopping and seeing a movie, they head home to find Ashanti waiting impatiently. She doesn't give her mom the chance to put her purse down before she jumps her with questions.

"What did they say?"

"The new films are clean. There is a small bit of calcification on my other breast, but no mass."

"Really? You're not lying to me, right?"

"I promise—no cancer."

"Yippee!" Ashanti jumps into her mom's arms and hugs her tight. She pulls back and asks, "So, when would you like me to make the appointment for the genetic test?"

Zya ruffles Ashanti's flowing hair then goes into the kitchen where Tina is standing, offering her a hot cup of tea. "I'm still shocked. I can't believe it."

"Maybe my films got mixed up with another patient's."

"You think someone is walking around with a four-centimeter mass in her breast, and she doesn't even know it?"

"Yeah, I guess so."

CHAPTER TWENTY-ONE

"Dom, hey, it's Patrick. I have a big surprise for Amber. I was going to wait, but I just can't. I know you all are going out for drinks tonight, so I thought with all of her extended family present, tonight is perfect."

"She's here, want me to get her for you?" Dominque asks, sitting at her desk.

"No, no, it has to be a surprise. Tell me where you're meeting tonight, and I'll show up unannounced."

"We're supposed to be going out tonight?" Dominque asks, confused.

Patrick's heart sinks and a hollowness creeps into his gut. "Amber told me she was going out with you girls tonight."

Dominque, trying to cover for Amber, comes up with something quick to say. "Oh, I can't believe they didn't invite me. I know they want to give me time with Tad, but they should have at least asked. Give me ten minutes, and I'll find out where we're meeting. I'll call you back."

With slumped shoulders and his head hanging, he says, "No, don't bother."

Stewart comes rushing through the door to change and get

ready to meet his phone-sex gal. "You're home early. Nobody to sue today?" He stops dead in his tracks, watching Patrick roll a diamond ring around the table. "Is that what I think it is?"

"It was," Patrick says, defeated.

"Man, you don't look too good."

"I should have known better. It was too good to be true. What was I thinking!" He slams his fist down on the table causing the ring to jump.

Stewart sits down next to Patrick at the table. "You all right, man?"

"I'll be fine; I'm just beating myself for thinking I could find an honest and caring woman. I won't end up like my dad. No woman will ever get under my skin again, NEVER!"

"Hey man, why don't you come with me tonight to *Jack's* for a beer. We can head over a little early and sit at the bar be-fore she arrives. Then you can tell me what you think."

"Thanks, but no thanks. I wouldn't be very good company. I'd tell you she was trash even if she wasn't."

Stewart quickly jumps into the shower, hoping Patrick's sour mood doesn't rub off on him.

After participating in his own pity party for over an hour, Patrick decides he's not giving Amber, or any woman, the power to stop him from living the way he wants. He knew the other shoe was going to drop. This is precisely what he told himself no woman would ever do to him.

Fed up with his inner turmoil, Patrick grabs his keys hoping he can make it to *Jack's* in time to let Stewart know he is there and where he'll be sitting. Just in case his lady in red is a dis-appointment.

He rushes into the bar, and after his eyes adjust, he sees Stewart sitting by himself in the back corner. As he walks through the crowd, he spots a woman wearing a deep-red dress coming from the other side towards Stewart. He's too late.

He tries to squeeze into the bar so he can get a better look at her, but it's so dark. He watches as she walks up to Stewart and notices a look of surprise on his face. She sits down, and as she turns around, the light above the table glows around her silhouette—*No! It can't be!* Patrick gets up and rushes out the door.

Debra knows she needs to decide. One she hopes to make before the baby arrives. She'll be so busy, there won't be any time for romance. Looking at pictures of both men, she wishes one of them would jump out and decide for her. Both of them are just so great. She should be happy to have two wonderful men to choose from, but she's not. It's becoming way too difficult and stressful.

She drops her head into her hands in frustration when her doorbell rings. She isn't expecting anyone. Probably more flowers. With her mind elsewhere, thinking about her looming decision, she walks to the front door and opens it. She steps back with her hand across her mouth and gasps.

"Will you marry me?"

"Yes, yes, I accept!" All Debra had to do was ask for a sign. And now, with him down on one knee asking, her decision is made.

He slips the beautiful diamond ring on her finger. The yellow stone is the same he offered her before, but the setting is now a very simple, yet elegant, solitaire.

"You changed the setting?" Debra asks.

"I want you to pick it. So this for now." Roberto enters the room and picks her up in his arms and twirls her, kissing her the whole time. As he puts her down to look into her eyes, the baby kicks him.

"Ohhhh! Little George—he likes."

Little George kicks again in excitement, and they both laugh. He does somersaults in what seems like a celebration. "Little George has never been this active."

She laughs as Roberto pulls her close and kisses her with all the love and passion you would expect at becoming engaged. She closes her eyes, enjoying the warmth and love. When she opens her eyes, she's stunned. For a split second, she thought it was Brian's arms wrapped around her.

Suddenly, a hot liquid trickles down her leg. But it isn't time yet, she still has another month to go. When she looks down, she isn't expecting to see blood.

"Come on, come on, Amber, pick up."

Amber left the office while Dominque was on the phone with Patrick, having slipped past her without being seen. She had to leave before Dominque stops and asks questions. *Damn you, Brandy for showing up now!* Amber has to get to her before she does any damage.

Amber's phone rings—it's Dominque. Avoidance feels like a better option than lying. She'll call her back tomorrow.

Dominque drives over to Amber's house, hoping she didn't screw things up for her, panicking as she weaves through rush hour traffic. After nearly an hour stuck on the road, she sees Amber's car coming up the street.

She waves her hands and honks, trying to get her attention, even rolling down her window, waving her hand out for her to pull over.

Is that Dom up ahead? Oh jeez, "Get down, she can't see you," Amber says to the person in the passenger seat. Amber looks down as if looking for something on the passenger seat as she passes Dominque's car.

Dominque can't believe she didn't see her as she pulls up into the nearest driveway to turn around. By the time she does, Amber's car is nowhere in sight.

That was close.

Finally giving up, Dominque heads home. When she opens the door, she finds a candlelight dinner awaiting her. Elegant crystal glasses and taper holders join beautiful china dishes over a lace tablecloth. A matching white china vase filled with white roses and other angelic flowers sits in the middle. "Oh, Tad," she sighs at the masterpiece before her forgetting about Amber.

She's overjoyed she hasn't ruined this gift from God—her relationship with Tad.

Tad comes out from the kitchen wearing an apron and carrying two glasses of wine. He looks at Dominque and immediately becomes concerned.

"Honey, you don't look so good."

She explains to him what happened with Patrick and Amber.

Tad thinks about mentioning seeing him at the jewelry store, but decides it's better left unsaid. She'll only feel worse. "You seem a bit pale to me though, are you feeling okay?"

"I'm a little tired. I think I've been pushing myself too hard." She smiles at him, spreading her arms before the table. "But this will definitely help me feel better." Dominque goes into a coughing fit. Another dizzy spell causes her to sit down where she's standing.

Tad rushes over to her. "I don't like the sound of that."

She touches his cheek, then stands up carefully. "Oh, you're so sweet. It's okay, really. I'm just a little dizzy; feeling a little run down."

"Why are you dizzy?"

"I haven't been taking my iron supplements. I keep forgetting. I'm sure I'm just anemic again."

"Let's forget dinner and get you into bed."

"How about we enjoy this unbelievable meal you made for us instead? If my iron is low, food is exactly what I need right now. Then I'll go take a hot bath."

"And then go to bed?"

"Is that an invitation?"

The ring rests at the bottom of her half empty wine glass. Since she's not feeling well, he postpones the question and takes the glass to the kitchen. As he stands up to get her glass, she looks up at him with a weak smile, then coughs uncontrollably.

He reaches for her water glass as she coughs and coughs into her napkin.

Finally, feeling a lull, she reaches out for the water.

Tad notices blood on her napkin. "Dom," he says, pointing to it.

Her eyes drop as the room starts to spin. She would have fallen over onto the floor if he wasn't there to catch her.

He picks her up, grabs his keys, and rushes out the door with her over his shoulder.

Ashanti has had a great day at school. Her mother is fine, she aced her calculus test, and her counselor discussed enrolling her into college courses this summer; she could graduate in her junior year. Her mom will be so proud of her. She's on her way to a full-paid scholarship to any school she wants. And she'll get to do it a full year earlier.

Since her schedule changed by staying after school to talk with her counselor, she walks home with no concerns. Her head is in a cloud as she floats home thinking about the movie she and Stacey are going to see later.

She takes a shortcut through the park, a few blocks from home when someone grabs her arm. Her head snaps towards them as they seize her other arm. They shove a dirty cloth or rag into her mouth as she opens it to scream. They drag her, while she's kicking and flailing, behind the huge, eighty-year-old ficus tree. When they stop, she's face-to-face with the bully from school.

"You just don't get it, do you? I told you to leave. We don't want your kind around here!"

Ashanti struggles against her captors to no avail.

"Oh no you don't. You're not getting away from me this time. You won't leave on your own, so I'll do it my way."

One kid pulls out a switchblade and opens it in front of her face.

Her eyes grow wide as she shakes her head back and forth —*NO!* Ashanti screams in her mind.

"Get her backpack," the bully shouts to the ones holding her arms.

One loosens his grip enough for her, with split timing perfection, to reach inside her opened backpack, and secure the gift from Stacey—the one she hoped she'd never have to use.

"Brian, you need to get to the hospital."

"Amber, what's wrong?"

"We don't know, the baby, Debra's bleeding. They're on their way over there now."

Getting Patrick's voice mail again, Amber finally leaves a message. "I wish you would answer your phone. I need you right now. Debra is on her way over to the hospital—it's the baby. Please call me back. I need you!"

Amber hangs up the phone and grabs her handbag. "Come on Brandy. This isn't exactly the way I wanted everyone to meet my identical twin, but I don't have a choice. We have to get over to the hospital."

"I have a disguise if that would make you feel better." Brandy pulls out a platinum blonde wig and shows it to Amber.

As soon as his phone beeps to let him know there is a new voicemail, he immediately deletes it. It's from Amber, and he has absolutely nothing to say to her.

Stewart, sitting next to him at the table, looks over and sees Amber's name on the screen. He made a promise not to say anything. But now, he's wondering if maybe he should. No, better not to say anything at all. He was over her before he met with her anyway, it won't make a difference.

The neighbors watch as the ambulance zooms away from the park. Nobody is exactly sure what's happened. The police officers at the scene are doing a good job keeping everyone away.

One of the neighbor's comment, "Must be a death. They only do that when someone dies."

They shake their heads, thinking how close this happened in the park where many of their children play.

Chapter Twenty-Two

Tina and Tracey are in the hospital waiting room, waiting for news about Ashanti. Amber has yet to arrive.

A middle-aged couple is in the corner; the wife is quietly crying in her hands, while her husband sits looking out into space with a firm scowl. He does nothing to console her, which seems odd to Tina. She's so glad she doesn't have someone like that in her life anymore.

A tall man in green scrubs comes into the waiting room. Tina, Stacey, and the couple all nervously look his way. He makes his way towards the waiting room; this is never easy…

- Who got hurt in the park?
- Is Little George, okay?
- Why did Dominque cough up blood?
- Will Amber and Patrick ever get together?
- Where has Brandy been?
- Will Zya and Tina's love last, or will someone come between them?

You will find the answers to these questions, and many more, in "Deja Vu: Here we go again…," Book II of the Unbroken Series.

Order today: www.MelodiousEnterprises.com

Stay-Tuned for special features not in the Unbroken Series, as they become available, along with other exclusive offers and writings, not available to the public.

https://www.MelodiousEnterprises.com/unbroken-readers.html

Please, before you leave a review.
The kindest thing you can do for an author is to leave them a review. *Be honest, but please be kind.* We've poured our hearts out over these pages—these are our babies. While we can't please everyone, we try our hardest to please the masses. Please be kind when leaving your review. Thank you!

Bio

Melody Saleh - Author/Storyteller/Escape Artist

Melody is a Florida native living in Fort Lauderdale with her husband while her daughter and family live nearby. She is an avid animal lover and philanthropist throughout South Florida. Having survived breast cancer twice (1998 and again 2008), she has a zest for life—always enjoying having her feet on this side of the ground.

"My happiest place is on the golf course; my second happiest place is spending time with my grandchildren. Twenty+ years ago, I didn't think that would be possible. Life is great!"

CPSIA information can be obtained
at www.ICGtesting.com
Printed in the USA
JSHW052231111020
8662JS00002B/12